I S H I
THE RISING

Taylor Barnes & Will Keane

3.1
PRESS

VENICE, CALIFORNIA

The authors would like to thank Tina Turbeville for contributing her considerable editing expertise. We would also like to acknowledge the friends and family who generously provided support and feedback throughout the process of creating this book. Thank you, we could not have done this without you.

3.1 Press
406 7th Avenue
Venice, California 90291
www.31press.com

Publisher's Note: This is a work of fiction. Names, characters, places, and incidents are a product of the author's imagination. Locales and public names are sometimes used for atmospheric purposes. Any resemblance to actual people, living or dead, or to businesses, companies, events, institutions, or locales is completely coincidental.

ISHI The Rising/ Taylor Barnes & Will Keane. —1st ed.
ISBN 978-0-6929233-1-3

For my daughter India, who inspires me
to envision a better world.
—*Taylor Barnes*

For my daughters Shauna and Jessica,
my two miracles.
—*Will Keane*

CONTENTS

"In no chess problem since the beginning of the world has black ever won. Did it not symbolize the eternal, unvarying triumph of Good over Evil?"

George Orwell, *1984*

ISHI
THE RISING

THE SET-UP

Memphis Tennessee, 1993

Gerald sat on the gray linoleum floor of the dimly lit liquor store, hiding from the owner, so he could read his favorite comic books without buying them. Huddled up against the back wall, he wedged himself between the ice cream freezer and an oversized malt liquor ad, with a spinner rack of comic books completing his hideaway. As he turns the pages, he notices the yellow light from the aging ceiling fixtures is casting a greenish tint to his brown skin. In his twelve-year-old mind, this makes him feel like the Hulk and he smiles to himself while he reads.

"Ding, ding," the front door bell of the liquor store chimes as someone enters. Gerald can hear a man's deep chuckle followed by the higher pitch of women laughing, and the sound reminds him of his mother. She would be disappointed with him if she knew what he was doing right now because she is a church going woman and she frowns upon any sort of dishonest behavior. She is working serving a party at Mrs. Ulrich's house. He is always welcome to hang out in the kitchen over there, but it makes him uncomfortable whenever one of the guests looks over and asks who he is, and the answer is, "Oh him, that's the maid's son." Neither he nor his mother had an identity beyond that in Mrs. Ulrich's home. He didn't want to go home and sit alone in a cold apartment, watching TV and eating potato chips until his mother got home.

"Ding, ding," the door opens again and the lazy, summer evening vibe of the store is disturbed by raised voices and yelling. He wants to ignore the sound and keep reading, but the argument is escalating. He tries to see what is going on but can't without revealing his hiding place. Two men are arguing, and the owner of the store, a Korean man, repeats several times in very heavily accented English, "Take it outside, take it outside! You no break anything! You break, you pay!"

One of the men sounds high on drugs, or alcohol, or both. "Maaan, your pussy ain't worth shit! I couldn't even get it up with that shit. Maaaan..." Gerald hears the man spit on the floor to punctuate his complaint.

The other man, with his deep, silky smooth voice, tries to diffuse the situation, "Brother, that's not my problem." he laughs, "We don't do returns." Then the girls laugh too. "Here, take some cash and buy yourself some beers."

He hears some scuffling, a slap, and then the sound of coins falling on the ground. "I don't want your shit money!" There is a short silence, and Gerald holds his breath while he waits for what will happen next. The women gasp in unison as he hears the distinctive "click" of a gun being cocked.

"Brotha, we don't need to go there, please, put your gun away." Gerald hears a crack in the silky smooth baritone voice, and the store owner has stopped yelling, which he suspects is because he's taken cover somewhere. He wants to get out of there too but is sure the only way to leave is through the drama unfolding in the middle of the store. "You see, that's what I like, respect... R.E.S.P.E.C.T. Respect! You show a brotha respect when he's gotta gun in his hand. I like that," says the drunk man.

"Man, do you want one of my ladies? Pick one. Hell, take both of them—on the house! Jus' put your gun away brotha." The other man is pleading now and all the smoothness has evaporated from his voice.

He can hear the heavy breathing of the two men as they struggle with each other, but only for a moment.

"Ahhhhhhhh! ahhhhhh!" the sound of the women's voices break into the room like a sonic boom.

"Pop, pop, pop, pop!"

Gerald jerks back as far as he can into his hiding place. The entire store is quiet except for the crackle of a neon beer sign. Out of the silence rose a slow whimper, escalating into a wail and finally, a wail that rattles Gerald's senses.

The screaming hooker takes off running away from the scene of the shooting. Her high heels make a clacking sound on the tile floor as she heads towards the back of the store in search of a hiding place. Whipping around the corner with the comic book rack she is surprised to find Gerald huddled in the corner, causing her to scream even more loudly.

Rambling wildly with her eyes darting everywhere, she says, "He shot him... he shot my man! God, he shot him!" She turns, pointing in the direction of the front of the store when, from behind her, a hand appears and moves her pointing arm out of the way. Curious who she is talking to, the crazy man with the gun steps forward to look.

"Well, look at what we have here. Don't you just look like a nice lil' ol' boy scout?" He studied the scene, taking in Gerald's hiding spot, and then scratches his chest in a slow back and forth motion while he thinks about this new development. He looks the boy straight in the eyes and very calmly says, "Bet you always tell the truth, don't ya?" Gerald just stares at the man, or more precisely at his gun, which he is casually balancing across his other arm. The gun dangles so lightly that he would've never thought he'd just killed a man with it moments before. But the crazy man's sweaty face, red-rimmed eyes and runny nose, tell another story, one that probably isn't going to end well.

"Well, don't ya boy?" asks the man, now getting a little agitated.

"Yes, sir," he answers, lowering his focus from the gun to his own tennis shoes.

"Yes sir, what?" sneers the man.

"I always tell the truth," Gerald barely chokes the answer out.

"Wrong answer my man." He pulls the gun around to point it directly at the boy's face. Gerald starts to cry, choking on his tears and squeezes his eyes tightly shut, anticipating the worst.

"Shut up… SHUT UP!" is the last he remembers hearing.

The gunshot should have ended his life instead it grazed the side of his head and knocked him sideways, causing him to crack his skull on the metal edge of the ice cream freezer. Gerald discovered later that as the crazy man pulled the trigger, the hooker pushed him, throwing him off balance, in an effort to save Gerald's life. The bullet only grazed his head, otherwise it would have gone directly into his brain. He always wanted to thank her, but she disappeared after that night.

******

When Gerald opens his eyes, he expects to see the gray, water stained walls of the liquor store, but instead he is surrounded by clean, pale yellow walls with sunlight streaking across them. He looks at the I.V. hooked into his arm and realizes he is in a hospital. Then his eyes fix on a TV screen hanging from the ceiling. He is fascinated by a show about the Russian chess master, Gary Kasparov, playing against an IBM computer. The sound is off, but he can't take his eyes off the action. As he watches the chess board a voice comes into his mind and says, "move the bishop to G3" and then Kasparov's hand moves towards his bishop. Gerald is playing the game in his mind exactly as Kasparov is playing it on the TV but one step ahead. His mother walks into the room, but he barely notices her because he is so engrossed with this new discovery. However, when she sees that her son is conscious, she runs to his bed and gathers him up in her arms crying, "Oh, oh, oh..., thank you God! Thank you Jesus! You woke up... you woke up!" Taking his face in her hands, she stares at him for a very long time and smiles through her tears. Finally, composing herself she asks, "Gerald honey, tell me you are OK. Talk to me," because up until that moment, she hadn't given him a chance to breathe, let alone talk.

He answers, "I'm fine, Mama." She starts to cry again when she hears his voice. "My head hurts but I'm fine." He wants to reassure her so she will stop crying. She takes a breath, smooths her hair, pulls herself together, and, in an effort to get things back to normal, says, "Can I bring you anything, baby?"

"Mama, can you bring me a chess set?"

Gerald's mother pauses, looks at him oddly, and says, "But you don't play chess."

"I know... but now I think I do play chess." He looks back at the TV screen, and the voices in his head continued to tell him every move Kasparov will make before he makes it.

******

That evening, a nurse comes into his room carrying a box. She pulls his bedside table around and proceeds to set up a chess set for him. When she lifts her gaze to meet his eyes she gives him the most dazzling and beautiful smile he's ever seen, and says in a soothing voice, "There you go little man." She helps him sit up in his bed so he can see the pieces on the chess board better.

"Thank you," says Gerald, who is now mesmerized by the game and its possibilities.

"It's a challenging game," the nurse says, "it's called the 'Game of Kings.' If you learn to play chess, with all of its complexities, you will have the key to any strategy you need to win in life!" She beams her enchanting smile, and even though her words are a little beyond his twelve-year-old mind, he knows he will remember everything she has said to him tonight, "You should look up Bobby Fischer and a chess match he played in 1956 when he was just about your age. It was called, 'The Game of the Century.' I think you will find his strategy inspiring—especially because early, on he lost his queen but still won the game." She smiled again, fluffed his pillow one more time, and said, "Do you know who you are?"

"Sure, Gerald Fowler."

She smiles sweetly, pats his arm in a gentle reassuring manner, and then she is gone.

A moment later, Gerald's mother enters the room carrying a plastic container. "Hi honey, I thought you might like something other than hospital food so I brought you some of my Mac 'n' Cheese."

"Thanks Mama!" Gerald grabs the container and a fork from his mother's hands and digs in hungrily. Nothing in the world better than his mother's Mac 'n' Cheese.

"Where did that come from?" His mother asks as she points to the chess set.

"You didn't get it for me?" Gerald asked.

"No."

"Did you tell the nurses I wanted one?"

"Honey, that was the furthest thing from my mind. I left, picked up your brother and sister, dropped them at home, and headed over here with your Mac 'n' Cheese."

"Ohhh...," now Gerald is very confused. "How did the nurse know to bring me a chess set?" he says softly to himself. He picks up the Black Queen and rolls the piece back and forth between his fingers while he thinks about that question.

"Well, I'm glad you got your game," says his mother as she bustled around the hospital room straightening things up.

"Yeah... It's the 'Game of Kings'," Gerald says.

CHAPTER ONE

THE SACRIFICIAL PAWN

The starless black night envelops the winter landscape of the rural Connecticut neighborhood, blotting out all the details except for a pair of headlights on a black sedan. It navigates through this community of the very rich, winding along roads piled high with freshly plowed snow.

As the sedan approaches a stone wall with an immense iron gate entrance to a long private driveway, the headlights go off, and it pulls to the shoulder of the road. Only two lamps, on either side of the iron gate, provide any light. A subtle, barely there "hummm" breaks the quiet of the countryside, it is the sound of electricity powering the security system's motion sensors. Four people emerge from the black car into the dimly lit scene, the last one is an immense man—double in size from the others. He is rolling a chess piece, the black queen, back and forth between his thumb and forefinger in a thoughtful manner. After a moment, he glances back at the car and tosses the chess piece onto the seat before he shuts the door. Each of the four men wears a fitted suit, with a hood and gloves. They are dressed in white from head to toe, which allows them to blend into the snowy landscape. Their night-vision goggles are embedded into the hoods of their outfits and obscure their faces.

The four approach undetected, and, with quiet agility, scale the gate and drop to the other side. The motion detector lights go off for a second, and the security guard in the office notices the glitch. He takes a moment to study the video but decides it's probably a rabbit triggering the system. Besides, it is too cold to go out and physically check the perimeter so he'll wait and see if it goes off again. He never notices the four people huddled in the snow just to the side of the entry gate.

Once they assume they are in the clear, the group runs at a low-to-the-ground trot, towards a large mansion in the distance. They stick to the shadowy corners of the snow to hide their footprints from the security cameras and have not uttered a single word between them—all communication is with hand signals and head nods as they move in unison. Once they reach the stone façade of the house, each person takes a position in front of either a door or a window. One of them attaches a small metal box with electrodes to the frame of a window. On top of the box, a computer screen comes alive and begins to rapidly scroll lines of code. The box taps into the private security system of the house. The computer displays the entire security setup along with the bypass codes, and the technician begins to tap and swipe the screen. Within seconds, he has disabled the system, but the cameras are still active so the guards are unaware that anything is wrong.

He raises his hand and does a three-finger countdown. On three, the window and doors unlatch, and each person enters the house without incident. Once inside, each taps a strap on their wrist, and their white suits turn to a reflective gray material, disguising them from the security cameras. The technician has brought the box into the house to scan for the heat signatures of the guards and one occupant. They wait as the guards make their rounds and then move up the wide curved staircase to the upper landing. From that point the group heads towards a bedroom at a far corner of the home.

******

Damien Marshall, Jr. (DJ to his friends and family) is asleep in his opulent bed, which is decked out with six hundred-thread count, Egyptian cotton sheets, and a silk comforter. He's dreaming that his body is rocking gently in a little sailboat on a lovely Tahitian sea. The rocking is becoming more violent, as if a storm is stirring up the waves. Somewhere in his dream, he realizes that the shaking of the boat is real. He wakes with a jerk as he feels hands grabbing his arms. DJ struggles to sit upright, but someone puts a hand over his mouth, and forces his head down on the pillow. He tries to focus on his attackers but can't see them, only the outlines of their bodies—there are four of them everything else is gray. DJ wants to scream but even if they did uncover his mouth, he is certain no sound would come out.

The intruders bind DJ's hands, tape his mouth, and throw a lightweight, reflective blanket over him to spirit him out of the building. When they reach the outside, they touch their wrists and their suits, as well as the reflective blanket, became all white. Walking confidently through the snow, they know the guard watching security monitor will never notice them leaving the grounds. Despite the tape on his mouth, DJ's teeth chatter from the cold, his socks are soaked from the snow, and his feet are starting to burn and go numb. They reach the iron gate, and two members of the group pull him up and over as if he were a sack of flour. A moment later, he is inside a warm car speeding away from his comfortable bed to who-knows-where.

The following morning DJ Marshall's secretary is unable to reach him by phone. When the security guard checks his bedroom, it is obvious that DJ has been abducted, but by that time, he is long gone.

12 months earlier...

The bright light of a computer screen fills an otherwise dark room and draws attention to a social media posting with a provocative headline about a new revolutionary movement taking over the financial districts of cities, such as New York, Chicago, Los Angeles, London, Paris, Frankfurt, and Beijing.

A nameless female blogger remarks, "Wow, things are really heating up out there! All these postings are about demonstrations in financial districts all over the world! It seems pretty organized... doesn't this worry you a little?" A disembodied man's voice answers from across the dark room, "The media always makes a bigger deal out of it than it really is. This is barely causing a ripple in the financial community. It's business as usual."

"I don't know..." the woman stops to consider the posts up on the screen and says, "there seems to be quite a bit of anger out there..."

"Maybe," the man interrupts, "but really, I wouldn't worry about it. There will always be angry people. Besides, our job is to observe not analyze."

******

Underground, in a hidden military bunker, an elaborate multi-screen live feed is watched by a gathering of people in uniforms. The same provocative headlines about demonstration, in the various financial districts flash across the monitors, along with commentary from several media "talking heads." On another screen, a high-security, overhead visual feed is delivered by either drone or satellite. One of the soldiers shouts, "OK—let's get to it! Time to train people! Out in the yard in five!"

******

"Where is my cell phone? Nobody ever knows anything—where is it? Hey! Do you know where my phone is? If I have lost it, it will ruin my whole day! My whole life is on that thing!"

"Try the bed."

"Right... Thanks..." I dive into the sheets patting every lump looking for it, "I have a crazy busy day ahead of me, and I just want to get out of here! Ah! Found it!" I hold my phone up triumphantly and then start scrolling through the messages I might have missed.

"Told you." DJ appears in the doorway of the bathroom. He does look good with his blond hair slicked back, those great abs and nothing but a bath towel. Mmmm—No! I can't get distracted. I have to get to work.

Thank goodness, saved by my phone, which is vibrating with an incoming call, not to mention I already have six missed calls. I turn away from the tempting sight of DJ to answer, "Christa McCaffrey."

It's Ellen, my staff assistant, and she is speaking so fast I can barely understand her. All I can make out is that the phone is ringing off the hook, people are being arrested, and there is a demonstration downtown.

"Ellen, slow down, please. Tell me how many people have called so far." She gives me the call log over the phone, and now I have the full picture. This is going to be a very busy day. "I have to make a stop on my way into the office but have the paperwork ready for me. I am going to dash in and head straight to the courthouse."

DJ is still standing in the bathroom doorway checking his messages, when he glances up from his phone and gives me a look that says, "You aren't paying attention to me..." and then breaks out that sexy smile. Any other morning I would totally jump back into that unmade bed, but today I need to remain strong. He's fixing his cool blue eyes on mine, "Babe, don't give it too much thought. I assume your office is going crazy with arrests from the march downtown." He turns his phone towards me so I can see a photo on the screen. "This is what sells the news. All that doom and gloom, fear mongering. The media is probably blowing it out of proportion. I bet there weren't more than fifty people there. Most people don't care enough to get out there and protest, much less vote."

I am considering his analysis and wondering what the number really is, so I look it up. "It's more like 50,000 people and they are making arrests," my phone is vibrating in my hand again, reminding me that I need to get moving.

I do a mental inventory; phone, briefcase, purse, shoes... am I forgetting anything? I look around the room and catch my reflection in the mirror above the dresser. I always feel odd seeing myself in all this opulence. DJ looks perfectly at home, but I feel like a fraud. My brown skin and curly hair look out of place to me, only my blonde streaks and the surprising dark blue color of my eyes, betray my white father's contribution. When I wake up in DJ's world, I feel like I am living my fake life and as soon as my phone rings, and I go back to work, I am living my real life.

My phone buzzes with another text update about the march downtown. "This entire protest feels a little more intense. Like a grassroots rebellion could be happening." I can't quite define this sense I have about these events it was almost like a voice was trying to tell me something, but I couldn't quite hear it. I shrug it off and turn to leave.

DJ is still standing at the door to the bathroom in his towel, so I comment, "Are you going to the board meeting like that? I'm sure you'll have everybody's rapt attention."

"Noooo…" DJ says, "I was thinking of going like this!" He dramatically drops his towel, and now totally naked nonchalantly leans against the doorway.

What a sly man, but I am going to keep my cool. "Fine. When you're arrested for indecent exposure, give me a call." I drop my business card on top of the crumpled towel. Now I can leave—we've had our fun.

"See you later?" DJ asks.

"I'm off to the Farmer's Market, then downtown to the courthouse. Maybe, are you asking me out?"

"Absolutely!" He beams that irresistible smile that I can never say "no" to.

"That sounds really nice, we haven't had much alone time lately—I will try to make it happen."

"Great! Mind if I dress casually?"

All I can do is give him a devilish smile—if I engage with that charming man any further I will end up back in bed and a lot of people might not get out of jail today. I leave the bedroom waving my hand over my head.

******

Walking out the front door, the sun hits my face, and I think that after six years on the East Coast it was good to come back to this beautiful California weather. DJ's garage looks like a new car lot and he always generously offers me whichever car I want, whenever I want it. This morning I am in a hurry so rather than call a ride, I grab the keys to a black Audi and take off.

As soon as I turn onto the canyon road my brain is on autopilot, taking each curve of the drive from memory. This is my moment to think. DJ in his bath towel still flashes into my mind, making me smile again, but I push it away. On the surface DJ is a dream man: gorgeous, smart, rich, and sweet. It all should feel right but... DJ is getting more serious, and I wonder if I fit in his world—could I do that life forever? Something is nagging at me when I am with him, and I feel like an ungrateful bitch because of it.

I need to focus on my driving as I come into downtown Santa Monica. I'm in a rush, so I head to my secret parking place that will get me in and out of the Farmer's Market quickly. I'll run in and grab some coffee, a salad, and something for the staff since we have a tough day ahead of us.

I step out of the car, the sunshine embraces me, and I think, "What a beautiful day!" This weather always makes it difficult for me to go to work. I don't really need to go to the Farmer's Market, it's just my way of procrastinating—I love to pretend that I have the time to cook a beautiful gourmet meal.

Walking down the alley, I notice the homeless people that are always there and think they are in odd contrast to the high-end stores and expensive cars that surround them. The police are everywhere as well. I've seen so much poverty and violence in my life but it seems to touch me a little less now that I am living in DJ's world. I don't know if that is a good thing.

I spend some time going from vendor to vendor sampling produce and chatting. I stop at my favorite tomato stand and behind the piles of succulent pink, red, and green tomatoes is a new face, a very attractive face. His stare is intense but he's not looking at me, he is deep in conversation with two other men.

Actually, all of them are pretty hot, and I think, "I should buy these tomatoes look at what they're doing for those guys!" My private joke makes me laugh.

The attractive "new face" is looking at me with the full force of his charm, and I feel a bit like a fly caught in a web. He's so pretty it's hard to look away. "Beautiful day isn't it." There it is—the smile.

"Yes, it's why I love living in California." I smile but stay cool.

"We have some delicious Japanese pink tomatoes to sample… would you like to try a slice?" He hands me the sample, and I take it without hesitation.

As I look at his attractive face, I can't chase away the feeling that there is something vaguely familiar about him. I slide the warm, sweet tomato slice into my mouth to savor the unique flavor and…

*****

Every time I breathe, I suck something into my nose and mouth, cutting off my breath. I am starting to regain consciousness and my heart is racing as I realize there is a hood over my head. I feel heavy, like my body is made of lead. I can almost see shapes if I try very hard to peer through the weave of the bag, but there is not enough light to make out anything clearly—I can't get my bearings. My stomach aches from the stress, I have no idea where I am, or what has happened to me.

The last thing I remember is the Farmer's Market and I was at the tomato stand. Now, it's freezing and I have a heavy, down comforter, wrapped around me. I sit up on a narrow metal bed, which squeaks with my every motion. Something is in the room with me so I hold my breath for just a few seconds, and then I hear it, breathing—someone is here with me.

The idea that I am alone with someone I can't see and don't know what they want from me should send me into a complete panic, but, instead I still feel calm. Maybe that's stupid, I don't know. Every muscle in my body is tense with readiness for whatever may happen next. I wait... and wait... for the person in the room to make their presence known.

Finally, I hear a slow scraping sound of a chair dragged along the floor, and footsteps walking towards me. I tried to peer through the weave of the bag, but I can only see pinholes of light. My breath bounces off the cloth, making it hot and sticky inside the hood. The footsteps are coming closer to me, and now they are so close that I can feel their body heat in the cold room.

"Are you Christa McCaffrey?" a man's voice asks. He smells like beer.

"Yes," I try to give my answer with as much force as I can muster under the circumstances.

"Good... good." He has a deep, soft voice.

Silence, I don't move a muscle because I have no idea what to expect next. He pulls the bag off my head, and I have to lower my eyes and blink furiously until I adjust to the light in the room. I hear the man walk back to his chair and sit down.

'Oh God!' I think as a slow throb starts to build behind my eyes. My head hurt like hell!

"I am sure you have quiet a headache coming on. It is a common side effect of what we gave you. I apologize, it was a necessary precaution... here," he hands me two aspirin with a glass of water. Even though they had drugged me before, I don't care and take the aspirin anyway. I am desperate to get rid of this pounding head. I need to be able to deal with what might come next.

I look around the room and see cinder block walls and very little furniture. That explains why the place is so cold. There were no windows either. I exhale and can almost see my breath hang in the air.

Finally, I focus on my keeper for the first time since he took the hood off. It is the attractive man from the Farmer's Market but he looks a lot less attractive to me now. I can't believe I fell for his smile and charm. Panic rises in my chest, but another part of me is ready to fight for my life if it comes to that. I'll be damned if they are going to sell me as a sex slave or worse. I would die first. I could try to buy his loyalty, but I need to wait and see what type of man he is. If he's a real psychopath, money will have no impact on him. DJ would pay very well to get me back. Maybe this guy already knows that. For the moment, I need to be quiet and let him do the talking.

Standing up, he starts to slowly pace the floor in a thoughtful manner, always looking back at me from time to time. "Christa, do you remember when you were in the foster care system and lived with the McCaffreys?"

What! Of all the opening questions he could ask, he wants to know about my foster care parents and my life as an orphan? I was certain this was about DJ, since he is the heir of one of the wealthiest fortunes in America. Now I am confused, but I answer him calmly, "Yes, I remember." The McCaffreys had trained and polished me with the intent that I would attend an Ivy League college, meet the right people, have the right career, and eventually have money and influence. They taught me to defend myself physically and mentally and to manage my fear in all situations. They were—in short my saviors.

"Why?" I ask.

"This will take some time to explain, but the McCaffreys trained you to be part of a revolution, specifically our revolution, the "Of the People" movement, or as the Feds know us—OTP. The McCaffreys believed the next revolution would put the country in the hands of the people who deserve it and who worked for it." He searched my face to see if I understood and agreed with him, "Is this some type of extreme, right wing militia group?" I ask. "Because I would have no idea what you would want with me—unless you need legal services." I am starting to feel a little bolder for some reason. I might stand a chance of walking away from this situation. This would not be the first tight spot I had talked my way out of; I had been in some tough situations in the past.

"Not at all, the 'Of the People' movement, or OTP, is made up of ordinary citizens from all races, religions, and economic backgrounds. We simply believe in true Democracy—maybe with a dash of socialism."

He flashes his first smile since removing the hood, and despite the circumstances, he is still very attractive. I feel like such an idiot for thinking that right now! Through it all, I still cannot shake this familiar feeling I have about him. I am very comfortable with him. Am I suffering from "Stockholm Syndrome" already?

"We are trying to restructure society to truly represent every citizen and provide a decent life for them. We won't be lied to, divided, or manipulated, as we have been in the past. But, we are not a revolt—we're a reclamation, taking our country back from the bankers, corporations and lobbyists… that's all."

He paused and held my eyes with his, probably a beat longer than he should have.

I could not believe what I was hearing, but strangely it all made sense. I flashed back to earlier that morning watching the demonstrations on my computer and the feeling I had that they were something more than they seemed.

The McCaffreys were wonderful people, with every one of the kids in our home cared for in a way that was highly uncommon in the foster care system. We had target practice, martial arts training, survival training, science, and basic building skills. We were encouraged to read every night and to discuss what we read at the dinner table. There was nothing we could not do. I never thought too much about it except that I was lucky to have that start in life.

"I'm sorry we took you the way that we did." His voice breaks into my flashback bringing me back into the cold room. "We weren't going to hurt you. We needed to get you alone, but we couldn't risk you being seen with any of us. So we took you from the Farmer's Market because there are no surveillance cameras in that area."

"Why couldn't I be seen with you?"

"Most of our members have dropped off the surveillance grid a long time ago so we could not be identified by facial recognition algorithms. We don't exist in the system—no record, no tracking. In your world, people like us trigger a lot of questions—especially since you are seeing Damien Marshall, Jr." He gave her a very steady stare with this last statement and then continued. "Essentially, because of your access to the Marshall family and others, we brought you here to recruit you. We need someone on the inside, and, whether you are aware of it or not, you were trained for this."

So there, it is… this is about DJ. None of this shocked me; ever since I started dating him, I wondered if something like this might happen. I sat quietly and took in all this new information. The McCaffreys had always said there would be another American revolution. They said the people would rise up and take back their government from a tiny group, the one percent, who were destroying everything with their greed. It was the reason I specialized in constitutional law and civil rights. Yes, I am dating a wealthy man, but his wealth has allowed me to grow my practice and help more people. DJ is of the same mind as I am about the responsibility the wealthy have to give back to society for the betterment of everybody—I couldn't have dated him otherwise. I looked at my captor's determined face, and something told me this would be a long cold encounter, but I knew I needed to be patient and hear this man out.

"Could you hand me my cell phone?" I ask.

"Why? I can't let you make a call—they could track you to this location."

"I understand that, but I suspect that what you need to tell me will take a long time, so if I call my boyfriend and tell him that I've been called into an emergency meeting at the office, he won't notice I haven't come home."

There was a very long silence, which I eventually broke. "Look, even if they do track me to this location, you could kill me long before they get here. You could have killed me by now. I understand that something made you desperate enough to grab me. Plus, you seem to know quite a bit about my early life, which tells me a lot of preparation went into taking me. In order to be able to hear you out and remain calm, I need this situation managed well. I know that taking me is probably not the brightest thing you've done, but now you have me, we should make the best of this situation. If DJ suspects that I was abducted, he will unleash a hailstorm of police and FBI on you. So, maybe we can avoid that and you can just hand me my phone?"

He stood there for a moment and then gave an exasperated sigh as he dug into his pocket and produced my phone and the sim card. When he gave it to me, I saw an almost imperceptible tremor in his hand and thought, "He's not as cool as he appears. He seems to have a conscience about what he's done."

I dialed DJ's number, steadying my mind so I could focus only on his voice and the lie I must tell. I didn't want him to detect even the slightest bit of nervousness and start to grill me. I might not hold up very well if he did.

I heard the ring and hoped it would go to voice mail but he picked up.

"Hey, Christa, I was just thinking about you. What time do you want to get together?" He sounded like he was on the golf course with his buddies and already had a couple of drinks. Good, he is relaxed.

"Aw, I am so sorry. I have an emergency deposition to prepare for and I'll have to finish tonight. I am staying late at the office. But I promise I will make it up to you this weekend."

"Shame, I thought it was a good idea. Well, the weekend works. What time do you think you'll be home?"

"I have no idea. It could be a late night; we don't have anything put together since this was sprung on us at the last minute. Don't wait up but I will check in with you later." The last part I added so that it was clear to my captor that I didn't intend to play this game indefinitely.

"OK... love you."

"Love you too."

I hung up and handed the phone back. "I'm all yours. Frankly, I am curious but can we start with some food, a drink and some names?"

"Oh, yeah, sure," he stumbled on his words, "I am Evan... Evan Cole, you know me better as 'Sparks'."

"Sparks?" Wow, the last time I saw him was as a kid in foster care at the McCaffrey home. I leaned back and took a better look at this gorgeous, athletic man with the wavy brown hair. Yes, there it is, just above his hazel eyes, a little scar over his left eyebrow from when I whacked him with a wooden sword over a decade ago. I felt my memory slide backward to a life I had not thought about in quite some time.

The McCaffrey's foster care home, 15 years ago...
Social Services has just dropped off a new boy at our foster home—he looked about the same age as me, eleven or twelve. He stood in the hallway staring at the floor and wouldn't lift his head. On that day all I saw was a shy, gawky boy, with long shaggy brown hair falling in his face. I felt something for him I knew I could trust my instincts, so I had through the group of kids that crowded around him to ask, "What's your name?"

"Sparks," he replied quietly.

"Sparks? Why Sparks?"

"It's where they found me... Sparks, Nevada.

"Oh" I said, "cool." He still hadn't looked me in the eye, so I got down on the floor, on my hands and knees, and twisted my head so I was looking up into that mop of hair he was hiding behind. Then I caught his eye, and we stared at each other for a minute before I saw a shy little smile creep across his lips. I was satisfied. "My work is done," I thought, I'd made contact.

After that, this boy Sparks, and I, were inseparable until the age of eighteen. He had been abandoned in Sparks, Nevada by his narcissistic mother. She ran off with a rich man, who didn't want his life complicated by a child, and never saw her son again. Sparks was always a brilliant science geek and a genius inventor. No foster care home could hold him if he didn't want to be held—until he landed at the McCaffrey's, then *he* decided to stay put. Once I went off to college, I never saw him again. He never made it into an Ivy as I did, he should have but was too dyslexic to pass the placement exams.

Present day in the bunker...

"Oh my God... it is you! Where have you been? Do you have any idea how much I missed you?" I jumped off the little bed and gave him a huge hug. It was a bit awkward to say the least, but I couldn't help myself. After all these years, here he is and I want to hear his story.

"Well, let's get some food, a bottle of wine, and let me hear your story. This should be good."

I could not stop grinning, because despite being abducted, drugged, and freezing cold I was so happy to see Sparks again.

*****

Phoebe Carlyle presses her ear to the door of the interrogation room. She had been Sparks' girlfriend most of last year, but almost from the moment they created the plan to abduct Christa McCaffrey, he began to pull away from her. Now, as she stands in the hall listening to their familiar laughter and chatter filter through the door, she sees the perfect opportunity to take care of the business which has brought her to the OTP compound in the first place. Perhaps she may even have an opportunity to pay back Sparks for dropping her as well.

For the last year, she has been developing the confidence of the OTP group to obtain access to the tech devices that Sparks had developed. He had created a cutting-edge weapon, but she didn't know what it was; he wouldn't talk to her about it. One night, after she had plied him with beers and tequila shots, he admitted he had created the perfect weapon for a bloodless war, and that is all she knows. If she can find this device, it will be worth a lot to the other side.

Phoebe thought back to when she had initially been attracted to Sparks, and the OTP, in a rebellious moment in her life. Once her father got wind of who she was hanging out with, though, he put the pressure on her to drop the relationship. She wouldn't, so her father asked one of his friends, a intelligence operative, to talk to her about how dangerous the OTP was. She still wasn't interested in abandoning the group because she thought she was in love with Sparks. Once his deeper feelings for Christa became evident, she contacted the operative in a moment of anger and jealousy and asked what she could do. He recruited her and trained her to be an informant. She was an adept pupil and a natural spy.

Phoebe's sole mission was to get into the tech lab and steal Sparks' inventions. Up until now, she had not known where the lab was. It was a well-guarded secret. If she hadn't been part of the team that abducted Christa she wouldn't even be in the underground bunker—they never gave her access. She knew this might be her only moment to take advantage of that.

She walks down the hall with purpose and confidence—appearing, for the sake of the security cameras, that nothing is out of place. Stopping in front of the lab door, she pulls out Sparks' key, which she lifted off him during Christa's abduction. At that moment, a fellow

OTP member, Sam, rounds the corner of the hallway and practically runs into her. Phoebe knows Sam finds her attractive so she stares him straight in the eyes and flashes a big smile to distract him.

"Hey Phoebe, I thought you'd be with Sparks doing the download with the new girl."

"Yes, well Sparks kinda has that all locked up. Three's a crowd you know...." She smiles even more broadly.

Sam is about to walk away when he notices the key in the door, "Phoebs, is that Sparks' lab key?"

Before he can get all worked up, Phoebe stops him by applying the full force of her feminine wiles. She moves closer to his face, holding his eyes with hers. "Please can we keep this quiet? I was hoping he'd be here alone so I could talk to him—you know, personal stuff—but he's still with that Christa chick. I didn't want to come off like a jealous bitch so please don't tell him I was here."

"I don't know, Phoebe. We are supposed to report anyone going into Sparks' lab..."

"I know, I know... *believe* me I know. I didn't go in the lab... I just stopped by. Sam, let's get out of here, please? We can hang outside and maybe take a walk in the woods? I have always wanted to know you better—we've been friends for a while but I really don't know anything about you."

Phoebe purrs the last few words in a quieter more seductive voice and watches as Sam starts to melt under the pressure. Grinning, she lightly touches his arm. She knows Sam would love to spend time alone with her, but what she needs is to get him out of this hallway and away from the security cameras.

"OK, I suppose that couldn't hurt. I'm still breaking a lot of rules but ... OK."

Sam smiles and follows Phoebe out of the bunker. Once alone in the woods, Phoebe whirls around and slices his throat. He falls on the soft forest ground surrounded by brilliant autumn leaves and quickly bleeds out.

"Oh Sam, bad timing," Phoebe says as she stands over his still body and begins kicking leaves on top of him. She has failed in her mission and knows she better get back to the compound before Sam's disappearance is noticed. She doubles back through the woods, just missing a group of OTP members doing their afternoon patrol of the perimeter. Phoebe has the perfect place in mind to hide out.

******

The cool air of the bunker brings me back to life. I am exhausted from the events of the last few hours. I lean my head against the wall, stare at the ceiling, and do a mental review of my situation.

It has been several hours, and Sparks and I have covered a lot of territory. From the OTP movement to give the government back to the people, to our childhood together in foster care, to catching up on what has gone on in the years in-between. I'm tired, but the conversation has energized me. To connect with Sparks again and regain such a private piece of my past has opened up a part of me that hasn't been accessible for a long time.

There is a soft knock on the door and I watch as Sparks goes to answer it—he talks to someone in the hallway and I hear him say, "Yes, I think we're ready."

A tall, stately gentleman with a powerful build enters the room. There is a quiet elegance about him as he studies me. He approaches me and holds out his hands, cupping mine in his and says, "Welcome Christa. Call me The Nomad, everyone does, I am the guide for this group. I'm certain this has all been overwhelming for you, but thank you for having an open mind."

The Nomad is not smiling as he speaks and his eyes intensely search my face as he delivers his next words. "I have one question to ask you at this time, and your answer is critical to where we are in the process. After this, we will meet again to start your training. What I want to know is, do you know who you are?"

What an odd question. I could have thought of a hundred other questions he might have asked but this is nonsensical. All I can think is, "Of course I know who I am you stupid fool!" When I look into his eyes though, I don't see stupidity or foolishness—I see wisdom and intelligence.

"Yes, I am Christa McCaffrey, law partner at Steven, Brunbach and Gar..."

"No, Christa, that is not what I'm asking," The Nomad broke in, "do you really know who you are?"

I stop—words escape me. I don't know what he is asking of me. I'm a girl who always has the right answer and likes to be one step ahead of everybody, and this is unnerving. I feel so frustrated that I stumble on my words, "I... I... I'm not sure what it is you're asking of me."

"That's fine, that is the answer I was looking for." He smiles for the first time. "We are not too late. Don't worry, you will know soon enough who you are. Just remember there is an army of higher consciousness out there." When he delivers that last bit of cryptic information, it fosters a thousand new questions in my mind, but a security alarm stops our conversation abruptly.

The Nomad and Sparks shoot anxious looks at each other and run out of the room together leaving me to wonder. A moment later, the door cracks open, and a striking red-headed girl sticks her head in the room.

"Mind if I join you? It's a little crazy in the hallway right now."

"No, I don't mind," I say, and think I can use the company because I really don't want to be alone.

She sits on the little bed next to me and leans back against the wall. She is very relaxed as she lets her arm dangle off to one side and says, "We might as well get comfortable; the whole compound is on lock down."

I think I hear something clink on the ground when she sits down, but before I can look and see what it is she gives me a very genuine smile and says, "Hi, I'm Phoebe by the way."

******

It seems a guard has gone missing. He's not reported in. This concerns The Nomad and Sparks because this guard was specifically assigned to the hall where the research lab is located. Sparks rushes to the lab make sure everything is in order, but when he gets to the door, he discovers his lab key is missing. Sparks knew the lab hadn't been entered—every entrance is recorded and he has an electronic alert if anyone opens the door after it's locked. Sparks decides to keep this information to himself because if his key has been stolen, there is a chance the thief will try to use it again. Either way, it won't hurt to keep it quiet for a little bit and see what happens.

After several hours of searching the compound for the missing guard, a militia soldier gives The Nomad a message that can only be heard between them. The Nomad looks like the weight of the world is on him when he holds up his hand and calls off the search. He retires to his office where he pulls the long, heavy drapes shut to create an air of privacy, containment, and shadowy calm while he sits and contemplates what has happened. Folding his hands into his lap, he assumes a meditative pose.

Sparks quietly enter The Nomad's private office, accompanied by the security director, Big G. G's first name was Gerald, but nobody has called him that after the age of 12, when he grew to be the 6 feet, 4 inches tall, and 250 pounds. He was often referred to as a "mountain masquerading as an African American man." G looks as if he'd been a formidable force on the football field at some point in his life, but this threatening impression is diffused by his little shadow of a dog, Gypsy. She is a many-colored Australian shepherd with one crazy blue eye that seems to only watch Big G. She follows him everywhere, hanging on his every word, always at the ready. Big G rescued her from the front porch of an abandoned house near a freeway in South Central LA. The dog had a broken leg, several deep gashes, and was starving. It was obvious she'd been thrown from a car and left to die, but, somehow she had managed to survive and find her way down to that porch. G decided she deserved a second chance and ever since he took her in, the two have been inseparable.

"We can't wait any longer." The Nomad interjects this midway into a conversation that he's been having with only himself up until this moment. Sparks and Big G know exactly what he means. "As both of you must know, we found Sam's body in the woods. We haven't determined who killed him, but it was murder—his throat was cut. Whoever this intruder is, they may still be here, or worse be a spy in our group, so be vigilant—this is too close."

The Nomad lets his words sink in and says, "If they have figured out our communication system that will have set us back years! I'm not certain they haven't. We need to begin the next phase. I've spoken to the Council, and they are in agreement. They have seen incidents similar to what happened here in other camps. It's time…" his voice trails off in thought.

Sparks listens but says nothing—Sparks knows not to interrupt The Nomad because he often receives guidance telepathically. It is something all of the Council members can do with each other.

It's what holds the opposition together and keeps them off the radar of the government and local law enforcement.

New York City, 1986

A "G'd" out man in a baggy jeans, bomber jacket, and a knit watch cap is trying to cross a busy street in Harlem against the stoplight. Cab drivers are screaming at him and flipping him off, but he just keeps walking, oblivious to the drama. He's carrying a guitar case, and his hand insistently twists the handle, over and over. His eyes are red because he's strung out and focused on getting to a pawnshop, where he plans to trade his only guitar for enough money to get a fix for the night. Once he sells it, he will let go of any hope of regaining his music career. He'll just be another junkie on the streets of Harlem. While he's crossing the lanes of traffic, a cabbie decides to get smart and zoom around the car stopped in front of him. There is no time—the junkie is standing directly in front of the cab and is hit head on. He is flung like a rag doll in one direction and his guitar flies in the opposite direction, to land smashed into a million pieces. A crowd gathers around his unconscious body, which lies in the middle of Amsterdam Avenue.

Darkness and confusion—the man can hear the crowd, but the sound feels miles away. There are only two voices he can hear clearly, his and a voice he doesn't recognize.

"Ah man, please don't le' me live through that! Please God—I can't take no more." The junkie's voice cracks with the pressure and pain of his existence.

"You don't have to suffer—you can move on, if you want to," says the stranger's voice.

"I can...what's the catch? No, no—jus' le' me go. This life has kicked my ass since the day I come into it! I'm out."

"I know you are weak and tired and feel like you can't go on, but giving up before your time isn't always a good thing—you might have to come back and do it all again."

The junkie interrupts, "I can't... I can't do this life again! Send me back then. I'll go..."

"Wait... hear me out," says the stranger's voice. "If you let me have your body to complete the work I need to do, your debt is paid. You won't have to come back to do this over again. All you have to do is agree to let me walk into your body right now. You move on."

"Yes, yes! I agree," says the junkie.

In that moment his broken body opened its eyes, but it was the spirit of The Nomad that peered out instead of the strung-out drug addict who had moved on.

A voice from the crowd says, "Aw, man, it's a miracle you're alive! Just hang in there bro, an ambulance is working its way here right now. Hang in there."

As The Nomad drifts back into unconsciousness, he whispers to himself, "No worries, I'm not going anywhere." Several hours later, he comes to in a hospital bed. A young nurse attends to his IV.

"Oh, you are awake. Well, aren't you the lucky man today!"

Her smile lights up the room, and her eyes are so clear she practically glows. She reaches out and touches the top of his arm where the IV tube is; the gentleness of her touch erases any pain he feels.

"It looks like you will be here to celebrate another year," she says with a little laugh in her voice. "Promise me a glass of champagne on New Years?" Her face lights up again with her brilliant smile, and then she is gone from the room.

The Nomad closes his eyes and starts to drift off to sleep when he hears them for the first time. He had been waiting—he knew they were out there. The other walk-in souls like him. Now they crowd into his head, chattering, and, through their words, his purpose becomes clear. New Year's Eve they will begin the plan. He thinks about the nurse with the brilliant smile and longs to feel that healing touch again when another nurse comes into the room to check his chart.

"Where is the nurse that was here a few minutes ago?" he asks. "I want to thank her for being there when I first came to."

"There is no other nurse on duty," she says dismissively. "We're short staffed tonight, so I'm it until midnight. I don't know who you saw—maybe you were still out and imagined her? It's not uncommon."

Confused The Nomad falls back on his pillow.

"Now that you are awake, can you tell me your name?" the nurse asks.

"No, I don't remember," he lies. He wants a fresh start as a "John Doe." "Call me The Nomad because I'm a wanderin' soul," and he smiles at the idea of it.

The nurse laughs, "Well you must be feeling better because you've got your sense of humor back." Picking up his chart and reading the top page, she comments, "I will say this, you are healing remarkably well considering the severity of your injuries. You'll probably be able to party with the best of them on New Year's Eve." She laughs again.

Several weeks later The Nomad, now on the mend after his car accident, enters a bar to have a beer and celebrate a new year and a new beginning. As he takes a sip of his drink, a voice behind him says, "Don't forget to order me a glass of champagne." He turns and sees the nurse with the radiant smile standing there. He can feel her thoughts in his mind saying, "The Council sent me; I am your guide to help you set up your group." Then, aloud, she says, "Do you know who you are?"

The Nomad says, "ISHI. I am ISHI."

She smiles and adds, "You are also part of an army of higher consciousness." Then the two of them toast the New Year. They sit in a corner booth of the bar until closing, planning and talking about the impending reclamation.

******

Present Day...

The sunlight has begun to fade, but The Nomad has allowed the office to grow darker without turning on a light. He is deep in thought and neither Big G nor Sparks wants to disturb him.

The Nomad's voice finally breaks the quiet of the room. "This breach was fairly brazen, which tells me the opposition is feeling confident. This is no longer about fighting under the radar—this is war, out in the open. There have been peaceful protests, but it won't stay that way. Our local police, backed by private finance, are stockpiling military grade weapons. They are more an army, rather than a public police force, and they are training for a war against their own people—not peaceful resolution. It is time to make a move."

The Nomad turns to Big G looking for the type of input that could only come from him. G has been misjudged all his life. Every time he opens his mouth, people expect a man of his color and size not to have an exceptional mind. Only The Nomad appreciates G's strategic brilliance. He has spent years studying philosophy, military history, and playing chess in Central Park with some of the best—including a secret game with the illusive master, Bobby Fischer. His way of looking at the world is always several moves ahead.

Now he assures The Nomad, "All the members have been prepped for their parts in the takeover." He has always liked to throw a little American history in with his plans to bolster the validity of his ideas, "You know the first American Revolutionaries claimed they won with only three percent of the population actively fighting. We've got far more than that." G seems satisfied with this fact, and he reminds everyone of the old saying that those who don't study history are doomed to repeat it. He is confident he would not make that mistake.

The Nomad digests all of this information and says, "Lets not get over-confident. Our opponent is a well-financed many-headed hydra and completely without ethics. For now, keep the training going, and keep your eyes open. We might have more spies—someone may have been coerced within the compound."

Sparks has been quiet through most of this conversation because all he can think of is his missing lab key. He may have lost it, but he feels certain that is not the case. He still hopes that by remaining silent he will flush the spy out because he suspects what was in his lab is the target, not him. The spy didn't succeed this time so he is certain they will try again if they think the lost key has gone undiscovered. After all, they have killed a man to try to get what they wanted. They won't give up easily. Sparks will be ready for them the next time. He speaks up, adding to The Nomad's speculation, "If that's true, we need to get Christa out of here immediately! If she's spotted by the spy, it could put her life in jeopardy."

"Yes, of course, I've already considered that. We can train her later when things are safe again. For now let's send her back to get intel on the security and location of Damien Marshall, Sr. That shouldn't be too difficult since she's dating his son. Get her home safely, and let's start digging."

******

I slip the key into the front door of DJ's house, and as I turn it in the lock and hear the familiar "click" as it opens, I remember when he presented that key to me. We were at dinner and he pulled out a jewelry box. Of course I thought he was going to propose, and I panicked and readied my "no" answer because it wasn't the right time in my life to become anybody's wife.

At that moment he had caught the look on my face and had started laughing. "Don't worry babe, it's not what you're thinking."

I remember a feeling of relief had swept over me when I flipped open the lid, and there was a gold-plated key with my initials, CM, engraved at the top.

DJ had said, "I want you in my life all the time, so here is the key to my house. If we ever do get married you can still use it because the initials will be the same." He had added the last part with a teasing glint in his eyes.

I'd thought for a minute and had countered with, "True, but who said I would change my name if I got married?" We both laughed. I'd kissed him and said, "Thank you, I love it!" It had been one of many good moments with DJ.

As soon as I walk through the front door, I have this feeling as if my head is too full, my body is exhausted, and I don't know if I feel safe or stressed. I throw my keys onto the front hall tray, and the sound seems even louder than it should because it is late, and the house is very quiet. Before I came home, Sparks prepped me for hours, but now all I can think about is a hot shower and the comfort of my own bed.

"Christa?"

I look up a little startled because DJ is coming down the stairs—I really hoped he would be asleep. Arghhh...I am so tired and I don't know if I can keep up a good front right now, but I will have to. I have rehearsed my story in my head and am ready for the Q & A. I need to appear as if I've just had a late night at the office.

"Hey you... what are you doing up? I hope you weren't waiting for me. I told you I was going to be late."

"No, no... I just couldn't sleep. I knew you weren't here, and for some reason I just kept waking up."

"Aww, that's so sweet... but I'm sorry you couldn't sleep." Give him a kiss, I think, and I lean forward and place a quick peck on his cheek as I pass him going up the stairs. "All I want to do right now is take a hot shower and crawl into bed."

I look at DJ's face to see if there is any hint that he might know I wasn't at the office, but I don't see a thing. "I'm sorry you couldn't sleep," I add.

"No worries, you're here now," and he grabs my hand to walk upstairs with me.

Even in my exhaustion, I think no time like the present to get a jump on my information-gathering, so I ask him how the board meeting went.

He shakes his head and reviews the meeting in his mind before answering, "It was strange. My father and his Chief of Security, Kimball, were very wound up. They wouldn't say why, but they demanded a lot of new security measures for both our corporate offices and our personal residences. My father was so paranoid that he said until all the new measures were in place he was taking Kimball and a small security staff and flying to our compound in the Bahamas. I really don't know what got into him... maybe he is starting to lose it from old age or something."

I feel a wave roll across my mind. This probably isn't a coincidence that DJ's father is suddenly paranoid about security just as the OTP compound has been breached by a potential spy. Somehow the two fit together; I just don't know how. I hope and pray that whoever that spy is has no idea I was there. His father has always been kind to me, but I have never given him a reason to be anything else. Kimball creeps me out, he is ex Special Forces, loyal to the bone, and has the dead eyes of a killer. Whenever he is in the room, I want to leave, he makes me very uncomfortable.

"Well, your father is entitled to some paranoia at his age—don't you think? What did your brother think of this plan?" I say this as I am undressing and heading to the shower. The distraction works easily on DJ.

"Oddly, Henry wasn't at the meeting, and that is very unlike him. I suppose you are right... Damn it, you're always right... about so many things." He smiles and follows me into the shower.

*****

It has been a few days since they found Sam's body, but there has been no connection to Phoebe. Sure, she was seen speaking to him on the security footage, but it did not show her leaving the building with him or anything else. Immediately after Sam's murder, she was seen in the holding room with Christa—on the pretense of protecting her. The genius move Phoebe made was leaving Sparks' lab key on the floor of Christa's room. There are no security cameras in there, so Sparks thinks the key fell out of his pocket while debriefing Christa. If he has any idea Phoebe was the one who took his key and killed Sam, he certainly isn't letting on. Phoebe feels her cover isn't blown yet.

She paces the hallway outside Sparks' lab. He is in there, and she wants him to invite her in, but she needs a plan—which she finally has. This is her last ditch effort to get one-on-one with him. She knocks on the lab door and waves through the glass window, so Sparks can see her. He is so engrossed in his work she has to do this a couple of times. Finally, he notices her and comes to the door.

"Hey, what's up?" Sparks says—not quite inviting her in.

Phoebe curbs her usual flirtatiousness because she knows it won't work on him. Only ideas and straight talk get his attention. "I had an idea about the communication system. Of course, I don't know all the details of it, but I thought this might work. Can I run it past you?"

"Oh, yeah... sure," Sparks stands back and opens the door wider for Phoebe to enter.

She glances around quickly as she walks in ahead of him. She tries to assess what is on his worktable without arousing attention.

"So," he says, "let's hear it... your idea." Sparks stands with his arms crossed ready to assess Phoebe in more ways than she knows. His guard is up, but, so far, he is on the fence about her. Initially he was physically attracted to her—who wouldn't be? She is an obvious beauty, fiery red hair, crystal blue eyes, and creamy white skin, with light freckles that add an air of innocence to her looks. To top it off, she has the lithe body of a dancer. The sex was always great with Phoebe, and that's when she is really dangerous—in bed. She looks delicate, but looks are deceiving. After they got past the physical attraction, her brain became the turn-on for him. To Sparks, her capacity to understand his work is her most seductive trait. However, not long into dating, the screws started to come loose. She is high-strung, with a hidden mean streak that didn't show until their first argument. Now, all Sparks sees standing before him is a crazy woman, desperate to get his attention and he doesn't trust her.

Phoebe gives Sparks direct eye contact as she begins to explain her idea. At the same time, she sizes up her options for making off with the information she needs.

"Well, you know the OTP camp in Nashville?" She begins to weave her little story. "They have a group of musicians that have begun posting music videos, and they are getting a pretty big following. They are message songs—the stuff people want to hear right now."

Sparks listens, nodding and wondering when she will get to the point, while Phoebe secretly strategizes how quickly she can lung forward, slit his throat, and clean out the lab of as much material as she can grab. "Well," she continues, with a sweet but methodical tone to her voice, "I thought we could work with them to embed a coded message in their music. What do you think?"

Sparks considers this idea—turning it over from every angle: development, implementation, ramifications, and options. Phoebe continues her surveillance of the lab, looking for duct tape, packing tape, rope, or anything to constrain Sparks. She also looks for a container to carry the files out of the lab—maybe a trash can?

"That has possibilities," muses Sparks, "I'm working on this new analog approach—well, not that analog is new, but this might work with that."

"Wow, that sounds amazing!" Phoebe moves around Sparks' workbench until she is standing next to him. At the same time, she is memorizing the contents of the table and trying to understand this new analog thing he is building. "Can you tell me how it would work with the music?" She hopes he will give her just a tiny bit more information and she might really have some valuable intelligence for her handler to pass on.

"At the moment we are targeting Marshall Industries…"

Phoebe immediately makes the connection between Marshall Industries and Christa McCaffrey—Christa is dating Damien Marshall, Jr., the eldest son of Damien Marshall, Sr. Now Sparks is worth much more to her alive. She wants more and starts to move closer to him when there is a very loud knock on the door to the lab. Phoebe and Sparks look up at the window, Big G is waving to them. Sparks moves quickly to let him in while Phoebe slides away from the worktable. She isn't about to mess with Big G. Sparks alone would be easy to take out but Big G makes it more difficult if not impossible. At least she has some good information to pass on.

"Hey Big G," she tosses off the greeting with an easy smile.

Big G doesn't acknowledge Phoebe. He doesn't like the girl; he has never liked the girl, and doesn't get what Sparks sees in her… except for the obvious. He thinks she is a phony and has never truly left her spoiled-brat, rich-girl roots behind. Since she offers him nothing in the way of business, or anything else, he just doesn't waste his time with her.

"What's Phoebe doin' in the lab?" Big G practically spits the words out.

"Actually, Phoebe had a great idea…" Sparks defends his decision to let her in.

Phoebe takes that as her cue to leave, "I just thought Sparks could do something with an idea I had, that's all. I'll let him explain it. I'm sure you guys are busy anyway." With that she moves to the door.

"Bye, Sparks."

She didn't even bother with a good-bye for Big G who already has his back to her. She glances through the lab window and can tell, just from his body language, that Big G is clearly unhappy that Sparks let her in the lab without security present. She knows she'll never get another opportunity like this again.

CHAPTER TWO

MIDDLEGAME

Ilean into the bathroom mirror to remove my mascara and stop short at the sight of my face. I see two of me, the mask of make-up I've put on every morning since returning from the compound and the other face hidden beneath the social smile who is a spy for OTP.

I can't believe all the secrets I am keeping on behalf of the movement. To say that my whole life has been turned upside down would be an understatement. I know when I look in the mirror I don't see all of me. Something is hidden—some part of my memory which I can't tap into. I think about what The Nomad asked me, "Do I know who I am?" I am still uncertain what he meant, but I'm aware I need to find the answer.

The Nomad had explained the uprising to me—just as my foster parents had when I was a kid. At the time, it felt more fanatical—all the talk about the disappearance of the middle class, the criminal bankers who went unprosecuted, and the destruction of the environment. Now, when The Nomad speaks about these things they have all come true. I've been living my lavish life with some guilt since I know many people who are failing through no fault of their own. It was obvious that society is failing them, failing to care for its own.

Here I am—nobody to confide in or to trust with my secrets. Certainly not DJ—he may be part of the problem. The secrecy has definitely begun to take a toll on my relationship with him. I am certain he thinks I'm having an affair. I try to assure him that my work has been the problem, but I don't know if he's buying it.

I admit that the more strings I discover that DJ's father pulls, the more distant I feel from him. I know that's ridiculous because I haven't found a shred of evidence connecting DJ to any of the company's unethical behavior. DJ's brother, Henry Marshall, is another case entirely. He has his fingers in many pots, and if it will make more money, he doesn't care what the long-term consequences might be. Fracking—sure, who cares that small earthquakes happen, or that, the ground water becomes contaminated? How about the "little" wars they finance, to boost their corporate interests in other nations? Protecting his banker allies is what is important to Henry. After all, most of them are his Ivy League frat brothers—a group of powerful, privileged men ruining the lives of millions. How much blood is on Henry's hands?

I have to stop turning this over in my head, it makes me feel sick to my stomach. It's too much to take in. I am relieved that DJ doesn't appear to be part of that inner circle of decision makers, but that does cause me to wonder if maybe, just maybe, I could trust him with all my secrets. Maybe I could even recruit him. I wonder if he'd support a movement that would unseat his family's power and money. Or, maybe I am just a controlling bitch, trying to keep him with me at any cost. Hmmm....

A hot bath should wash away my anxiety and relax my muscles. I have a party to attend tonight with the entire Marshall family and I need to be ready to face them. I slide into the hot water and my senses begin to dull. As I relax, the buzz of my phone interrupts my moment alone. I really don't want to answer it, but, whoever it is, they are being very insistent. I try to ignore the buzzing, but they won't go away. Finally, I can't stand it anymore, so I reach over and check the phone to see who it is. A photo of ruby slippers, like the ones that Judy Garland wore in the movie, "The Wizard of Oz," along with the text, "Dorothy's come home :-)" is on the screen.

"Ahhhh!!!!!" I can't jump out of the tub fast enough—I throw on a robe and race downstairs trying not to slip and break my neck on the way. I pull open the front door to find Gary Indiana Goodwin (yes that's his name, his parents had a love of Broadway musicals and a sense of humor). Gary, the most talented, brilliant, and utterly fabulous queen a girl could have for a friend! Modeling the ruby slippers coquettishly for me, in jeans, he finishes the whole look with a t-shirt inscribed with the words, "Welcome to Gary Indiana" across the front of it.

"The irony of that shirt is not lost on me," I say with a sarcastic tone. Indiana had made it legal to discriminate against LGBT people at one time.

"Oh, honey, I knew you would get it! Your wickedly sharp mind never misses a thing! Speaking of that, what do you think of the shoes? Retro chic, are they not?"

With that, he sweeps past me into the house. Whenever Gary shows up, it's like a cat that has been lost for months and presumed dead. Suddenly he appears at your door, purring away as if he never left. Gary makes himself at home by heading into the kitchen, grabbing the first bottle of wine he finds and pulling open every drawer until he finds the corkscrew. Gary is never deterred from getting what he wants—and right now he wants to share a bottle of wine with me. He is ready to chat—or as he would say "dish." Either way it will be a big, gossipy, catch-up conversation.

How am I ever going to get through a bottle with my old friend and hide all my secrets from him? I know I am going to confide in him. I need to talk to someone, and Gary has held my confidences for years. We went to law school together at Harvard and back then he wasn't out of the closet because his conservative family was footing the bill for his education. He was their only son and the "heir to the throne." Gary loves to say, "A queen can rule just as well as a king." When he finally came out, he had just graduated, and his father cut him off financially. This actually set Gary free; he decided to make a U-turn in life and enrolled in culinary school. Once he became a chef, his bluestocking roots and Ivy League education opened doors to some of the most prestigious homes in America where he was sought after for not only his culinary skills but also his ability to plan and organize any event effortlessly. This drove his father crazy because he was often attending events for which his son was the celebrity caterer.

"Your timing is perfect!" I tell Gary.

"Of course... that's what my last boyfriend said," he adds with a sly smile. Looking at my robe, "Nice outfit... get out much?" He catches the look in my eye and says, "Wait a minute... you *really are* happy to see me, aren't you? What is going on here?"

I don't know how he does it, but he can always read my emotions like a book—nobody else can, not even DJ.

"So much is going on, I don't even know how to summarize it all or where to begin."

"Then steer me to the stove, and we'll cook and talk. That's always the best way to tackle a difficult conversation. Don't you think?"

He already has his hand on my shoulder walking me towards the kitchen. He isn't taking "no" for an answer.

"Can't, I have this gala to go to tonight. A party for DJ's father, so it's a command performance for the family. I would much rather hang with you, stay in my comfy robe and sip wine all night." I smile because I have never felt so appreciative of my friend as I did in this moment.

"Fine! I get it doll—you don't need to ask twice, I will be happy to go with you!" Gary gives me a devilish grin.

"I don't remember asking you, but, now that you suggest it, that is a brilliant idea! DJ will be busy with the family and their business associates, and you can keep me from being bored to death! You will have to lose the ruby slippers and the Gary Indiana shirt though."

"No problem. I am like a Girl Scout, always prepared. I brought the perfect suit, just enough sparkle to get the tongues wagging." Gary is loving this, he is ready to rattle a few cages. "But first, a girl's gotta eat. Let me whip up a little frittata, and we'll finish this bottle." Gary had already starting pulling out the iron pan and the eggs.

As he whisks the eggs, sautées vegetables, and throws together a salad, we drink and I unload the entire story about The Nomad, finding Sparks, the militia, and what they want me to do. By the end of the conversation, I have turned him into an enthusiastic recruit for the OTP movement. It feels so good to finally have at least one ally in my world.

******

Gary and I enter the ballroom, and we are greeted by a thousand sparkling white lights, wrapped around beautiful orange topiary trees. The tablecloths fabric, which is not white and not gray, seems to change colors as we move around the room. The 1930s Art Deco Italian marble floor has a subtle sheen to it that is the result of hundreds of hours of dancing. It is a graceful and elegant setting with its floor-to-ceiling French doors that open onto the balcony to reveal a sweeping view of the lights of Los Angeles. The musicians play a wide of array of popular, classical, and jazz tunes, keeping the crowd happy and relaxed. Circulating among the guests is the catering staff who all look like extras from a movie—some of whom might actually be. Of course, there is the requisite famous actor or actress to keep the luster high.

I look at Gary and have to smile at his deep, eggplant-purple tuxedo and pink shirt. It was pure Gary, elegant with a twist. He drew any attention away from me, as a sea of well-coifed, blonde heads in black dresses turned to check him out. I spot DJ across the room standing in a circle with his brother Henry, his father Damien Marshall, Sr., and some business associates I don't recognize. Kimball, The Marshall Corporation's pit bull Chief of Security, stands guard to the side of the group. Dragging Gary across the room, I walk up and kiss DJ "hello." The group is sizing Gary up when Henry Marshall says, "Gary, it's been awhile, but I see you haven't lost any of your very unique style over the years."

Gary looks Henry up and down, purses his lips together, sucks in his breath dramatically, and says, "And I see you haven't gained any over the years." They attended law school together so he can get away with chiding him because Gary graduated top of his class while Henry had a significantly lower placement. You just don't mess with Gary—he's too sharp.

I punch Gary in the shoulder and whisper under my breath, "Behave!"

"That was me behaving." Gary says.

I sigh—there is no controlling him.

The men in the circle take up their business conversation again and I am already bored. I look back, and Gary has drifted away from the group, for which I can't blame him. There have to be more interesting people to talk to or he could be in the kitchen checking out the competition.

Henry decides to focus on me, "You're looking well, Christa. I see you're finding time to workout."

He looks me up and down as if I am a prized cow. The thing I find intolerable about Henry is what an entitled pig he is. Rumors continue to circulate that in college, he was abusive to more than one girl, but nothing was ever proven. Still he reeks of misogyny. DJ is shifting his hands in and out of his coat pockets because he doesn't know what to do with himself. His role at Marshall Industries is marketing, and if they aren't talking about branding, advertising, or social media, he is out the loop conversationally.

I don't recognize the other two men that Henry and his father are so intently focused upon, but they look either financial or judicial. They are discussing the ethics of quashing a peaceful protest with force. Isn't that an affront to the Constitution? Of course I think it is, but I keep my mouth shut because I learn more when I don't engage. "Know your enemy," I always say. They debate the "protection of the people" as if the majority of Americans are children that can't take care of themselves. The conversation morphs into an indictment of modern journalism and it's lack of objectivity. One of the men cites the recent media coverage of a peaceful protest and the backlash it created with the public, as an example. He says the lopsided press coverage needs to be "managed" because it can cause enormous financial damage for their businesses. I feel like a fly on the wall—they don't seem to care, or remember, that I defend the wrongly incarcerated and welfare mothers of the world, pro bono.

I look away from the circle of men to find Gary deep in conversation with a stunning young woman. Leave it to him to find the most beautiful girl in the room and befriend her. He probably knows every detail about the gorgeous designer dress she is wearing. I decide to join them—I'm sure it is a much more entertaining conversation.

As I walked up, Gary says, "Christa! I am so happy you ditched the old guard for us!"

The young woman turns to meet me, and beaming a beautiful smile says, "Hi, I'm Phoebe Carlyle."

I am stunned—yes, this is definitely the same girl with the unmistakable red hair and brilliant blue eyes that I'd met in the interrogation room on my first day at the compound.

"Why is she here?" I wonder, "Is Sparks here too?" I control my emotions on the surface, but I still can't rid myself of the idea that she is so close to my world, and that makes me nervous. Phoebe flawlessly feigns meeting me for the first time; nobody would have guessed we had ever met before—not even Gary.

"Gary has been telling me some great stories about the two of you in college. You have had some adventures! I wouldn't mind an adventure or two; life needs to be spiced up from time to time." With that statement, she flashes a smile in Gary's direction.

"Gary," I say through clenched teeth and smiling my best phony party smile, "shame on you... you've been sharing our secrets!" God only knows what he told her, but this is not the woman to loosen his tongue with. Especially considering all the secrets I divulged to him earlier that evening. I did tell Gary about the woman that visited me in the interrogation room. But I didn't go into detail with him, so at this moment he has no idea that Phoebe Carlyle is a member of OTP, and I want to keep it that way.

"Don't worry hon, I didn't tell her *all* of our secrets." He gives me a knowing glance and a big laugh.

Phoebe and I start to laugh with Gary, but I look at Phoebe, and just for a second I see something in her eyes. It is a cold, hard, calculated look—the look of a psychopath. I've seen it plenty of times on the faces of incarcerated women I work with at the prison. It's her calculated charm, coupled with the ease with which she tells her lies, which causes me to suspect Phoebe might be the spy at the compound. It all makes sense. I don't have any hard proof, but I can feel it in my gut. Still, why is she at this party? It is a long way from the OTP compound.

"Phoebe, how did you wind up at this oh-so-exciting soirée?" I asked.

"Oh, my father, he drags me to all these things. I guess he's hoping to marry me off to some successful hedge fund director." she adds with a laugh. "He's the man standing to the right of DJ, Owen Carlyle."

"He's an investment banker, isn't he?" I ask.

"Among other things." Phoebe looks me straight in the eyes with that answer. "Damien Marshall, Sr. and my father go back years. They are in bed together on so many deals I am surprised their wives can find room in there at night!" She laughs, and Gary joins her.

"I have heard his name but I am surprised you and I have never met until now."

I want to see where Phoebe would go with this lie.

"Yes, well, I've been off the radar due to a relationship I was in. He was a sexy, tech geek who didn't like to socialize. But I'm here now," she says, "his loss, your gain!" She raises her champagne glass in a toast.

"Well, I am happy you are here. You saved me from going to the kitchen and talking shop with the chef!" Giving Phoebe an air kiss, Gary adds, "Maybe we should blow this party and go to the Formosa Club for some colorful drinks with little umbrellas!"

"Oh, God, yes!" says Phoebe.

Both of them turn and look at me, hoping I won't throw cold water on their plan. "That sounds like a perfect idea. Let me see if DJ will release me from my social duties. Just give me a minute."

I really don't need permission to leave the party—I just need a moment to decide if I really want to be alone with Phoebe. I don't think she is dangerous, just manipulative... I'm not even positive she is a spy. Maybe a little more time alone with her will help me decide.

I walk up to the circle of men around Damien Marshall, Sr. and hear Phoebe's father say, "...choking off the funds to develop weapons."

Damien Marshall, Sr. says, "Yes, that works too," then he glances in my direction and says, "Owen, lets talk about this later."

Turning towards me he launches into his usual plea, "Christa, are you ready to give up being a bleeding heart and come work fewer hours for more money?"

DJ's father has been trying to get me to work as their in-house counsel almost from the moment I started dating his son.

"Well, you never know… I may be softening my stance on that idea." I give him a charming we-shall-see look and ask, "May I borrow DJ for a moment?" Without waiting for an answer, I hook my arm through DJ's and guide him away from the circle of men.

When I turn my back on the group a chill runs up my spine, so I look over my shoulder and catch Kimball watching us. That man has the eyes of a shark, no emotion. It is impossible to read him. I turn back to DJ, "Would you mind if I slipped away from the party? Gary and I want to head over to the Formosa Club. I'll stay if you feel like I am abandoning you." I lightly run my hand up and down the sleeve of his tux in a reassuring manner. I always feel I need to show DJ that he matters most to me.

"No, No. Go… if I could go with you guys I would. But, I would be missed; you will be missed less. If I can get away early, I'll text you, and maybe we can meet up later?"

"That would be nice, but I know how your father is so I won't hold my breath." I kiss him, sweep a piece of blonde hair out of his face, and I leave.

"It's a go." I say to Phoebe and Gary, "Let's collect some tiny umbrellas."

******

Sparks stands in front of a small group of OTP militia dressed in civilian clothes and carrying signs reading, "ONE LAW FOR THE BANKERS—ONE LAW FOR US."

Sparks looks his group over approvingly—a good mix of men and women, mostly young, but all of them trained in combat and surveillance. "Remember, tonight is just a fact-finding mission. It's a peaceful protest. Do not engage! Keep a very low profile. Wear your caps and hoods, and be aware of the surveillance cameras at all times; they might use drones, so try not to look up and let your face be identified. Use your digital cameras to take photos, NOT your cell phones. Make sure your phones are off, and pull out the sim card once you are within sight of the protest. Be aware that they will be scanning the protestors with facial-recognition software and tracking local cell phone calls. Check yourself and your clothing and make sure you are not displaying any labels or identifying tattoos or piercings. It is important that we are ghosts in the crowd. Does everyone understand?"

"Yes, sir." Twenty voices reply in unison.

"Good." Sparks continues, "Our job is to document the private security response to a threat. Another group will be handling the disruption. Our job is to fan out around the building and get photos of the guard's faces, their gear, the weapons they have, and take notes on their response time to a crisis. Chances are they're trained to handle these events in the same manner every time, so this is our opportunity to see what that training is. Photograph any special equipment that you don't recognize. We want to evaluate everything. As long as we stay behind the barrier with the other protestors it should be an easy in-out."

Sparks and the recon group pile into a dark van and head to the protest site.

******

What is that sound? We are headed to the front of the building to pick up our car, and there is shouting up ahead. As the doorman let us outside, I see a huge crowd of protestors,

which wasn't there when we arrived. They appear peaceful, chanting slogans about equal justice for all. Private security provided by Marshall Industries is circling the estate in a ring of guns and muscle. I lean forward and ask the guard directly in front of me, "Is this a safe situation for the people inside?"

"Don't worry Ms. McCaffrey," obviously he's been well prepped because he knows who I am, "everybody is fine. We have plain-clothes security inside and all of these men are military trained. They have experience with crowd control. We expected something like this."

"Thank you. That puts my mind at ease," I lie. It doesn't calm my fears at all. I look around at the security setup as Gary, Phoebe, and I wait for the car. Off to the side I notice a guard in front of a small electronic screen. On it is the complete floor plan of the building with little red dots all over it—which are moving. It takes me a minute to realize what I am watching, but then it dawns on me that every important person in that room is "chipped" with a tracker. I wonder if I am—even though I don't remember ever having one put on me. Maybe nano chips were slipped into our drinks. I doubt that—more than likely it was an implant of some sort. There is one red dot on the front porch and three of us grouped together. I decide to test it to see if I was "chipped." I take a step towards the screen and pretend to fiddle with the heel of my shoe. No, the dots on the porch don't move. Thank god, I'm not being tracked. I notice a red dot moving on the porch towards my location and I turned to see Phoebe walking up. Phoebe is "chipped!" I stand up quickly and block the screen so she can't see what I have been looking at.

"Can I help you with that?" she asks chirping with sweetness, which now I don't trust at all.

"I got it, thank you. The strap was coming loose, that's all."

The car has been brought around and Gary is waving to us to come downstairs.

"Pop, Pop, Pop," a loud sound comes from inside the building. The guards spring into action and two of them quickly whisk us inside the car and pound the roof yelling, "Drive, Drive, Drive! Get out of here!"

Gary punches the gas a little too hard, and we all fall forward and then back again inside the car. Lurching down the driveway of the mansion, we eventually get to the exit gate, and I can see more protestors surging onto the drive, making it difficult to go forward quickly and get the hell out of there. I can feel the anxiety start to rise inside of me. In the middle of this chaos, I am piecing together some facts, and I don't like what I conclude. I am in the car with a woman who is most likely a spy and has already killed a man. We slow down and I take a moment to look out the back window at the house and the crowd. That's when I see him, Sparks, among the protestors. Our eyes locked and then Phoebe turns to look out the back window too. The car starts moving again and I watch Sparks' face as he notices Phoebe sitting next to me. He has a look of shock and panic. At that moment, I know unequivocally that Phoebe is the spy. The car is moving quickly now and I steal a glance at Phoebe to check if she has spotted Sparks, but it is obvious she has not.

******

"Why is Phoebe in that car with Christa!" thinks Sparks. He wants to warn her, but he knows that would be impossible.

When Sparks first joined the "Of The People" movement, he erased any trace of his foster care background, so no connection existed between him and Christa McCaffrey. He worries that she is in trouble, and he knows with certainty Phoebe is the spy who has infiltrated their compound. He can only hope that Christa has figured that out too. Phoebe was never supposed to socialize with Christa because her rebellious background is public record, and she is probably on some government watch list, which will draw the wrong type of attention to Christa. Sparks wishes he'd never fallen prey to Phoebe's seduction and recruited her into the group. That type of human error he can't afford. Everything is dangerous and complicated because of her now.

Sparks has other priorities though. Their disruption of the Marshall Awards Gala may not have come off without problems, but he can't be sure. He knew the gunshots he'd heard inside the house were not part of the plan. He now needed to keep an eye on his own people and hope that Christa can take care of herself.

15 minutes before—inside the mansion…

Damien Marshall, Sr. and Owen Carlyle are engaged in conversation when a waiter, with a tray of drinks approaches the circle of men. Each man reaches for a glass, but when they do the waiter pulls out a vile of pig's blood from inside his jacket and throws it on them yelling, "You have blood on your hands!" The blood splashes across the white tuxedo shirts of, Damien Marshall, Sr. and Owen Carlyle and splatters their faces, which are frozen with looks of shock and horror. The OTP had planned that security would wrestle the waiter to the ground, arrest him, and the coalition would bail him out in the morning. Meanwhile his action would get some press and disrupt the event.

The plan went sideways though, when the waiter reached into his pocket, his hand motion catching the attention of Kimball. When he threw the blood on the men, Kimball pulled his gun and fired three rounds into the young man just as he was shouting his damning words.

Security rushed the area and swept Owen Carlyle, Damien Marshall, Sr., and his sons Henry and DJ, into a "safe room" while they assessed the situation. DJ tried to call Christa to see if she made it out of the building safely, but all cell phone signals were being jammed until the situation was under control. He would have to wait it out and hope she was all right.

In the late news report, it would be covered as a protestor for the ethical treatment of animals who disrupted the party disguised as a waiter. He was tasered by the local police and taken into custody. There were no injuries. His death would go unreported.

******

Gary, Christa, and Phoebe pull their car up to the front of the Formosa Café in West Hollywood and emerge into a group of very drunk and very glamorous drag queens. Gary gets out of the car handing the keys to the parking valet while laughing and blowing air kisses all around. "Ladies, you look faaaabbbbuuuulllous!" The drag queens smile their superior smiles and sashay away purring, "Ooo, thank you honey."

The Formosa still has the flavor of old Hollywood in the '60s, and the walls are covered with faded signed photos of Sinatra, Bogart, Gable, and assorted beauties—some famous like Ava Gardner and Marilyn Monroe, and others long forgotten. The lighting is dim, the seats are comfy, and the drinks are strong. The three slide into a booth at the back of the room, and Gary orders a round of Mai Tai drinks with little umbrellas.

Phoebe looks over at Christa as she sips her drink and pretends to get a little tipsy—in reality, she has the alcoholic tolerance of a man five times her size. She is sizing Christa up and devising a plan to take her out. Christa has been a problem for a while because of the inside information about Marshall Industries which she has been passing along to OTP. Some of it has been very damaging; however, Christa is good at covering her tracks, so there is no link to her. Her connection to DJ Marshall makes this a much more delicate situation. Phoebe isn't ready to blow Christa's cover within the movement, so she chose not to out her to the Marshalls. Nobody knows what Christa has been doing except Phoebe, and she feels it is an easily remedied situation which she plans to correct tonight.

Phoebe is sure Christa is on to her and she needs to be eliminated now. Christa doesn't seem to be buying Phoebe's girlfriend act as she did at the party.

She starts to build her plan in her mind... she could follow Christa to the ladies room. Once in there, she will lock the door, subdue Christa, and inject her with a paralytic drug—which she carries in her purse to be used in tight spots such as this one. Her plan is to call a cab with Christa's cell phone and have it pick her up at the back door of the club. She would tell the driver Christa is too drunk and to please drive her home. She'll pay the driver in cash. By the time the cab arrives at Christa's house, she will be dead on the back seat from an apparent heart attack. Meanwhile, Phoebe would return to the bar and tell Gary that Christa went home early because she wasn't feeling well and said that she would see him in the morning. The two of them would then go on and party for several more hours. Yes, thought Phoebe, a pretty flawless plan.

******

I get up to go to the ladies room and of course Phoebe comes too. What is it about women going in pairs to the ladies room? The bathroom is empty, and when I walk in, I hear the faintest "click" and a voice, which I don't recognize as my own, is in my head saying urgently, "She's locked the door." I look around the room for potential escape options, and there are none, only a

very high window and a locked door. All I can do is pretend I didn't notice what she's done and see what her next move is. I walk up to the mirror and start to fix my hair and put on more lipstick. Phoebe follows up behind me to do the same, plopping her little handbag on the sink edge and digging around for a lipstick. We aren't speaking. I wash my hands and turn to the paper towel dispenser when I hear the "swoosh" of her skirt moving quickly across the ground. The strange voice in my head says, "She's coming behind you, drop now!"

Without hesitation, I drop to one knee. I have no idea what Phoebe intends to do, but I know I need to slow her down, so I reach back and chop her in the knee cap with as much force as I can. She buckles, and as she comes down, I move around and grab her right hand, which, to my surprise, is holding a hypodermic needle. I chop into her elbow with my hand, and her arm flies back; then I forcefully guide her hand to jam the needle into her scalp.

Phoebe falls back with a look of shock on her face, and says, "I underestimated you..." as she crumples onto the floor of the ladies room unable to speak because the drug is already taking effect.

I quickly grab the needle from her head with a paper towel, put it on the ground, and stomp it into little pieces, then flush it down the toilet. I check Phoebe's pulse, and it's weak. I know she probably won't survive the ambulance ride to the hospital, but I call 911 anyway. I unlock the bathroom door and text Gary that something horrible has happened and to meet me at the ladies room.

******

Phoebe dies on route to the hospital. Her father was waiting at the ambulance entrance confirming my suspicion that she was a spy and had a tracker embedded in her, like the other guests at the party. There is no other way her father could have known that Phoebe was on her way to that hospital.

As soon as I can, I will have to get this information to Sparks. The location of the compound is clearly compromised now.

The rest of the night is a complete blur of endless hours sitting in the hospital emergency room, giving statements to the police.

ISOLATING THE THREAT

After a successful night of gathering intel at the Marshall Industries party, the OTP team returns to the compound. Slipping into the crowd unnoticed, they had been able to observe the security force in action and they now have some insight into how they operates under pressure.

For Sparks, the more pressing concern is Christa. He was unsettled after seeing her in the car with Phoebe, but his concern intensified after he heard Phoebe had died that night. He wants to get in touch with Christa, but he can't think of a way that will not link the two of them together. It isn't good enough that all he can do is hope she is safe.

Sparks paces the length of his lab repeatedly trying to come up with a solution—a safe way to contact her. Then an idea occurs to him, it poses a minimal risk, and it could work. Over the last several years, a coalition of OTP groups has taken over the outside wire maintenance contracts for different telephone companies throughout the country. Under this guise, they have been installing their own public pay phone system in strategic places to create a network for analog communication. Until now, the system has been waiting in the wings to be debuted. The phones look identical to any regular phone except the cord to the handset is blue instead of silver. This is how a member can identify an OTP phone in the field.

Sparks has a complete map of the location of every pay phone in the network. If he pings Christa's cell phone, he can pinpoint her location, and as soon as she moves near one of his phones, he could make it ring an SOS distress signal. Then it will be up to Christa to recognize what is happening, which was a big "if."

The system is untested, though, but it's the only option he has. Now is a good time to field-test it. He needs to know that Phoebe has not leaked any critical information. Sparks has no doubt, that Phoebe is the spy and had access to critical information about their operation, how they communicate, and parts of the plan for reclamation. Phoebe is dead, so if nothing has been leaked, they are OK—otherwise OTP has a huge breach on their hands. Christa was the last person with Phoebe and she will know what Phoebe knew. At least, he hoped she would. He pulls up Christa's cell phone information, pings the tower, and overlays the coordinates onto his map. She is in the emergency waiting room of the Hollywood Hospital, and there is an OTP phone in the lobby. Now all he has to do is wait for her to move closer to the phone.

******

The bright lights coupled with the overtly cheery fabric of the chairs in the emergency waiting room makes me want to shrink into a dark corner. Light and bright are the last things I am feeling right now. All I can do is pace because I can't sit still. I have too much adrenaline coursing through me. I know I am headed for a crash, but it hasn't happened yet. I find a hallway, which is a little out-of-the-way and not so well-lit, just the place

I must calm myself. I let my head rest against the wall and close my eyes to cut down on the amount of stimulation coming into my brain. I long to feel calm.

"Ring, ring, ring," the damn pay phone next to me is freaking out—intermittent rings—and just when I think it has stopped for good, there it goes again. Out of frustration I decide to pick up the handset and quickly slam it back down again. That should put an end to the incessant ringing. Gary shoots me a look from across the waiting room that silently asks, "What the hell are you doing over there?" I look away and close my eyes.

The ringing starts again, and again I pick up the receiver and hang it up, more gently this time. A minute later, it starts again; I think I am about to lose it, when a pattern in the ringing catches my attention—there is something familiar about it. One, two, three short rings. Then one, two, three long rings. Then one, two, three short rings again. It is Morse code—an SOS! Is that possible, or am I just exhausted?

I decide I will pick up the receiver, but I turn my back to the waiting room so I won't be noticed answering the pay phone. "Ring, ring, ring." On the third ring I grab the phone receiver and put it to my ear but I don't speak—I wait.

A voice says softly, "Christa?" I stop breathing for just a second because I know that voice.

"Sparks?" I whisper into the receiver.

"Yeah. God, I am glad to hear your voice! Is everything OK? I've already heard about Phoebe."

"Wait... how did you know I would pick up this phone?"

"I'll have to explain that later—we must talk fast. I knew something wasn't right when I saw Phoebe in the car with you. She wasn't supposed to be at that event tonight."

"I know. Long story, which I will tell you later, but Phoebe was definitely your mole. She tried to kill me, and I had no choice but to kill her," I whisper. "I made it look like an accident, and so far it seems everybody bought it."

"Hmmm... OK, I had a feeling it was something like that. Are you OK?"

"I am, but probably still in shock."

"I think we should put a little distance between OTP and you, just until we know you aren't compromised."

"I'm fine, and I am pretty sure my cover is secure; the Marshall's don't seem to suspect me at all."

"Listen Christa, we don't have much time, and I need you to do something. As soon as you know when and where Phoebe's funeral will be, book a room at the Washington DC Hyatt Regency under your name for five days. Tell DJ and your office that you are required to go to Washington for a classified meeting with a client. Attend the funeral and duck out a little ahead of the crowd. Tell DJ you're going directly to the airport from the funeral. Take a cab to Polly's Waffle House on Jefferson Boulevard, it's on the way to the airport. Once you are at Polly's, make sure your phone is disabled; go directly to the back hallway, and exit to the alley. We will be waiting for you. Do you have all that?"

"Yes, DC, Polly's Waffle House on Jefferson, back door exit... got it."

I glance back at the waiting room and see DJ outside the building headed to the glass entry doors. I quickly hang up without saying goodbye. What a brilliant maneuver on Sparks' part to find me via the pay phone and use Morse code to get my attention. I am happy he has my back. I look up from the pay phone and there is DJ. He spotted me the moment he walked into the lobby. Waving his hand at me, he walks over with a very somber expression on his face.

"Christa!" DJ hugs me. "What a horrible night for you! I can't tell you how shocked we all were when we heard what happened to Phoebe. I didn't even know she was with you until I heard it on the news. You just said you were going with Gary."

"Oh yeah, I did, didn't I..."

DJ was probing without knowing it, and I must be careful about what I say to him right now. "I'm fine. I didn't know her at all. Gary met her at the party and invited her out with us."

"Ohhh..." he pauses and thinks about this, and adds, "Let's go home. We can talk about this when you're rested."

"That sounds really good right now. We have to grab Gary—he's staying with me—well us—for a few days. He's pretty rattled from tonight, and I think he will appreciate staying with friends."

"Of course," says DJ. With that, he grabs my arm and heads me towards the waiting room to find Gary, who is at the far end, sprawled out on one of the chairs, and looking utterly exhausted. "Come on, Gary, time to go home," I say.

Gary follows us out wordlessly. It is just as well, there isn't much to say, or much we can say. I know at some point in the coming days, I am going to have to relive the details of Phoebe's death, but tonight I don't want to worry about it. The tough conversation will be with Sparks and The Nomad when I tell them how I read Gary in on the movement without their permission. I have no idea how that will go over."

******

The brilliant blue California sky and the warm breeze blowing in from the desert seem to laugh at the gravity of the day. The weather is in opposition to the sea of black clad mourners standing by Phoebe Carlyle's grave.

I could have felt guilty, maybe I should have felt guilty, but Phoebe's casket is a reminder that it easily could have me in there instead. The entire Marshall clan is in attendance in a show of support for the loss of one of their own. DJ's mother, Sheryl, is making a rare family appearance. She prefers to spend her time doing yoga, beauty maintenance, and shopping. From all my encounters with her, I have never known her to care about much else. She is too thin, in my opinion, and who knows what lengths she goes to stay that way. Her scarecrow frame is topped with a dramatic black hat and oversized black sunglasses. Standing next to her is Henry's wife, Annie, or as I like to think of her, Sheryl Marshall's "mini me," wearing a slightly less dramatic hat and dark glasses as well. Henry stands with Annie, with his tight jaw; braced hands and the ever present look of an asshole on his face—even at a funeral. DJ's father is appropriately somber, in an expensive black silk Italian suit and equally expensive dark glasses, which make him, appear distant and inscrutable. Phoebe's father, Owen Carlyle, who I recognize from the party and later at the hospital, is very composed, but it isn't difficult to see why. Standing next to him is Melissa Carlyle, his wife and mother of Phoebe. She has to be supported physically by him because she is an absolute mess, and it is obvious they have sedated her. But that hasn't stopped the bursts of wailing and sobbing. I really can't blame her; after all, she is there to bury her daughter, and each outburst cuts into me like a knife stab of guilt. I certainly don't let it show on my face—I can't. In the row behind Marshall and Carlyle is a man with military posture and the attitude of an intelligence officer, taking everything in behind his dark glasses. Finally, there is the Marshall Industries security officer, Kimball, who is already eyeballing me as DJ and I join the crowd of mourners.

We stand here, the sun beating down on us, growing increasingly uncomfortable in our black clothing. My mind isn't on the ceremony in front of me; instead, I am rehearsing what I have to do after the funeral. I have already told DJ that I want to leave before the wake to get to the airport on time, so he is prepared when I start to walk away from the gravesite early. Owen Carlyle lightly grabs my arm as I stand, saying, "Don't leave yet, please." I sit back down; I can't exactly refuse the grieving father, can I?

Still, fear shoots through me when he grabs my arm. I replay the events surrounding Phoebe's death like a fast-forward film in my mind. Was there a camera in the bathroom that I hadn't noticed? No. I'm sure there wasn't. Had anyone been outside the door? I really don't think so, but I can't be certain. Nobody tried the door the entire time we were in there. The stalls were empty. I assure myself that there is no way Owen Carlyle could know the truth about his daughter's death.

DJ shoots me a worried glance and says under his breath, "I thought you needed to leave for the airport."

"I do, but Mr. Carlyle really wants me to wait," I whisper back.

"Won't you miss your flight?"

"No, I have a little time. Out of respect, I'll wait for him."

Just then Carlyle, Damien Marshall, Sr., Henry, Kimball, and "the suit" walk over, surround me, and effectively block my exit to the street. I quietly pull out my cell phone and input my request for a cab into my app all the while making small talk with the group.

"Christa," Mr. Carlyle's face is expressionless as he looks at me, with the exception of the intensity in his eyes, which are probing my reactions, "thank you for being here. This must not have been easy for you since, well... you found her..."

Mrs. Carlyle bursts into tears again, and we wait for her to compose herself.

Carlyle continues: "I want to thank you personally for trying to save Phoebe, calling the ambulance, and riding with her to the hospital. We never really got a chance to speak that night...." He lets the last words just hang in the air with all the implications of what watching his daughter die must have meant to him.

"Of course, you don't have to thank me. I am very sorry for your loss Mr. and Mrs. Carlyle..."

Mrs. Carlyle breaks down again, and DJ cuts in, "Christa really must catch a flight, and, unfortunately she must leave for the airport now."

"My cab should be here any minute." I turn to look up at the street and thank God, my ride is just pulling to the curb.

I say my good-byes and turn to leave, when I almost run directly into Kimball because he is standing so close behind me. He feels like a block of ice, or more accurately an iceberg—it's what's under the surface that is the real danger. He slowly moves aside never taking his eyes from me and once again giving me a creepy feeling. I can sense him watching me as I walk to the cab. Trying not to break into a run is difficult because I am so anxious to get out of there. My brain keeps repeating, "Walk faster."

I tell the driver, "LAX, but we will make one stop on the way," and I give him the address of Polly's Waffle House.

We pull into the parking lot of Polly's Waffle House, and I turn off my phone and pull out the sim card. I have cash in my hand, which I give to the driver. I tell him to drive to the American Airlines terminal at LAX. If anyone asks later, I instruct him to say that's where he left me and not to mention the stop at Polly's. He is fine with that since I pay him five times his actual fare.

Pulling open the glass front door to Polly's, I am thrown back in time as I enter a classic '60s-style coffee shop with a plastic, slightly space-aged feel. It's a family-friendly place for Saturday morning waffles with the kids, complete with paper coloring mats and crayons at every table. Glancing around, I spot the back hallway that Sparks mentioned, enter it and find the exit door at the end.

Punching open the door, a blast of warm air and sunshine envelops me. Parked in front of the door, is a dark van. The door slides open, and there is Sparks with his engaging smile. "Perfect timing," he says, "get in!"

I climb inside, and, to my surprise, Gary is there along with Big G and his dog, Gypsy. I start to say something when Gary interrupts, "Party over here!" He pats the seat next to him and then shoots a challenging glance at Big G who gives him a stern look. Gary looks him up and down and says, "You and your muscles would be a lot more fun if you were more charming!"

Big G's expression doesn't change as he leans into Gary's face and says with a deep, growling, almost threatening voice, "One mustn't look at the abyss, because there is at the bottom an inexpressible charm which attracts us."

He holds Gary's gaze for a very long moment then leans back looking straight ahead and folds his arms across his chest, making his massive biceps look even larger.

Gary sits there for a second and then he smiles. "A man who threatens by quoting Flaubert! Fascinating... ummm, ummm." And he bats his eyes at Big G.

Once again, there is no controlling him and all I can do is laugh. The van heads out of Los Angeles, the first leg of what will be a long and twisting journey through the center of California.

******

The next morning, as the sun is rising over an isolated California valley, they arrive at their destination…

Christa and Gary step out of the dark van into a rural landscape of rolling green and golden hills, surrounding a beautiful farm with groves of twisted oak trees. The sun casts angelic beams across the meadows, making the entire scene look like a dream. They are meeting here rather than the OTP bunker. They have changed location as a precaution after Christa discovered that Phoebe had an implanted tracking device.

Sparks explains that The Farm, as OTP calls it, is a remarkable example of how they are trying to build a model for a new society based upon sustainability and sharing. There is solar power, a gray water system, an organic vegetable farm, chickens, goats, a stream stocked with fish, and the only method to buy and sell is via bartering. The members are artisans of various trades: engineers, metal workers, carpenters, tailors, weavers, gardeners, bakers and chefs. Everyone has skills that The Farm requires. This was the experiment to create a blueprint for a new society.

While they stand there taking it all in, a sweet-faced older woman walks up to the group and introduces herself as Estella. She says she manages the kitchen and has heard that Gary is a trained chef. She invites him to join her later for some "culinary fun." Christa and Gary smile—especially Gary. He wants to watch Estella cook right then, but that will have to wait.

Gary exclaims, "I love her! Where did she come from?"

"Estella is a real gift for The Farm. A very talented chef—she had a successful restaurant in Los Angeles," says Sparks.

"All traditional Mexican recipes from her family who were from Oaxaca. For 30 years, she built that restaurant, even after her husband suddenly died from a heart attack. She worked it with her three kids and put them all through college. Her guacamole was legendary! The neighborhood improved, and real estate developers came in; long story short, they squeezed her right out of her business. There was nowhere for them to go, so they ended up with us. Her eldest daughter, Jasmine, is now an attorney and provides legal representation when OTP members are arrested during protests or for any other legal issues we might encounter. It has worked out well for everyone."

"I am going to have to talk to that woman before I leave! At the very least, I'm sure she has a great recipe for molé sauce," says Gary, and Christa knows nothing will deter him from getting it.

"We must to get moving; The Nomad is waiting to talk to both of you." Sparks and Big G guide us down a little dirt path to a large bunker behind the main farmhouse. Inside, The Nomad sits in a leather chair surrounded by several large computer screens, on which multiple people were broadcasting news from locations all over the United States.

"Please, take a seat," says The Nomad. Gary and Christa sit but Sparks and Big G remain standing, which is unintentionally intimidating. Sparks glances at Christa, and then keeps his eyes on The Nomad.

"Christa, thank you for uncovering Phoebe as the mole and risking your life to protect us. Revealing the tracking system has been invaluable. But—that said—you have seriously breached our safety by revealing the entire movement to Gary without clearing it with us first."

The Nomad speaks quietly, but the seriousness of his words cannot be mistaken. Christa and Gary shift uneasily in their chairs, not sure where this conversation is headed. Sparks stands completely still, looking straight ahead. Big G does the same. The quiet of the room is thick with anticipation. What is The Nomad capable of, and what type of recourse will he take with Christa and Gary? Nobody utters a word—each choosing to wait for The Nomad to speak again.

"Normally, it takes months to vet someone before we will approach them to become a member of OTP." The Nomad speaks in a level tone of voice, "We had to rush the process for Gary because you chose to discuss our organization, and your role in it, without prior permission. Believe me, if the information we gathered on Gary had not met our standards— if anyone in his immediate circle of friends or family seemed to have a hook in him for any weakness, such as drugs, alcohol, gambling, sex, we'd be having a very different conversation. He is clean and we can go forward with an offer for him to join the group. We just don't want another Phoebe—what she could have done to us... She could have brought down the entire organization." He pauses, looks hard at Christa and Gary, and then continues, "We checked Gary out, and not only did we not find anything to suspect him of working for the other side, we also found every reason why he should be working for us."

Everybody relaxes a little, and Gary, with an audible sigh, makes no attempt to hide his relief.

"Gary, you will have to go through some training like Christa did. Your access into the homes of several corporate CEOs, will be very helpful for gathering information on their movements and travel plans. We'd like you to focus on recruiting spies within their household staff," says The Nomad.

Gary nods in agreement, and his eyes grow wide in anticipation of playing James Bond. He already plans to run right out and buy a martini shaker for the part. Everyone in the room can see it is killing Gary to contain his enthusiasm.

A tall, athletic squad leader comes in and asks for the trainee. The Nomad nods towards Gary, and the man says, "Please follow me, we need to get you fitted with a firearm and set up with some hand-to-hand training this afternoon."

Gary shoots the most hysterical eye roll of delight at Christa and mouths under his breath, "Oooh baby, look at me... hand-to-hand!" If the atmosphere wasn't so serious in The Nomad's office, Christa would have broke out laughing.

"Sparks, please handle Christa's debrief." And, with that, The Nomad sends them out of the room.

******

The Farm is so peaceful that all the sounds of nature seem amplified. There is a gentleness to the atmosphere. The air is clean, and I feel like I am drunk from the light-headedness it causes when I breathe in. I don't want to go home—I want to stay here forever and slow down to a more human pace of living. Sparks and I walk toward the main farmhouse, but neither of us is speaking.

The more time I spend with Sparks, the more connected to him I feel. Sometimes I swear I hear him thinking, and then he will say the very thought I heard. Yet, it is more than that, he is easy to be with. The few conversations we've had have been natural. I find myself looking forward to the briefest of moments with him. DJ creeps into the middle of my thoughts, and I have to remind myself of how much I am betraying him by spying on his family. I cannot compound that by becoming attracted to another man. Once I remind

myself of that, my thoughts about Sparks come to an abrupt end. It is moments like this that I appreciate my mental ability to compartmentalize my thoughts.

Sparks interrupts my internal conversation. "We're going to the basement," he says, while pointing to some steps on the side of the house. "That's where my lab is. It'll be a good place to do the debrief."

I nod and follow him down the steps. Sparks opens the door to his pristine research lab and I think, "so this is where the magic happens."

Sparks stops in the middle of the room, takes a deep breath, turns to me and states, "Look, for what its worth, I thought you handled the Phoebe situation exceptionally well. I don't know many seasoned officers that could have done better."

"Thanks." I look into his hazel eyes, which shift between blue and green and find myself staring. My admiration and emotion reflect back to me from the expression in Sparks' eyes, and suddenly it feels awkward because I don't know how to respond—so I look away.

Sparks continues talking, seemingly oblivious to the moment we just had. "When I saw Phoebe in the car with you, I was sure she was operating off book and that nothing good was going to come of it."

"Yeah, well, she had me somewhat fooled." I'm not proud of that statement, and I look away again.

"She had everyone fooled. We found Sam, a militia guard, in the woods under a pile of leaves—throat slit. He was last seen with her, you were lucky. Maybe if we had put the pieces together sooner... But I'm not sure. Only Big G seemed to have her number—he never liked her but that was because Gypsy never liked her."

"Good instincts, that one has," says Sparks. We both laugh at the thought of how much that little dog controls the heart of that huge man. I look around the lab—I don't know what I am looking for. I guess I just want to learn a little more about Sparks by taking in his work environment. Neat, almost obsessively so, everything has a label. He had headphones—probably loved music. I seemed to remember he used to play the guitar—and there it was, a black guitar case propped in the corner of the room. I guess he hasn't changed all that much.

"We can sit over here," he says walking towards a black couch against the wall. "Actually," he laughed, "it's the only place to sit."

"Sparks, before we get started I have to ask—is Gary going to be OK in training?"

"Are you kidding? Did you see the look on his face when the trainer came in and said he needed a firearm? He was like a kid at Disneyland! He'll be fine, trust me."

With that last statement, he pats me on the shoulder, and his touch suddenly creates tension in the pit of my stomach. I deflect the feeling; but I don't want him to take his hand away, "I do trust you, thanks."

OK, let's get started." Sparks pulls out an old-style hand-held tape recorder. He explains that, with the exception of one hour a day, there is no Wi-Fi at The Farm. He goes on to explain that the computers in his lab—as well as throughout the compound—use air gapping (or computers that have never been connected the Internet) to create a secure, private network. Sparks clicks the recorder and says, "Why don't you just walk me through the events of the night Phoebe died as you remember them."

I describe the way I first met Phoebe at the compound, the snippets of conversation I'd heard at the party, leaving the party with Gary and Phoebe, the protest outside and how the Marshall Industries' security reacted to it, and hearing the shots inside the building. Sparks questions me for more detail when I tell him about discovering the trackers on the security guard's computer screen. Specifically, he wants to know everything I can remember about the monitor and what was on it.

"This is new information. We assumed they were tracked via their cell phones. We considered they might be chipped but didn't have the security equipment to scan for it—that's a priority now. We'll use this to our advantage since they don't know we are aware of their tracking system. My next job is to figure out how to disable the trackers without knowing exactly how they work. It's doable. This is important. They have been talking about requiring every baby born in the U.S. to have a chip put in at birth. As you know, this is a violation of privacy and civil rights. If I can crack the code on these tracking devices, it may help the rest of us in the future. This is good..." His voice trails off in thought. I look at his face, as he is lost in this new problem to solve, and I consider, once again, how handsome Sparks is.

I notice his brown wavy hair curled around his neck and ears. His eyes—such a subtle mix of green, gold, and brown—not only change color with the light, but also when his mood shifts—and they are framed by long dark eyelashes any girl would be envious of.

One of the clearest memories of my childhood is the first day Sparks showed up at the McCaffrey's group home. Everybody chattered about the run away. Sparks had left every home he was placed in, and he was only 12-years-old. He'd already taught himself to drive a car, rewire a security system, and make a cell phone do things you wouldn't think possible. No wonder an ordinary foster home couldn't hold him. But the McCaffrey home was far from ordinary—I guess that's why they put him there.

From that point on, we were inseparable.

Despite being a brilliant geek, the Sparks sitting in front of me today, is physically fit from all his militia training. In fact, he's become quite a catch. "A sexy, tech guy who didn't like to socialize," as Phoebe had put it. I blurt out without thinking, "Were you involved with Phoebe?" I am immediately embarrassed as the question leaves my mouth.

Sparks pauses before answering, he is thinking. "Yes—it was a while ago."

"Oh…" I feel like a total idiot! Why did I ask him that! Now I had made the entire conversation between us completely awkward.

Of course, I can't stop thinking that Phoebe had used the word "sexy" to describe Sparks. I fight my own attraction to him, when a moment later, almost as if he had read my mind, Sparks turns towards me and squares his shoulders, looks directly into my eyes with a frank and mesmerizing look, and says, "She meant nothing to me." He keeps looking into my eyes—searching for permission from me to reveal more. I find myself staring at his lips and wanting to know what it would be like to kiss him.

I feel my stomach clench as my emotions get the better of me. I can't turn away from him. I have to, though. I can't do that to DJ no matter how attracted I am to Sparks—and I feel very attracted to him at this moment.

I shift backwards a little and mutter, "Oh, OK, I guess that worked out."

Again, I immediately regret this statement—how insensitive of me! Phoebe is dead, and I say, "I guess that worked out!"

I can't win—I am a complete idiot. I have no idea what to say next, and for a trained trial attorney, this is a new one. I scramble for words, "If we are finished, maybe I should walk back and see how Gary is doing?"

Clearly the moment is lost. Sparks leans back and says, "Yeah, I think I have everything I need," and he shuts off the recorder. He takes one more opportunity to study my face, as if he is memorizing every curve and shadow. Now I feel pressured and defiant, so I stand up abruptly, and he follows suit.

I really am not upset that Sparks seems attracted to me—it is the exact opposite, I am very comfortable with him—and that could be a problem if I don't watch myself.

******

Sparks offers to drive Christa to the San Francisco airport. She had been booked on a flight from Washington DC, and an OTP member is flying in her place. The itinerary involves a flight change in San Francisco, and Christa will now board at the layover, flying the final Los Angeles leg. They drive down Highway 1, and a layer of fog is creeping in, clinging to the Redwood trees, and settling in little patches where it can't escape. The landscape is gray and quiet except for the sound of the car moving through it. Christa and Sparks talk in their relaxed and candid way with the cadence of old friends—skipping from subject to subject. Favorite bands, first serious loves, bad hairstyles, high school prom dates, where they have lived over the years, favorite foods—anything to fill in the gaps of information missing from the years they haven't been in touch.

The car follows the twisted coastal highway and occasionally they fall into silence. San Francisco and the airport are now quite close and the time of parting as well.

Sparks finally says something, "Look, we have some very sensitive work to do together, and I want to be sure we're cool. You know what I mean, right?" He stumbles around with this and he knows he is being less than direct, but he wants to clear the air before he sends her home.

"We're cool, no problem." Christa knows that Sparks is trying to back pedal the attraction between them, and she appreciates this. She is OK because she knows she isn't going to let anything happen, no matter how tempted she might be.

Sparks looks relieved, "We're almost at the airport, if you want to turn on your phone, it should be fine."

Christa pulls out her cell phone and the sim card and pops it in. The phone makes the familiar powering up beep. Sparks pulls into the drop-off zone for departures, and both of them get out of the car to say good-bye. They know it might be awhile before they will get time together again, so they hesitate, not knowing quite what they want to do. Then Sparks reaches out and gives Christa a long, warm hug good-bye. Out of habit or concern, she reaches up and moves a piece of hair out of his face, then they look at each other a beat longer than either intends, and they smile because they can still see their 12-year-old selves reflected in each other's eyes.

"Gotta go," Christa says and gives Sparks' arm a friendly squeeze. She turns and disappears into the crowd of travelers—back to her life.

******

Everywhere at the airport people are taking selfies and saying goodbye. Having one of these moments is a young, newlywed couple—holding up their phones and smiling for the camera. In the background of their pictures are a couple, a man and woman. The woman sweeps a piece of hair out of the man's face as they look at each other with very tender expressions. The newlyweds pick the photo they feel shows their best faces, and, with a click, they upload the picture to multiple social media platforms, hashtagged "#truelove #SanFranciscogoodbye #homewardbound".

*****

Taking another sip of his mocha-almond-latte, extra hot with an extra shot, the computer analyst settles in for another boring session of trolling the Internet for information. He pulls off his plaid overshirt and smooths his beard in a contemplative way as he stares at the screen.

"Beep, beep." His computer alerts him to a possible data match. He doesn't get excited—this happens 20 times an hour. He moves closer to the screen to examine the material and yells, "We've got a hit!"

The analyst waves his supervisor over to his terminal and explains, "I was scanning recent uploads from different social media sites, and a photo taken about an hour ago at the San Francisco airport met the basic facial recognition criteria. I pulled the photo and ran the full diagnostic, and it's 99% positive. The photo is Christa McCaffrey."

The supervisor pulls out his phone and makes a quiet call. Fifteen minutes later, Kimball strides into the room. He takes one look at the photo and has no doubt it is Christa in the passenger drop-off zone of the San Francisco airport. The photo's hashtags make it obvious. "Has she been to DC at all?" Kimball wonders. "But why San Francisco?" However, what is far more interesting to him is the man with his back to the camera. He asks for other angles on the scene, but there are no straight-on shots. Kimball looks at the smile on Christa's face and how she is touching this man's hair, and he knows he finally has some dirt on her. This is the evidence he must have to bring DJ on board and encourage him to cooperate with a full interrogation of Christa. A slight, cruel smile appears on Kimball's face as he anticipates breaking this news to Damien Marshall, Sr. He mumbles to himself, "Gotcha."

CHAPTER FOUR

CAPTURE OF THE BLACK QUEEN

♟

Henry Marshall walks, or rather stalks into his office, ready to pounce on his prey." The dirty work is always left up to me," he thinks. His father doesn't want to be bothered if Henry can handle it, and DJ—well, DJ is just clueless. Henry speaks his assistant's name to an empty room, "Jeri?"

"Yes, Mr. Marshall?" comes a voice from the walls.

"Get me Kimball and Marianne Lewis—have them come to my office immediately."

"Calling them now, sir," and the voice evaporates.

Henry stops his stalking long enough to look out the window of his high-rise office. From up here everything looks attainable; you can't see the people, the problems, or the money—none of it. It is impersonal and distant, which is the way he likes it. He has found it easier to make decisions that may impact society if he isn't looking at the individuals. The view also makes him feel powerful. However, presently he is tense and can't stop clenching his jaw muscles. There is a problem, a big problem, and he is determined to take care of it.

A knock on his office door interrupts his contemplation, and, without turning around, he says, "Come in." Kimball and Ms. Lewis, the company's media liaison, enter the executive suite. Still not turning to look at them Henry says, "We need to get in front of the Phoebe Carlyle thing. Something in my gut tells me Christa McCaffrey is lying about how deeply involved she actually is. I'm not sure about Gary Goodwin, so we can leave him alone for now."

He turns around and looks both of them in the eyes. "The 'incident' that happened at the fundraising event the other night—that can't happen again. I want the protestors discredited; associate them with some type of fringe terrorist group, or pick specific leaders in the movement and smear them. Whatever disinformation you can push out there, do it. Nobody must take their message seriously. It may be time for a media diversion, a sex scandal—something. Marianne, I need vigilant monitoring of all media. I want to know every move these people are up to!"

Both Kimball and Ms. Lewis continue to stand at attention; they can see Henry is just getting started. He stalks the office floor again—back and forth with long strides, hands clasped behind his back, as he devises his plan aloud. "I don't want to be too overt about taking down these protestors. Keep that in mind, OK." He stares at Marianne in a very defiant manner and says, "Get the security footage from that night, and try to identify as many people as possible. Then let's have a little fun—manipulate some bad luck, arrest warrants, diversion of funds from their bank accounts, illicit photos; keep the pressure on. I want them so busy trying to keep their lives together they can't target us. You can handle that, can't you, Kimball?"

"Yes sir." Kimball says without hesitation because to hesitate on anything Henry Marshall asks for, will trigger a tirade of anger.

"Marianne, make certain the Marshall name is not associated with the death of Phoebe Carlyle or the recent protest at the fundraising event. We don't want anyone connecting any dots to us. I don't want to see our stock fall a single point because of this. Get it?"

"Yes sir." Marianne also answers without hesitation but with a little more trepidation because it was a well known fact that Henry Marshall is a sadistic pig when it comes to women. He would take any opportunity to torment her and eventually fire her for the tiniest infraction. He always hires very attractive women—such as the three who held the position before her. There is no fighting him; he is Marshall Industries, his father's right hand man. He's too powerful; all she can do is put up and shut up until she can't take it anymore. In the end, everybody tolerates Henry for a line on their résumé. Once they leave Henry Marshall's employ on good terms, doors fly open and opportunities are everywhere because Henry has his fingers in many pies. If you leave on bad terms, you will never work anywhere but behind the counter of a fast food restaurant.

"Marianne, you can go. Kimball, stay a minute."

Marianne turns and leaves but even as she relaxes a little, she can feel Henry's eyes on her ass as she walks out of the room. She can't leave fast enough.

Once he hears the latch of the office door close, Henry speaks again, "What do you have for me?"

Kimball starts his brief. "I've had security doing research on Christa, and we have reason to believe that she was involved with Phoebe's death, but I don't have proof—yet. We've tried to keep tabs on her and found that her recent trip to DC may not have happened. We spotted her in the departure drop-off zone of the San Francisco airport with an unidentified man."

Henry raises his eyebrows when he hears this bit of information. This is news to him. He assumed she was completely loyal to his brother. As for the rest—he has never trusted Christa coming from a foster care background with the wrong type of friends and the wrong type of upbringing how could she ever truly be trusted around so much affluence? Possibly, he'd finally get a chance to prove his theory.

"Maybe she's having an affair. Hmmm…"

Henry continues speculating about Christa. "No matter, we need to flush her out. She's still seeing my brother, so until we have solid proof, we won't have his cooperation. This is delicate. My father likes Christa; until he has more information, he will continue to include her in family affairs. For now, I want full surveillance on her. Use whatever we have to stay on top of every move she makes."

Kimball nods that he understands.

"And I know I don't need to say this, but this must to be untraceable to us. I want surveillance everywhere—even when she's in court. OK?"

"Yes—got it."

"All right—go on and get back to me when you've got something."

******

For weeks, I have fed information to the militia. The way I transfer it is fairly simple and low tech. Whenever I hear something I need to pass along I go to a website for a Nashville blues band called Tin Horn, click on the first song for download, and next to the song will be an I.D. number. I find a landline telephone with a touch-tone keypad, and dial the I.D. number.

That number routes to a hijacked phone line that picks up the dial tone code and connects me to an OTP operator who lets OTP know I am ready to transfer some information.

The transfer of info takes place the next morning at the end of my regular run. I always stop for coffee. Outside the coffee shop are often homeless people asking for money. This morning the hand off is to a homeless man. He approaches me asking, "Can you spare some change, I need to feed my dog." I reply, "What kind of dog do you have?" and he answers, "A mutt but part Chihuahua."

The entire conversation has been pre-scripted by the OTP operator. If he varies even one word, I am to walk away. He holds out a calloused hand and stares directly into my eyes in a manner that makes me uncomfortable. I quickly look around at the people outside the coffee shop to double check I have the right man. Nobody else is paying attention to us, so I turn back to the homeless man and hand him the folded dollar bill with my handwritten notes inside. He grabs it and stuffs it into his pocket; a moment later, he pulls his cart around the corner and disappears.

This time the notes are from various meetings and parties I have recently attended with DJ. I pass on information about the Marshall Industries corporate office building and the specific floors which are secured using biometrics to randomly generate barcode keys. I also have the names of the five people who can issue the security passes. This information paints a clear picture of what OTP is up against should they choose to breach the private offices of Marshall Industries' main building. I am proud of my spying abilities. I'm better at this than I thought I would be. Although, every time I am in the middle of a hand-off, my heart races with the fear of being caught. I have no

idea what Marshall Industries would do to me, but I suspect it wouldn't be legal.

Ever since Phoebe died, I have felt very nervous but less so as the days went by. At first, I was worried that Phoebe had blown my cover, but nothing happened, so I am starting to relax. Life feels like it is getting back to some version of normal again.

******

Gary returns to his loft by the beach after the long weekend on The Farm. He looks forward to popping open a wonderful bottle of Merlot and ordering takeout from his favorite restaurant. As he unlocks the front door, his mouth is already watering at the thought of a lovely chocolate mousse for dessert. Humming to himself, he sets his bag down in the front hall. As he reaches for the switch to turn on the hall light, a lamp clicks on the living room.

"What the hell?" Gary says loudly as he peers into the living room. He needs a moment to adjust to the light. "Who..." and then he sees him, sitting as if he owns the place with a smug smile and arrogant posture, Henry Marshall.

"Henry! What the hell are you doing in here?" There is so much more he could have said, but he holds back because this is such a confusing and invasive act by Henry.

"Hello Gary, did you have a nice weekend?" Henry gazes steadily at Gary's face, looking for any expression that would betray him as lying.

Gary pauses; he sizes up Henry's attitude and determines Henry knows something, so he decides to be glib in his response. "Wonderful! What's not to love about a weekend full of near naked boys with perfect six packs? Of course, you would have been bored half out of your hetero mind by it all. So I guess it's all in the eye of the beholder." With that statement Gary throws him a coy smile and adds, "I don't think you committed a B&E to ask me about my weekend. What's on your mind?"

"Did Christa join you on your 'wonderful' weekend?" Henry asks in a sarcastic tone.

"Christa? Oh honey, she does appreciate a good view but she would have felt very alone," and Gary laughs. "I don't think a gay man's weekend would be her style. Besides, she was probably off with your brother holed up in some glamorous *pied-a-terre*."

"Hmmm... Whatever you say Gary." Something in Henry's voice, a certain confidence, makes Gary's skin crawl. The questions, breaking into his place, the intimidation, are high-handed and he knows Henry would only risk all that if he is certain he has something on Christa. Gary needs to get Henry out of there before he asks any more questions and Gary betrays himself or Christa.

"Henry, I really don't get this, but the next time you want to grill me why don't you just text me? If you don't mind, I really want to order some dinner before the restaurant closes and unwind from my wonderful weekend." He moves to the front door and opens it. He stands there holding the door waiting for Henry to walk out of his house.

"I like to ask certain questions in person—it allows me to not misinterpret the answers," Henry says, while ignoring Gary's obvious invitation to leave.

"Still, this is illegal last time I checked." Gary pulls the door open a little wider.

"I needed you to understand we can get to you whenever we need to." Henry delivers this last statement with a withering glare as he finally moves to leave. Calmly, he begins to walk out the front door but stops midway, looks back and says, "Nice place," then continues walking.

Once he shuts the door, Gary looks around and speculates from Henry's last words, how long he had been there before Gary arrived home. Doing a mental inventory of what might be potentially incriminating evidence, he can't think of anything. Finally, he relaxes uncorks that bottle of Merlot, and pours a glass as he orders dinner. Still, he is bothered by Henry's visit, so he proceeds to tear his place apart looking for surveillance equipment that he is certain Henry has planted there.

He hopes he is just paranoid and won't find anything, but instead he finds several audio bugs and a couple of cameras. He knows he must call Christa immediately. She needs to be warned to watch her back if Henry is on to her. He debates whether to risk calling her and decides an innocent person would have found Henry's behavior odd and would have called Christa right away—which he does. Her voice mail picks up which is actually better because if their calls are being monitored, there is no chance she will say something about the weekend, which would be exactly what Henry needs to go after her. "Christa, I just walked into my house to find Henry sitting in my living room. I think he's finally rounded the bend, honey! He made no sense at all, not to mention breaking and entering my home! I am exhausted—going to bed early. Let's meet for coffee tomorrow. Love you!"

Gary is comfortable that anybody listening to this call will feel he is innocent of any collusion with Christa. He is very worried for his friend, and, until he gets a chance to meet with her in person, he has a feeling she might be in danger. Somehow, he must get word to Sparks.

******

Sparks agitatedly paces the floor of his lab because he is concerned for Christa. He has heard about the stunt Henry Marshall pulled with Gary, and that Henry suspects Christa hadn't been in

DC. Maybe he was only fishing, but it was a bold move. So far, they have not been able to reach out to Christa and warn her—it is too dangerous. He headed to The Nomad's office to meet with him and Big G on a strategy to get Christa out of Los Angeles and away from Henry Marshall before anything happens to her.

"Sparks, please, sit," The Nomad says, gesturing to a chair in front of his desk.

"I..." He doesn't want to sit because he is so furious, but he does because The Nomad insists. "I can't tell how they know, but they know she's working with us. I feel it."

"Yes, I think you are right," cautions The Nomad.

"What will they do to her if they think she's knows anything about us? We'll never find her because they'll disappear her off the face of the earth!"

"Christa knew and accepted that risk when she took this on, but she is trained to handle this type of situation. We need to trust that for now. Obviously Damien Marshall, Sr. doesn't trust her either or Henry never would have received the go-ahead to start hunting for evidence."

"So why don't we... I don't know... get rid of the threat?"

"That day is coming but we will do it in a way that works for us. We don't play by their rules. Patience." The Nomad sits calmly waiting for Sparks to regain his composure.

Sparks doesn't calm down, instead he bolts out of his chair and starts wearing a hole into the floor. He then rants: "I, I've been working on something... it's good... it's almost finished... it could give us the edge." He looks at The Nomad, "I have been working on a gun, a new type of weapon. It uses the electrical activity of our cells and brains against us by slowing our response down to a near-death level. All action stops for a short period, and the person hit by the pulse is in suspended animation and can't move. It doesn't kill them—it just makes them helpless. It's silent—only the lowest level hum, barely audible to the human ear. Another plus is, after the pulse wears off, the person can't remember what happened to them. I haven't been able to explain that side effect yet. It's as if they were frozen in time. I know it's untested in the field, but I want to use it to get Christa to a safe place."

"I agree, she isn't safe." The Nomad takes several minutes to think about his next statement because he wants to talk to Big G without Sparks anxiously pushing his own agenda. "Sparks, please step outside for a moment—I need to talk to G alone."

Sparks hesitates, but then quickly leaves the room hoping that the sooner The Nomad speaks with Big G, the quicker they can get moving to protect Christa.

Once Sparks is outside The Nomad asks, "What do you think?"

While G thinks about his answer, he reaches down and gives Gypsy a few gentle strokes on the head; she closes her eyes and thoroughly enjoys the attention. "I think Henry Marshall played his hand too soon. If he hadn't confronted Gary and continued to watch Christa covertly, she would have eventually led him straight to us." Big G's voice is a soft, deep rumble as he plays the options out for The Nomad. "I have to ask, because he's not a stupid man, what did he expect to gain by confronting Gary? Maybe his only intent was to 'flush the prey from the bushes'."

"My thought exactly," says The Nomad. "That is the only thing I could think that he would gain. So far, we have not been able to reach out to Christa, and she's hanging out there unprotected, ignorant to what Henry is up to. Hopefully Gary can get to her."

"The entire thing is a setup to draw us out," says Big G, "but they don't know who we are or what our agenda is."

The Nomad makes a pyramid with his fingers and rests them on his forehead while G speaks. He looks up and says, "I believe we must consider Henry Marshall for our first swap."

G nods. "Other OTP camps have done it successfully, so we know how important it is that we don't fail. We cannot fail, says The Nomad. G nods again. There is a pause in their conversation, and for a moment the only sound in the room is the heavy breathing of Gypsy as she sleeps at Big G's feet.

"Let's take a run at them and let Sparks use the new weapon. But we need to be clear that if this fails and we set off a chain reaction there will be losses. On the other hand, I don't see how we can't answer Henry's aggression. His suspicions are bringing him very close to us, but, as far as we know, he's unaware of our plans for a reclamation—if they were discovered now, it would be too soon. Years of preparation would go to waste. So let Sparks fight them—it's what they expect. Give then what they expect, and it will lull them into a false sense of success. That will work to our advantage," says G.

"Yes," agrees The Nomad, "but we need to acknowledge that Christa will be in danger once we make this move, and if we can't get her out of there, we will have to walk away for the sake of the movement." The Nomad delivers this last sentence with a tone of sadness in his voice. He clearly doesn't want that outcome.

"Yes," G says solemnly. The light is fading in the room and casting everything in the warm orangey color of sunset. Both men are quiet for a bit, as they anticipate bringing Sparks back into the room to tell him the plan. "I believe the target should be Henry Marshall, not Marshall, Sr., since he seems to be working alone to catch Christa." Big G warns, "Sparks' new weapon better be exceptional because Henry won't be an easy target."

The Nomad and G look at each other for a moment, and both give nods that imply it is decided that they will do their first swap with Henry Marshall. G still nodding says, "Let's get Sparks in here."

******

Sparks, Big G, and four militia soldiers, move through the early morning darkness outside Henry Marshall's estate dressed in black clothing designed to hide their heat signatures from infrared scanners. They move undetected. Sparks has confirmed one last time that Henry Marshall is inside. A voice in Sparks ear com says, "He arrived an hour ago, confirmed, the target is on the property." Armed with prototypes of Sparks' new 'gun,' which he has tested and tested again—Sparks focuses on the fact that it needs to perform flawlessly, and he is convinced it will. To be certain there were no imperfections, he personally built each gun they are using with a 3D printer in his lab.

Sparks moves forward, quickly disarms the electric gate, and pushes it open. To make is less likely they will be spotted by security, they run along the sides of the driveway where the shadows are the deepest. The plan, as Sparks knows it, is to grab Henry Marshall from his bedroom, take him underground, and interrogate him. Afterward they will pump him full of drugs, which should scramble, if not completely wipe his memory, and deposit him back home. To an outside observer, it might appear he suffered a stroke because the drugs will disappear from his blood stream within an hour or two.

They know taking Henry Marshall is going to blow the movement wide open if it is discovered. They are prepared with a plan for retaliation which has been in place for a long time. All of them hope it won't come to that.

Sparks has a personal motivation for this operation. Christa is still in the dark—she has no idea what is about to go down with Henry. She could potentially be in even greater danger than she already is. He can't focus on that right now.

The team has split up and is running towards the house when Sparks hears a faint sound behind him. He turns and there is a security officer in full combat gear, with his gun drawn, charging directly at Sparks. Sparks can't pull his stun gun, so he has to engage the officer. He needs to turn himself into a moving target rather than freeze, so he drops to the ground and rolls towards the man. Before the security guard can determine what is happening, Sparks grabs one of his attacker's legs, and once he is off balance, kicks him the groin—the one area he determines might be vulnerable. Sure enough, the man bends forward in pain. Sparks takes this opportunity to reach out and grab the man's gun arm, pinching the nerves in his wrist until his hand momentarily paralyzed, loosening his grip on the gun. Sparks easily removes the gun and throws it into the bushes. The man, still in pain, drops his head, which Sparks butts full force opening a gash in the security guard's forehead. Blood, gushing down his face, obscures the man's sight. He instinctively reaches up to wipe the blood from his eye, and Sparks deftly lands a kick directly to the guard's windpipe, rendering him incapable of making a sound and gasping for air. He next moves behind the man and kicks the backs of his knees causing him to drop to the ground. Then he wraps his arm around the man's neck and starts squeezing. In an unforeseen move, the security guard pulls a knife from his vest and slashes behind him hoping to hit Sparks in the chest, but only succeeds in cutting him deeply on the shoulder. Sparks drops his bleeding arm, but keeps the pressure on the man's neck with his other arm, and a moment later the man passes out from lack of oxygen.

The entire encounter only took a few minutes, but now Sparks is in pain and needs to tie off the cut to his arm before he loses too much blood. He pulls the man's earpiece to listen to Marshall's head of security. He is ordering guards to fan out across the property and shoot to injure, not kill. The Marshall private security force was ready for them! The whole thing is a trap! They want to take them alive to get information. Three soldiers come upon Sparks hunched over the unconscious guard listening to the man's earpiece. They draw their guns and point them at his head. Sparks raises his hands, lowers his eyes, and prepares himself for the fact that these men may not respect their orders not to kill him.

He sits there…and sits there. Nothing happens.

He looks up, and the men are still pointing their guns at his head, but from behind them steps Big G and his men—all three with their stun guns drawn.

"Well, what do you know… these things actually work! Lucky you!" Big G smiles. "This is one hell of a weapon you invented." Abandoning their mission, they make a run for the front gate. They almost make it when they encounter Kimball who is blocking their escape. He stands defiantly, with a cold stare on his face, and then Sparks realizes he isn't moving.

"Oh yeah, he was the first one we zapped," says Big G. "Let's get out of here before that motherfucker comes to!"

They escape to the street—the entire operation a bust. Sparks knows he won't be able to protect Christa; she is on her own.

******

The courthouse hallway is cool and relatively quiet for a weekday. I look around at the aging art deco light fixtures, the

oak benches, and the wood paneled walls and think, "If those walls could only talk they would have some stories to tell."

"You can't fool me or my father." From behind me, a voice breaks into my thoughts. I turn to look at the speaker and see Henry Marshall with his predictable arrogant attitude. "Maybe you can fool my brother, but not for long," he continues.

I look at him with a cool expression despite my surprise at his unexpected presence, "Henry, have you lost it? What are you talking about?"

He moves into my personal space, a little too close to my face and says quietly, so only I can hear him, "I know you weren't in DC."

I know my eyes must have flickered some recognition of the truth for a second and I quickly try to hide it, but a second is all Henry needed. He walks away, leaving me in a panic, trying to decide what to do next—run or stand my ground as if nothing has happened. DJ might believe me and back me, but the pressure from his family, especially his father, would be enormous. I'm still not certain I can count on him to stand up to them, no matter how much he loves me.

I have no choice—this is now a very dangerous place for me to be, I'm going to have to run—there really is no option. How will I leave my life behind, and where will I go to start over? I hope the OTP farm compound is an option—I'd be with Sparks, and I know I can trust him. That may be a safe option for me but not necessarily for them.

*****

Seated in an opulent, beautifully-upholstered red leather wing chair is Damien Marshall, Sr., the patriarch of the Marshall family. He is motionless while he enjoys the blue-sky view from his office window, which makes him feel above the whole world. Allowing himself a rare treat, a fine Cuban cigar, he rolls the rare tobacco between his thumb and forefinger, occasionally putting the cigar to his lips and taking a large puff of smoke which he would release and watch it lazily spread across the atmosphere of his office.

Henry, trailed by Kimball, enters the room with enough agitated energy to destroy the peaceful moment for Damien Marshall Sr.

"I hear we caught our spy," Damien Marshall, Sr. says, still puffing on his cigar and reluctantly turning away from the view.

"Yes, we did… it was Christa," answers Henry with a small note of triumph in his voice. This puts him one up on DJ in his father's eyes and he is enjoying the moment.

"Well… your brother isn't going to like that." He continues to puff away on his cigar.

Henry smiles. Kimball says nothing.

Damien Marshall, Sr. looks at Kimball, "Bring her in… and, well ,you know, Kimball… Don't…you know…if she is working with them, we want to know what she knows; she's useless to us any other way." He blows some smoke rings into the air and contemplates them as they dissipate into the room.

"Yes sir. Ahh… there is one other thing…they have some new hi-tech weaponry. She might know something about it, and that would be extremely useful. It's a pretty impressive weapon. I'd like to get my hands on one of those guns."

"OK, well get on with it then." Damien Marshall, Sr. waves them out of the room so he can finish his cigar in peace.

*****

I run into the closet and throw on some jeans, tennis shoes, and a t-shirt with a hoodie over it. I try to make myself look

as nondescript as possible. I look in the mirror to scrape my hair into a quick bun, and looking back is a young woman that I think looks like she just may be in over her head. I madly throw things into a suitcase and race from the house. I decide I will drive part way out of town and from there catch a bus or train to another city. A voice in my head tells me to try the coffee shop, maybe someone there can get a message to OTP. This doesn't make sense to me because the system doesn't work that way, but what the hell—at this point, I need to rely on my instincts.

I pull up in front of the coffee shop and look around for anyone, but there are no homeless people out front, so I decide to go inside. I order my drink and chat with the barista about her newly-dyed pink hair then sit down to wait for my coffee. The only other customer in here is a well-dressed professional man also waiting for his drink. He has his back to me, and he is looking through a pile of local newspapers stacked against the side wall.

"Don't look at me. You can't appear to be talking to me." It is the nicely dressed man speaking. I turn away from him even more, but I recognize his voice immediately. It is The Nomad.

"The Council has gone silent—we need to cut you loose from the protection of the movement. I need you to know you will be all right, and we will find you no matter what happens. Henry is onto you, that's why we must back away. Tap your finger on the counter twice if you understand me."

I tap twice.

"OK, good. We will be relocating the compound and taking protective measures. We are certain the Marshalls will come for you—be brave, you are about to find out who you are. Know this, when the time is right, we will find you."

It is quiet for a minute, and then I hear the door to the coffee shop slap shut. I turn to look but he is gone. God, I feel very alone right now. How have I allowed myself to get involved with OTP so easily, and now my entire life has come unstrung. I have no idea what DJ will think when he finally figures out that I have left him, not to mention what he will do when Henry tells him the truth about my spying. DJ has only been good to me, and I never considered how much pain I would cause him if a moment like this should happen. Of course, the family will turn him against me.

The moment has passed to try to recruit DJ. "Almond latte for Christa," says the pink-haired barista. I pick up my coffee and head to the car. Pulling out of the parking lot, lost in thought, I consider what kind of life I might be running to.

******

Henry Marshall is in his office surrounded by the leather-bound, great works of literature he's collected only because he feels they make him seem smart and wise, not because he appreciates them for their artistry. Looking at the gold embossed titles reminds him that he has read many of these books, and he is an educated man—all an affirmation of his intelligence and superiority. Christa is not going to get the better of him; she will never "out-think" him. He mentally formulates his plan to slowly torture her; knowing that he has the full blessing of his father only makes the scene much more gratifying. He will squeeze until she divulges her lies and deceptions, and afterward he will throw her out like the trash that she really is. He has never liked Christa and her superior, do-gooder attitude. That includes her smug faggot friend also, but he'll have to wait to grab Gary because there is no solid evidence linking him to this rebel movement. Still, just once he would like to get the better of Gary Goodwin.

He gives the plan to grab Christa one last play in his mind, just to be certain he has accounted for all the possible outcomes. If he pulls this off without any difficulty, and gains valuable information from her, he will have his father's favor and potentially the leadership of the corporation upon his death. Always the end game—who will inherit the 'throne' is the motivating factor, since he isn't the first-born son he must work harder to keep his father's faith. So far it is working because he is first in line to inherit control of Marshall Industries should his father pass away, Christa was his insurance that he would stay first in line.

"Kimball!" Henry yells for his security officer - it is time to bring Christa in and find out what she knows.

******

I need to head for the nearest train or bus station. I think I should drive toward the far end of the Valley, taking the canyons rather than the freeway. There aren't many lights in the canyon, and the road twists back and forth on itself as it winds its way up to Mulholland Drive. This plan feels safer to me. I can see the ridge of the hilltop and the lights of the Valley stretching out for miles before me. This sight always takes my breath away. Normally I would have pulled over onto one of the dirt turnouts to take in the view, but tonight I need to keep driving. The road is empty, and the quiet of the mountain ridge road gives it a lonely feeling up here. Only one other car's headlights flash occasionally behind me as I round each bend—each time reminding me that I am not completely alone. I'm making good time, and soon I will head across the valley floor to the other side where I can make a safe exit.

Glancing in my rear-view mirror, it seems the lights from the other car are starting to catch up with me. I accelerate a little so I won't slow them down, but not too much because of the curves in the road. Almost immediately, the lights are on top of me, and a black SUV plows into the back end of my car! My car jerks and skids for a moment, but I'm still in control. My sweaty palms slide on the steering wheel and my heart pounds as I accelerate to try to get away from the SUV. A moment later, the car is on the side of me on a two-lane curving mountain highway. I can't see through its tinted windows, so I have no idea who is trying to run me off the road. The car swings into mine, and I really panic this time because it is a shear drop to the canyon floor on the other side of me. I need to hold on—I refuse to die this way!

The SUV hits me again, and this time the force causes my car to skid along the dirt shoulder—but I am running out of shoulder! Oh God, I am sliding toward the edge. I desperately press on the brake, but I can't get the car to stop. The car is inching over the edge, so I throw my arms in front of my face in a futile attempt to shield myself from the fall—but a moment later, I am still in the driver's seat, and nothing has happened. I peek through my crossed arms to find that my car has come to a stop, but it is halfway suspended in air over the side of the mountain, while the back end still rests on the road. My mouth is opens to scream, but no sound comes out. I freeze. I don't dare move.

They are so quick and efficient. They unlock the car door, cut my seat belt, and rip me from the car so fast that I barely have time to think about what is happening to me. As my legs come flying out of the vehicle, there is a metal groaning sound from my car as it goes over the edge, falling silently for a second, and then hitting the bottom, exploding upon impact.

Two men tape my mouth and hands and throw a blanket over my head, shoving me into their SUV like a piece of luggage. I know my first alternative was a fiery death, but I'm not sure this option is going to be any better. My heart still pounds hard, so I breathe deeply in an effort to calm down. If an opportunity to escape should present itself, I need to be able to think logically.

I hope for a stop, but they keep driving for a very a long time. I have no idea which direction we are headed or anything about where they might be taking me, and the further away they drive the less hope I have of being found. My purse and my phone have been destroyed with the car—nobody knows where I am and there is no way to track me. About now, I am kicking myself for not taking the freeway. At least that would have been a more public area, and my abduction might have been caught on a traffic camera. In the canyons, there is nothing but wilderness and blackness for miles.

Finally they've come to a stop, and, with the blanket still over my head, they roughly haul me from the car and lead me into a building where the only thing I can discern is that it must be big and empty because there is an unbroken echo of our footsteps as we walk. I ache all over from the accident. I can feel the muscles in my back, and my legs want to spasm from the stress. A door opens and with a heavy metal sound, it clangs shut behind me. Leading me inside to a smaller room, they push me into a chair and secure my wrists and ankles with plastic ties. They pull the blanket off my head, but the room is dark and I can't make out my captors. They have taped my mouth, which prevents me from asking the millions of questions swirling in my confused mind. It's fine, it would be better if they spoke first, but nobody has made a sound, so I have no voice to identify them—nothing. I can feel myself wanting to hyperventilate, so I focus on my breathing and successfully center myself again. Out of the darkness, they douse me with a bucket of ice-cold water. I am drenched, and my clothes are soaking wet. I hear the clang of the metal door behind me, and I know they have left me alone in the dark room. It takes no time at all before I am shaking and shivering, and my jaw is clattering so violently that I think my teeth might break. I can't warm myself. The spasms of shaking are unbearable. I try to visualize myself warmer with heat rising up in my body. My stomach muscles are tight, and I feel nauseous from the stress, but I continue to visualize heat rising in my body. Eventually the visualization relaxes me just enough that I pass out and travel to my dream world for a moment.

I am standing in a large park with tall trees, rolling grass hills, and a lake in the middle. It could be Central Park in New York City. In front of me is a teenaged, African American boy playing chess with a much older white man. They are going toe-to-toe in a game of speed chess and have attracted a large crowd. Quite suddenly, the older man captures the boy's Black Queen. In that moment, the boy looks directly at me and starts to mouth some words but I can't hear him! What? What are you saying? Then I can just barely make it out, "I know who you are."

******

Sparks, and The Nomad, watch the hustle of activity as the OTP bunker is packed up for a move. Once the Council heard that Phoebe may have compromised their security, the decision was made to transfer the bunker to The Farm location. Sparks is not happy about the energy going into the move and nothing being done to save Christa.

"We have to do something! We can't just leave her there—they will kill her!" Sparks is not thinking straight since it's obvious he's currently motivated by pure emotion.

The Nomad's eyes are filled with empathy, but his words are hard, "We warned her. It was all we could do—and at tremendous risk to us. We must leave her, for now. The Council has decided. But it's also for Christa to finally understand who she is and how important her role is with the movement."

"I don't understand any of that," says Sparks, the volume of his voice rising. "All I know is that they will torture her and take her as close to death as they can, to try and learn what she knows. I have to do something! Please..." He sits down dejectedly because he already knows by the look on The Nomad's face that nothing is going to happen.

"You'll do nothing, Sparks." It is a rare moment to see The Nomad so forceful and insistent. "Anything you do now will not only result in Christa's death but the deaths or suffering of thousands of other people as well." He stops and lets this information sink into Sparks' mind.

In the background, Big G is lost in thought—staring off into space and moving his hands as if he is engaged in some type of activity. Sparks and The Nomad notice him for the first time during their conversation.

Big G mutters what sounds like nonsense, but his eyes grow brighter. There is almost a static charge in the air from the activity in his brain. Holding his hand up, he starts to twist it from side to side as if he is holding an object. He says, "She's the queen, the black queen. She was sacrificed but we can win—we can win because of that."

Sparks looks at The Nomad with a quizzical expression. The Nomad motions him to not say anything.

"It's the game of the century. They got greedy by taking her out of play. They think they've crippled us. They'll be aggressive now, but we can reposition our forces and go for a plan they will never see coming. Get them from the inside out. We can still fight.

They will expect the protests and outward threats of bombings or social disruption. They think Christa will give them the power they need to break us. They got greedy. That was an emotional move and it will bite them in the ass!" Big G breaks his reverie and turns to focus on The Nomad and Sparks.

He explains to them that he is referring to the chess master, Bobby Fischer's, famous "game of the century." In it, Fischer sacrificed his black queen halfway through the game shocking everyone. Technically his ability to win became far more difficult without her. He went on to win the game with his remaining pieces because of his superior strategy but also because his opponent probably relaxed a little knowing Fischer's queen was gone.

Big G believes the current situation mirrors that game. Christa is the black queen, and captors might let their guard down as they interrogate her believing that they have now found the means to crush the OTP. The movement's strategy will be to not fight the expected fight. We will fight them from the inside out."

The Nomad immediately gets what Big G is driving at, and it is a daring and risky plan. The words he had heard so many years ago when he first walked into that musician's body in Harlem came back to him, the same words he had said to Christa when he first met her, "There is an army of higher consciousness waiting out there." He knows what needs to happen next.

"G, I really don't know what I would do without you." The Nomad hugs the big man, and Sparks watches the entire scene mystified.

"And Christa? " asks Sparks.

The Nomad looks at him and says with conviction, "If you want to save Christa, you'll have to do nothing at all. As long as they believe she can give them information, they won't kill her.

We must not hint that we might be changing our plan because of her capture. We must not react—no matter how difficult it is. Do you understand?"

Sparks struggles with himself for a moment and then nods yes.

"One more thing… did Christa know the full story about the analog com system?"

"No, I only contacted her the one time on the pay phone at the hospital. As far as she is concerned, that was a one-time trick. She never knew about the network."

"Good—because the time has come to get the word out."

CHAPTER FIVE

KNOWING IS EVERYTHING

"Ambitions debt is paid."

Across the world, the people are waking from a long, ignorant sleep.
They can see clearly now that their governments only serve a few.
Eighty-five people control 90% of the world's wealth and
they will do whatever they need to hold onto it.
The people are peacefully marching in the streets. Austerity has been
enacted by governments to safeguard the wealth of a few. Austerity is
only for the poor and the disenfranchised
because the wealthy are living anything but austere lives.
The level of greed, which is openly displayed and never punished—
the struggle to put food on their tables,
and roofs over their heads—shocks the people.
The people are pointing their fingers at the moneylenders and want to
make them pay for their crimes against society.
The people are rioting to punish the corrupt police who "protect and
serve" only the rich, while the rest

are pushed into private prisons or violent death.
The people are turning to desperate violence
to protect their natural resources from becoming another
commodity to line the pockets of the 85.
Into this hopelessness has descended the new order, the new leadership,
an "army of higher consciousness." Souls that have come to create
revolutionary change before all humanity,
and the planet, perish because of a greedy few.
The eighty-five have barricaded their lives away from the masses.
Behind walls and security, out of touch with reality, they continue to
wreak havoc through their laws, their raping of the land, their "God-
like" manipulation of nature's biology, and their avarice.
The eighty-five who have bought and sold our freedoms
right out from under our noses. They control the media so truth is
unrecognizable. They control our education so wisdom is unheard of.
They control our laws so justice has disappeared.
Keep us stupid, fat, and apathetic, and there will be more for them.
They laugh behind their polished mahogany doors
at the ease with which they control the people.
The debt for their gross ambition will be paid,
and the people are ready to collect.

******

I have been sitting, soaking wet, in this cold, metal chair with a pool of water at my feet for what feels like hours. Time is impossible to judge because nothing remarkable happens. No window to the outside, no light, alarms, changing of the guard, no life at all. Just an endless moment that could be minutes or hours. I feel light-headed and achy, and my thinking is so fuzzy I can't make sense of any of this. I've tried twisting my wrists and ankles against the plastic ties that bind me to the chair, but they're too strong—they just cut into my skin. Now, all I can do is wait for their next move—and there will be a next move. Of course, I have questions, but the biggest one is who took me and what they want with me. They haven't killed me, so I'll assume they want something I have, probably information on OTP. My logic is trying to work overtime right now as I piece this story together.

I think I have dozed off again... my head droops on my chest and I feel groggy as I shake off the tiredness. I hear footsteps outside the door to the room. Completely awake now, I sit tense and still with anticipation as someone unlocks the door. The room is flooded with daylight, and my pupils can't dilate fast enough—I am temporarily blinded. My head hurts from the visual overload of light, and I focus on the floor. I am squinting at the cracks in the concrete, when a pair of men's, black leather shoes come to a stop in front of me. I look up to try to see the man's face, but the door shuts, and I am plunged into total darkness again. Only this time I am not alone, and I work very hard to stay calm and to anticipate what may come next.

I hear his footsteps as he circles around me like a predatory animal. Still, he has not said a word. My complete vulnerability is overwhelming, and I continue to mentally strategize my options to protect myself. Probably the worst option I can come up with is flipping my chair backward to potentially crack my skull open on the concrete floor—it would be effective, but I need a more workable solution, and I don't see one. All I can do is hide my fear and play along with my captor.

He continues to circle me, slowly putting one foot in front of the other, and his soft leather shoes make a swooshing sound on the concrete. Occasionally he moves closer to me and I smell the light scent of his expensive cologne that mingles with his hot breath on my neck. I want to crawl out of my skin and escape this reality. I futilely try to imagine a face or a physical description to him to make him flesh and blood rather than a, silent demon.

Without warning, he touches my face and I involuntarily flinch. He slides the back of his hand slowly down the side of my face, caressing my cheek. My mind starts to race as I consider a new option—he might want to rape me. I have naively focused on the idea that he wants information about OTP; it never occurred to me that his agenda would be more perverse! Every muscle in my body is rigid while he continues to slide his hand from my neck, down my collarbone until he reaches inside my blouse and fondles my breast. My stomach muscles tighten, and I think I am going to be sick, but I continue to be as unresponsive as a stone. I employ a trick I developed in childhood. I imagine I am a rock with no nerves, and it usually works. I feel he wants me to lose control and panic. Fear is his weapon, and if I prevent my repulsion and terror from rising to the surface, I can deny him a weakness he could exploit. If he knows he has elicited fear in me, that could be more of a turn-on for this sick bastard. Flipping my chair back and potentially taking myself out is starting to look more and more like a better option. I can live with what might come next. I must.

I hear him snap his fingers a couple of times, and out of the darkness appear two men who proceed to cut the plastic ties binding me to the chair. Just as I am about to breathe a sigh of relief, one of them holds my arms and the other quickly unzips my wet jeans and pulls them off me. Oh God! Are they going to gang rape me? I can't even... Now, shivering cold, in only a t-shirt and my underwear, they tie me to the chair again and disappear into the darkness. All is quiet for a moment but I don't dare relax because I know he is still here.

I hear him again, his expensive shoes, moving to the side of me. He slowly slides his hand up the inside of my thigh. My legs are tied to the chair, and all my instinct wants to do is pull my knees together, but I can't. I unconsciously pull against the ties in a vain attempt to close my legs, but he continues to move his hand further up my thigh, and my only thought is, "Make him stop! I can't go through this!" Almost as if he heard my plea, he stops just short of sliding his hand inside my underwear and totally violating me.

"So brave," the sneer in his voice cuts through the darkness and adds the slightest humanity to this horrible moment. It is comforting, in an odd way, that he has finally spoken—now he is just a man, and maybe I might get a chance to defend myself.

"There is nowhere for you to go, and nobody will find you. It's really up to you, Christa, how long this inquiry will last." He lets the statement hang in the air; obviously, he doesn't expect an answer since I still had the tape on my mouth. "We know you have been working with the uprising, and we want to know what you know, including all the information you passed on to them."

He deliberately speaks softly, so I have to strain to hear him. A subtle sadistic tone to his voice sounds vaguely familiar, but I can't place it; my head is too scrambled.

"I know we will have to break you—otherwise you will never give us anything. I really would prefer not to go there, but I won't pretend that I'm not going to enjoy watching you fall apart." He laughs just slightly at this last statement, and to emphasize his joke he places his hand on the inside of my thigh again and caresses it. Panic rises inside me but I push it down because my resolution to not show him I am afraid is stronger than my fear.

Just as I think I can't stand him touching me another second, he takes his hand away. I begin to exhale when I suddenly feel cold metal press against the skin of my thigh and being slid along my leg until it rests against my panties. Then I hear the sound of the hammer being cocked on the gun. "Who is this sick, perverse asshole?" I think.

He pulls the gun away, and even though I want to breathe again, I don't trust him. His point has been made, he will do anything to get me to divulge the information he thinks I am privy to.

"I need you to feel how serious I am and that we will obtain your intel by any means available to us. I am going to take the tape from your mouth and ask you a question. I remind you that nobody will hear you if you scream, so you shouldn't waste your energy. If you cooperate you won't die—now."

He rips the tape off, and my mouth and cheeks burn as the adhesive tears away a little of my flesh. I can't touch my face to try to relieve the pain, and tears well up uncontrollably in my eyes.

"Who are you working with?"

It seems like a simple question, one that I can throw a name at to buy myself time. I flash on The Nomad, Sparks, Big G and Gary. They are my fellow soldiers and I know all of them would lay down their lives for me if in a similar situation. I can't give them up to this asshole no matter what he might do to me! I am scared to remain silent, but I have no other choice. In this moment, I realize that, if necessary, I really would "rather die first." How many times have I used that phrase casually referring to a dress I didn't want to wear or food I didn't want to eat? Now I am experiencing the phrase literally. I remain silent and his question feels like a knife hanging in the darkness, waiting to end my life or the lives of my friends.

"I thought this would be your reaction, but it's the wrong way to go. You'll see in time it will be better to cooperate."

While he is talking, there is a buzzing sound, but I can't tell from where it's coming. Before I can fully comprehend what's about to happen to me and perhaps brace myself, an electric taser gun is set to my wet skin on the inside of my thigh, where moments ago he was caressing me. The current shoots through my cold, shivering body, burning a path through my muscles and veins until it felt like my hair is on fire. I can't control my muscles and jerk involuntarily until the chair rocks violently. However, no chance that it is going to tip backward because he reaches out and steadies it. He isn't about to let me crack my head open and take the easy way out.

He pulls the taser back, and I slump forward, still shaking violently. Tears threaten to spill out of my eyes and my fingernails dig into the palms of my hands in an effort to divert my mind from the torture my body has just gone through. I am completely overloaded emotionally—fear, anger, sadness, loneliness, confusion. I feel despondent, fearing that this may never end, when I hear one of those black leather shoes step towards me again and the buzz of the taser. That is the last thing I remember—everything goes black.

Release, I feel free, no pain. I float above my body in the dark room. I see myself curled forward in the chair below and my torturer leaning over me. Although I am unconscious, he is still applying the taser, and my body is flopping around involuntarily. I try to see his face from my overhead vantage point because I really want to know who this sadistic prick is, but the room is too dark and he has his back to me. Still, I keep trying to focus on identifying him when a voice from behind me says, "Christa…"

I turn, and see a woman floating in the air with me. She has very long dark hair, which courses out around her. She is wearing some type of beaded and fringed dress that looks Native American. This should have struck me as odd, but she seems so familiar to me—I feel we have met before, in fact, I am certain of it. Intuitively I feel I can trust her. She says, "You know you can't stay here. You must go back to that body."

"I can't go back to that! He's just going to kill me."

"He will not kill you. But you are about to go on a journey to find out who you are, and you need to embark in that body."

I am pulled back in my body by a terrible force, but I am still unconscious, locked in the deepest part of my mind. I can't feel the outside world or the pain I am experiencing. Instead, my spirit, or my soul, begins to slip backward in my memory.

******

I stand in a dingy kitchen, looking at a very little girl, probably about six years old, huddled on the floor crying. A man is raging and periodically lunges towards the sobbing child, and threatens her with his fist if she doesn't "shut up." There is a woman in the kitchen who is somewhat immobilized with fear. She is thin and frail, with a faded elegance to her exotic African features, she pulls on the arm of the angry man, even though she has no strength. He drags her along the floor as he lunges forward and grabs the little girl, picking her up by the throat causing her to choke and gasp for air. The woman screams over and over in the background—unintelligible sounds of anguish and pleading. Finally, the child stops breathing, and the man tosses her like a rag doll against the wall and never once looks back to see if she is alive. She falls lifeless to the floor and doesn't move.

I see the spirit of the little girl run away from her broken body on the kitchen floor and head directly towards me. A familiar voice speaks from behind me in this memory, and I turn to see the woman with the long dark hair. She says to my spirit, "Take that body, and, when the time is right, I will come to you and remind you of the work you came to do." She holds her hand out to the little girl's spirit. The girl hesitates at first to take the woman's hand and looks to me for permission. I nod OK, she reaches out and both are gone. In the same moment, I am pulled into the child's lifeless body and gasp to consciousness. I hear the thin frail woman in the background saying, "Oh thank you, thank you God."

The man has passed out on the kitchen table, and the woman quickly sneaks me upstairs and tucks me into bed saying, "OK baby, you sleep well, and in the morning you will have forgotten all about what happened tonight. It will just be a bad dream. Please baby, please forget." She cries softly for a moment as she lays her head on my chest and listens to my little heartbeat. Then she turns out the light and kisses me good night.

Once the house is quiet, I run away. No identification, no idea whose body I am inhabiting, I just run. Nobody will look for me—it will be too dangerous for that timid little woman who is my mother to come after me and the man, probably my father, doesn't care enough to try.

During my journey, I am not alone, the woman with the long dark hair guides me along the way until I am on the doorstep of the McCaffrey's foster care home. She then disappears. I have forgotten all of this—how I became Christa McCaffrey. I have forgotten that even then I had a purpose and resilient spirit destined to enact change. Now, I realize that all my life I have been aware that I wasn't alone, and, with that revelation, I can hear the voices of other walk-in souls like myself. The members of the Council, The Nomad—they are there guiding me, speaking to me, and I hear my own voice say, "You are ISHI."

The woman with long dark hair appears in the midst of the cacophony of voices... she is the closest to me... my personal guide. "I am Fallingtree, I have been with you since before you came into this body and I will be with you through every moment of this life journey as well. Know that you will survive and you will make a difference."

I remember The Nomad's question when we met, "Do you know who you are?"

Now, I have an answer... a resounding, "Yes, I am ISHI."

******

Damien Marshall, Sr. is seated in his private library, decorated with well-worn but expensive furniture and items collected from lifetimes of family money passed from heir to heir. Through the leaded glass windows is a view of the mansion grounds, which is turning shades of gold and pink with the setting sun. The oak paneling of the library takes on a warm patina as the light bounces off the polished wood. He speaks to a man in a dark suit with a distinct military posture. He is the same government spook that attended Phoebe Carlyle's funeral.

"This is an organized rebellion. They want to get rid of the present economic structure. We cannot allow that. They don't even believe in Democracy—they are socialists for God's sake!" He paces a little, but it isn't his style to get too agitated, probably because he can always throw money at the problem and it will go away.

The man in the suit stands there not saying a word.

"We have moles in the anti-government movement. Time to conduct some disrupting of our own—inject some violence.

We don't want another Gandhi or Martin Luther King rising up from the masses. Their next public rally is in Chicago where they will be gearing up for a big march on Washington, I want the momentum stopped there. We need to discredit and crush this before it gets out of hand."

The man in the suit still says nothing but it is obvious by the occasional slight nod of agreement that he is taking in every word, despite the militaristic and otherwise motionless manner in which he stands.

In an uncharacteristic move, Damien Marshall, Sr. turns and slams his fist on his desk out of frustration over how far this rebellion has already progressed unchecked. He has already thrown a lot of his money, as well as his associates' money, to finance military grade weapons for local police departments in an effort to create a small militia that is in their pocket. He has the cooperation of not only the FBI but also the financial community to make certain that this rebellion will be shut off at every turn.

"I want the FBI on this. We have domestic terrorism laws that can be used to dissemble this group. Why hasn't this been done already? Don't tell me about the constitutional right to assemble. Not with terrorism on the rise—Homeland Security takes precedent."

His question is for nobody in particular and the man in the suit doesn't answer.

"Convey my wishes to the director and to local law enforcement in Chicago. Let them know if they need anything, I will provide it. We'll talk soon." He shows the man in the suit to the door and returns to his desk.

The room grows darker now as the sun sets, and Damien Marshall, Sr. turns on a desk lamp. He pulls a Satellite Phone from a drawer, dials a number and waits.

"Listen," he starts in a hushed tone, "I'll put the FBI on this, but if we don't handle it right now, we'll have a group of martyrs on our hands rather than terrorists." He pauses and listens to the voice on the other end. "Yes, I know... I don't want them messing with our resources either. We are very close to having all the pieces in place. We need to take them out of the game before the treaty is signed. They have no idea what they have stumbled onto. I am confident we can squash this fairly quickly. We are working the data on them and it will be fairly easy to manipulate. Watch the news, you will know when its taken care of."

He listens for a moment longer and puts the SAT Phone back in his desk drawer. Typing a password into his computer suddenly causes an entire wall of his office to transform into several video screens, streaming live from places all over the planet. This is Marshall Industries' private satellite feed, which is capable of pinpointing exact geographical coordinates, and can zoom in with such precision that one can see blades of grass on the ground if needed. All of the feeds Damien Marshall, Sr. monitors are because he has a stake in the economies or the governments of these places. At the moment, he watches citizens fighting in the streets of Turkey and pays close attention to how the internet is fueling this—and, of course, he considers how to co-opt it for his own uses. He has his eyes on local elections within various governments for the purpose of making sure his people are in place. The recent disappearance of an influential industrialist in Texas has caught his attention, and he has several feeds dedicated to gaining information about this situation as it unfolds. The Texas billionaire is chipped, but so far this man remains missing, which raises some serious questions. He knows this man well and has done business with him. Old oil money—this man knows the game better than anyone. He is also an integral player in the upcoming trade treaty, which is top secret. For him to disappear off the map did raise some serious questions. For now, all Damien Marshall, Sr. can do is watch and wait.

He reflects on Christa and his suspicion that she is a spy. Maybe she knows something about the disappearance of this man. It's part of his motivation for taking her for interrogation. He hopes Henry will make it worth the sacrifice. He pulls the chain on his antique desk lamp, the room goes dark, and he sits there for a while thinking about his vision of the future and what it will take to get there.

*****

Every light in Sparks lab is on, causing the space to feel less than tranquil and more as if it is on fire. His shirtsleeves are rolled up, and he wears a white lab coat as he intensely works on a new project—a fabric that can change to reflect the surrounding environment, essentially a cloaking device. So far, his experiments have failed, but he knows a breakthrough is imminent, so he keeps pushing. Working long hours, barely eating, barely sleeping he knows if he can make this work, it will give OTP a distinct edge in the combat field.

Their protest marches and rallies have begun to gain momentum, the first phase of the uprising is clearly underway. Social media forums are burning up with commentary and spreading the word. Some will be shut down, but Sparks and his tech counterparts will create new forums in their place. The movement's profile is growing, making them all targets; they know they need to be ready.

Sparks is lost in thought as he analyzes the electrical and geometric integration of the tiny molecular-shaped "scales" he is developing. He is deep into solving how they will simultaneously reflect a 3-D object when the phone in the lab rings, breaking his thought process.

He is being summoned to a meeting. Immediately he drops what he is working on and rushes to The Nomad's office.

"Sparks, I am glad you are here. We have had some news about Christa." The Nomad is calm but very serious as he delivers this information. "We have a couple of sources who have been able to verify how she may have been taken from her car in a remote area. So far, nobody has had eyes on her so we can't confirm if she is still alive. One other thing—Henry Marshall had something to do with her abduction. We think he put the order out to grab her, but we have not confirmed it—that's just a rumor at the moment. We have no idea if DJ is involved but we know Damien Marshall, Sr. must have sanctioned it if Henry did take her. He wouldn't make a move this bold without his father's blessing."

Sparks takes in what The Nomad has said, and he begins to quantify the ramifications of Christa's disappearance. If Henry had her it could compromise the information they have received from her, plus she knows the inner workings of many aspects of OTP—enough to let Damien Marshall, Sr. know they are highly organized. Sparks is ready to get in the field and retaliate but wants their next move not only to be smart, but brilliant. He trusts The Nomad to know what they should do. Sparks remains quiet, unemotional, and completely analytical upon hearing all of this. "What's next?" he asks.

Big G leans forward, and in his low, bold voice he answers, "We have been thinking of a few options, but one would be to take a hostage of our own and force an exchange. Similar to what is happening in Texas right now. Texas is the beginning of the reclamation. The plan involves the capturing of the leaders of various corporations and banks and forcing a near-death experience to happen so we can open a door for an ISHI to walk-in."

"An ISHI?" asks Sparks. Everybody stops speaking and Gary looks at The Nomad to answer this question.

"I am an ISHI. You could say we are extra-terrestrial, but we are inter-dimensional too. We have existed along side humans for thousands of years," says The Nomad. "We are much like you, but we only exist on what you would call the soul level. There are others, and we are connected telepathically. We have always helped humanity when a crisis arises—Earth is our home too. Presently the ISHI have been 'walking in' or, trading with human souls all over the planet because times are so perilous. We are here in great numbers right now because there is so much work to do, and we only hope we are not too late."

Sparks is amazed but not very surprised by The Nomad's revelation because he has always known The Nomad is a unique individual. That he is from another world just confirms it. Sparks has so many questions about the ISHI, but he can see The Nomad is anxious to talk about business. His questions will have to wait.

The Nomad continues," Now we need to focus on the task at hand. This will be a big take-down, and we will have to pool our resources and manpower with other OTP groups."

Sparks asks, "Are we talking about one of the Marshalls?" Thinking out loud he adds, "They are well protected, except DJ. ... he might be a possible target, and his father will want him back. If this is the plan, then I am working on something in the lab; if I can perfect it, it would dramatically reduce the number of militia and weapons we would need to pull this off."

"That is exactly what I had hoped you would say," says The Nomad. The three of them work together for the rest of the night devising the final leg of their retaliation.

CHAPTER SIX

EN PASSÉ

♟

Gary drives up the Santa Monica Canyon headed for DJ's home. Eucalyptus trees line the driveway, throwing dappled sunlight across the windshield. He has felt helpless since Christa's disappearance and he can sense she isn't OK, but any move on his part will reveal his involvement with OTP, putting them at risk. From the beginning of their friendship, he has always had an intuitive link with Christa, and that ingrained connection is working overtime now. What should his proper response be to maintain his innocence in the eyes of the Marshall family? He concludes that if he wants to appear as if he is in the dark about Christa's other activities, he will have a proper freak-out.

Gary pounds on the front door of DJ's home, demanding to be let in, until DJ angrily opens the door to observe Act I of his "freak-out."

"Gary!" DJ starts but isn't allowed to finish his sentence.

"Oh my God!" wails Gary, "You poor thing!" He wraps his arms around DJ, hugging his stiff body and then pushes him to arm's length to assess him. "You look like hell. I came here looking for Christa, but I have my answer from the look of you."

He sweeps past DJ, pushing the door open so he can enter the hallway. "I've been calling that girl, texting her, emailing her, with no answer." He says all of this while starting to ascend the stairs to the second floor. "Did you two decide to go underground for a couple of days? Fighting? What is it?"

Gary does not wait for an answer; he keeps climbing the stairs. "Never mind, it's none of my business…besides my girl will tell me everything eventually. I just need my friend right now! I'm having a shopping and spa crisis!" He turns and faces the upper landing and yells as if Christa might be sleeping in the upper bedroom, "Honey, wake up! I hope you're decent because I'm coming up. Throw on some Louboutains, and let's go shopping."

"Wait!" comes DJ's voice from down below. "She's not up there."

Gary stops on the staircase and turns, then with his best beauty-queen walk, starts to descend the stairs, "Oh. OK. Where is she then?"

DJ just looks at Gary blankly.

Gary knows this is the moment for the grand climax to his emotional freak-out. "DJ? Where is Christa?" He continues to look straight into his eyes as he walks towards him.

DJ doesn't say anything but looks as if he is going to breakdown any second. Gary notes his reaction so he can tell Sparks later that it doesn't seem DJ is involved with Christa's disappearance. Still, Gary has to play this out just in case he is wrong. He rushes DJ and grabs him by the shoulders, shaking him and says, "Why can't you answer me? Where is she?"

He let's go of DJ and smooths the front of his own shirt to compose himself. He starts to walk around the front hallway in circles and then he rushes from there to the dining room to the kitchen to the living room to the library as if he is looking for Christa. DJ trails behind him saying, "She's not here, Gary. Really. I haven't seen her in a few of days."

Gary stops and looks DJ in the face, "A few days! What have you been doing all this time? A FEW DAYS! Have you called the police, the FBI, anyone? Why didn't you call me? Have you checked the hospitals? What have you done? Shit, DJ... A few days?" Gary continues to stare at him with a look of unbelieving horror. Hearing DJ's answer sharpens the reality that Christa is missing. Now Gary is very worried. "You don't know anything. Oh God! She could be hurt or... dead."

With that, Gary collapses into the nearest chair, fighting back the hot tears that are welling in his eyes. He swallows hard to compose himself again. Then he lunges from the chair and starts beating on the emotionless DJ, yelling, "What are you doing? You need to find her!"

DJ grabs Gary's hands and restrains him. He is devoid of any emotion at that moment and his face is impossible to read, but, just for a second, Gary sees the look of a Marshall in his eyes—a look he's often seen on Henry's and Damien Marshall, Sr.'s faces—a look of "I'm in control and you don't mess with me."

"Gary. You need to calm down. This isn't helping." DJ waits for Gary to appear collected and, then he releases his grip on his hands. "It's being handled. I've let my brother and Kimball know. In the meantime, we are waiting for a ransom note before we consider contacting the FBI. We are keeping everything very quiet. You know how these things go down in families like ours."

Gary nods. He knows very well. In DJ's family, scandal and the appearance of vulnerability are avoided at any cost. The impact on their stock prices is always more important to a family like theirs. Even though Christa isn't a family member, she is seriously involved with DJ and that makes the Marshalls vulnerable.

"We tracked her GPS and found her car, but it had crashed and burned at the bottom of a canyon. We assumed her phone was destroyed, so we don't have a trail to follow at this time."

Gary gasps at this news, "No!" He puts his hand to his mouth to stifle his voice because he doesn't know what he might say next, but his eyes are wide with terror, and DJ can see what Gary is feeling all too clearly.

"She wasn't in the car—they didn't find a body in the wreckage." With that, Gary lets out a very deep sigh of relief.

"Thank you! There is hope she's still alive. Maybe she is wandering around with no memory. Serious trauma often causes memory loss. Have you checked the local hospitals?" asks Gary.

"Everything that can be done is being done." DJ reaches out to pat Gary on the arm and reassure him but Gary grabs him in a huge bear hug and starts crying on DJ's shoulder.

"Yes... I'm sure you are doing everything you can," Gary says between sobs. He looks up from DJ's shoulder and surveys the room uncomfortably. His job is done here. He's given a performance worthy of Meryl Streep; it's time to leave. "Well, I suppose I am just in the way now. I have an event to get to— time to put on my brave face. You must let me know the minute you hear anything! You have my cell. I will drop anything I am doing and come running if you need me."

"Of course, I will call you the moment I know anything. You're a good friend." DJ forces a smile.

Gary awkwardly hugs DJ one last time and leaves without saying another word.

Once Gary is inside his car, he scrolls through the messages on his phone. He half hopes there will be one from Christa, but there is nothing. He thinks to himself, "Christa, you are one tough babe, but right now I am afraid you're in over your head."

Gary takes a moment, then starts his car and heads to his job— another big society event. He thinks, "Thank God I will be busy this evening; it will take my mind off of worrying about Christa when there is nothing I can do."

******

Gary pulls his car into the wide circular drive of the Cape Cod style mansion in Brentwood. As soon as he parks his car, Carmen Anderson, a beautiful brunette socialite in her 30s comes running into the driveway wearing a see-through red caftan over a black bikini. Her expensive mule sandals click-clack on the antique brick drive.

"Garrrryyyyy!" She stretches out the consonants and vowels of his name to show her desperation as she runs towards him with her arms outstretched. She gathers him up in a grateful hug, giving him an air kiss. "I'm soooo glad you are finally here! I'm going crazy without your practiced eye."

"We can't have you going crazy otherwise who will throw the party of the year?" Gary says with his most disarming smile. "Never fear the Calvary is here!" and with that, Gary laughs and hooks his arm into Carmen's, and says, referring to the famous Harper's Bazaar fashion editor, "I love the red on you! Very Diana Vreeland."

She kisses him on the cheek and says, "We need to get inside. I am afraid they are already making a mess of the flowers without you there."

Carmen Anderson is married to Weldon Anderson, CEO of CBI Corporation. Nobody can exactly define where Weldon's money comes from since his family had been earning fortunes in various industries for decades. Her home is worthy of her position in society as Weldon's wife—beautifully decorated; it has been featured on the pages of many society magazines. They are clearly part of the one percent of the wealthiest families in America, occupying just the sort or home in which Gary is most welcome. Weldon has known Carmen since she was a hostess at a popular restaurant in Beverly Hills, where he spent thousands of dollars just to be able to flirt with her until she agreed to date him and eventually become his third wife. Weldon is fond of saying, "Third time's a charm," and Carmen is a charmer. She has cajoled millions out of Weldon's unsuspecting friends for charity, all the while befriending their wives to become one of the most powerful fundraisers in the city.

Gary is Carmen's right-hand man for all of her events, and she pays him double to be on call for her. He caters everything from a small intimate luncheon of powerful Hollywood wives to a post-Oscar-Ceremony gala event. He has been by her side since her wedding, and she relies upon his judgment. Because Carmen values him, Weldon values him too. When Gary arrives at the Anderson home, it is as if he is family. He has the run of the place—no room is off limits, and nobody worries about being candid in front him. Today is no exception.

As Gary moves about the house setting up the flower arrangements and rearranging furniture to be more conducive to conversation and traffic flow, he hears Weldon on the phone in his office. Most times Gary pays no attention to Weldon's tight jawed voice because his conversations tend to be incredibly boring, but this time a few words catch his ear: "Marshall Industries is…" His voice cuts off for a moment, but Gary keeps listening while pretending to fix the flowers in the hallway, "Yes, they were," Weldon continues, "but now Damien Marshall Sr. is attending."

Attending what, wonders Gary; does he mean tonight's event? Gary stands still, hoping to catch every word.

"That's right. Yes, it is a big get. Everyone will want his attention. Hmmm... uh huh... We have a jet at the Santa Monica Airport ready to go tomorrow morning. I'd love to head out tonight, but my wife has me committed to some event at our home. Tomorrow it will be you, me, Owen Carlyle, and Damien Marshall, Sr." Weldon is quiet as he listens to whomever is on the other end of his phone conversation, "Yes, 9am; see you there. You know which hanger? Right, see you tomorrow."

Weldon hangs up, and before Gary can get away from the door, he comes out into the hallway. Gary quickly picks up a vase of white Chinese Mums and says in his most frivolous and non-threatening tone, "Aren't these just divine?"

Weldon looks up but appears lost in thought. "Oh yes, Gary, very nice," he mutters and leaves the house. Gary has always found that people underestimate his intelligence when he behaves that way, because he is gay, they almost expect it. This time it works to his advantage. He knows he has stumbled onto some valuable information, and he can't wait to get to a safe location and send a message to OTP.

*****

Big G is standing in the middle of large, windowless conference room, which has computer terminals and screens, and one central interactive screen. There are several desks around the periphery leaving the center of the room open. The Nomad and Sparks stand on either side of him as they watch G digest the latest intel about a plane that will be carrying several important executives, including Damien Marshall, Sr. He has his arms crossed, a clear sign that he is in his head, plotting strategy, calculating the moves ahead, and seeing "the game."

G is still calculating, replaying chess moves in his head as he substitutes real people for the pieces. "They have Christa—they've taken the Queen out of play. Their guard is down. They think they have crippled us. We need to push them—push the King."

"Damien Marshall, Sr.—he's the White King. We need to put him on the defensive and make him respond to our moves! He expects us to respond to his and try to rescue Christa. To panic…" G stops to look at Sparks and The Nomad, and then says resolutely, "We take the plane."

Sparks is immediately on top of that idea, but The Nomad needs more convincing. "If we do, we should only take Damien Marshall, Sr. and leave the others."

"Really?" questions Sparks. "But won't it put a hole in their plans if we take all of those men? We have the means and the opportunity."

"True, but, like the Texas plan, we only need one at a time." The Nomad continues, "Since Christa was taken, we have worked on a plan to take the rebellion off the street. We are getting nowhere with protests and waiting for legislation. We need to release a 'virus' into the very center of their organization. Now they have provided us the opportunity."

"A virus? Are you talking about biological warfare?" Sparks asks, not believing The Nomad will ever condone such a thing.

"No, not a physical virus—the ISHI—they are waiting in another dimension to come in and do the work to save humanity and the planet. They need bodies as vehicles in this dimension. But an ISHI can only enter a body if they are invited by a human soul. Most often this happens when the human doesn't want to go on living. The only way the transfer works, is if the human soul wants to be released. We plan to force the souls of a few powerful individuals in industry and government to give up their bodies and invite an ISHI to step in. We don't pretend this process will be non-violent because it won't be—but at this point it is necessary. Once the ISHI entities are in place, they will communicate telepathically, creating a global network that cannot be monitored by any government or corporation. We will work with humans to revolutionize the culture into something that will benefit the planet and humankind."

"But I thought they could only walk-in during a near death experience?" says Sparks.

"It's true that the soul must want to leave the body because it's dead or dying. I do not pretend that this will be a pleasant solution, but we will have to force the body to near death, perhaps more than once, to make the soul decide to leave. It's an option we never considered before, but these are desperate times, and we need leverage to correct the imbalance in the world. Otherwise, we lose, and humans lose in a very short period of time. Perhaps only one more generation."

"Let me understand this... We take Damien Marshall, Sr., force him to the brink of death until his soul agrees to leave his body, and then we guide a new soul—an ISHI soul—into his body. That soul will then go back into the world looking like Damien Marshall, Sr. but will run his company with the direction of the ISHI. Is that the plan?" Sparks asks.

"Yes," answers The Nomad. "This will work because they will only see us taking him as a hostage to negotiate Christa's return. Once we swap hostages the ISHI will have a presence in Marshall Industries. This plan is currently happening around the world, with heads of corporations, governments, and banks being abducted to create an opportunity for an ISHI to walk-in. You saw what happened in Iceland when they prosecuted their bankers, that was an ISHI movement," The Nomad stops to gauge Sparks' reaction.

Sparks takes a deep deep breathe, and lets it out slowly then says, "That's fucking brilliant! If this works, they will never know what hit them. It's the perfect bloodless coup! They are a souless bunch, so let's hope they have a soul to swap. Geez…" Sparks just stands there shaking his head and adding it up. Meanwhile Big G is still calculating the odds.

"The key is the white king. He is protected. It won't be easy."

"We'll need the help of another OTP militia group," The Nomad adds, "I know one that has several members working at the Santa Monica Airport. We'll team with them to commandeer the plane and grab Damien, Sr.," He looks at Sparks, "Let's get ready, this has to happen tomorrow at 9am. We have the element of surprise on our side; let's make it work."

******

Dawn is casting long shadows over the Santa Monica Mountains and the dark sky is rapidly giving way to the rising sun. Down on the ground, at the Santa Monica Airport, OTP is preparing to execute the abduction of Damien Marshall, Sr. The OTP members file into a hanger at the far end of the runway and wait for their instructions.

Sparks and Big G enter the hanger with a squad of ten men. They are met by the OTP members of the airport group to rehearse the plan of attack. They have three hours to get everything into place. The airport division of OTP has already substituted pilots, ground crew, and cabin crew for the Anderson jet flight crew. An airport ambulance has been provided to transport Damien Marshall, Sr. to a private medial facility of which only Big G and The Nomad know the location. Every person on the tarmac this morning is part of their group. Once the Marshall entourage arrives, the plan is to spray them with gunfire and create an ambush. Unfortunately they will not be able to use Sparks' immobilizing guns because it is doubtful they will have an opportunity to get close enough to their targets. They don't like this, but they know blood will be spilled today.

Santa Monica Airport, 9:00am

Three limousines arrive on the tarmac and head straight for Anderson's jet. The three cars stop in a line in front of the jet and the doors open. Sparks and his team start their approach towards the limos. They are not certain which car Damien Marshall, Sr. is in, so they wait for the men to emerge. The baggage handlers approach the cars—each one an OTP member with a handgun hidden in his or her waistband. Everything seems to be going according to plan. The stairs to the jet are lowered, and the pilot stands at the top to greet them as they board. He is armed as well, using his position on the stairs to gain a higher vantage point during the takedown. The ambulance waits in the distance for Sparks' signal that Damien Marshall, Sr. is ready for transport. Sparks thinks it is all moving along smoothly, but he still takes one last protective glance around the area because he knows a lot is riding on this operation, and he doesn't want anything to go wrong. Everything appears where it should be, but when he looks towards the hanger where the militia held its strategy meeting, he spots a female OTP member walking quickly to the back of the hanger. He tries to remember if this is in the plan, but it seems to him, everyone should be on the tarmac. He studies her—a young woman, short radical black hair shaved on the sides. Her face is odd—almost grotesque—as if one half is sliding downward. She has a slight limp, but, despite that, she is walking fast. Suddenly she stops in the middle of the hanger and looks over at all of them on the tarmac as if she is assessing the setup. She just stands there. Even from a distance, Sparks can see a horrible, ugly expression on her face, and in that moment he knows something is terribly wrong. Then she turns and continues to head for the back door of the hanger.

Sparks looks towards the limos, feeling a welling sense of danger but the next series of events unfolds so rapidly he is powerless to stop any of it. A barrage of bullets comes from inside the limousines. Sparks knows they have been set up, and he looks at Big G who nods in agreement that they should retreat to save as many lives as possible. The first man shot is the pilot, and he falls face forward down the stairs. The flight attendant comes running to the door of the jet, gun drawn, and she falls to a bullet as well. Damien Marshall, Sr., Owen Carlyle, and the others have never been in the limousines. In their place is a army of private soldiers, heavily armed, and decked out in Kevlar bulletproof gear. Ammunition almost bounces off their vests, while they pick off the OTP soldiers like birds on a wire. To Sparks' horror he watches as the baggage handlers, the men closest to the cars and the plane, have nowhere to retreat to, and the soldiers cut them down with automatic weapon fire. Those who could escape this blood bath are already running behind Sparks to the hanger. The OTP truck is parked in back, and that is the only way out. Sparks busts through the back door with one thing on his mind, get to the car.

"POP, POP, POP!"

Sparks falls on the concrete, not understanding what has just happened to him. He feels pain and wooziness; he's been shot and is lying in a pool of his own blood. He looks up, and the black-haired woman he had spotted earlier is standing over him with her gun aimed at his skull. He hears the gun cock and it is clear she is going to squeeze off one more shot, so he shuts his eyes and braces himself for the inevitable. A few seconds of silence pass and then there are voices all around him.

"Hang in there. Put some pressure, here! Come on, come on!" he can hear Big G frantically giving orders and several hands lifting him from the ground. A hot fire cuts through Sparks' body as they move him and then blackness takes over.

******

Damien Marshall, Sr., watches much of the airport insurrection on his private satellite feed, from the comfort of his wood-paneled office. His intelligence has been one hundred percent correct and he knows he has dealt a significant blow to the movement. He has some dead bodies and a bloody, failed, kidnapping event, which he can pin on OTP to create domestic terrorism chatter. The entire thing is playing to his favor, and he is very pleased. In a few days he will release the information that a paramilitary movement called, "Of the People," or OTP, was responsible for the attack. Which is the truth. But what the public will not know, is that Marshall Industries private security force have abducted and murdered people within the OTP movement long before the OTP orchestrated the attack at the Santa Monica Airport. Disinformation at its best. This is a good day for Damien Marshall, Sr. He pulls out one of his Cuban cigars from the ornately-carved silver cigar box and decides to reward himself with a smoke.

CHAPTER SEVEN

CHECK BUT NOT MATE

I open my eyes but there is no difference—all I see is darkness. My sense of time is gone—it could have been hours or days or weeks that I have been unconscious. I am descending into a crazy state because of a lack of sleep and continuous pain. I feel hands in the darkness. First they grab my wrists, and then they are cutting the plastic ties, freeing my arms and legs. I guess I'm not a threat anymore—besides, I am too weak to run. The man in the black leather shoes has tortured me on and off for hours or days, and it's all begun to blur together in my memory. He has asked me questions about things I know nothing about, such as a man in Texas I have never heard of and an airport terror attack. Oddly, he is not asking me about the things I do know, such as the location of the militia camps or any of their internal workings. But, despite my not knowing the answers to his questions, he continues to interrogate me, slap me, choke me, douse my head in water until I can't hold my breath anymore, administer electric shocks, deprive me of sleep and when all else fails—out of frustration—he uses me like a punching bag. Then he tosses my bruised and battered body back in a cell, giving me just enough time to recover so I can be tortured all over again. It is a hellish cycle, and I can't see how it will end except with my death.

I never could have survived all of this without Fallingtree. She has been with me since it began and guided me out of my body every time. We watch each episode from above, dispassionately, where I do not feel the pain being inflicted upon my body, where I don't scream out the names of people I don't want to betray. Sometimes I would die just for a moment, but they would put the paddles to my chest to make my heart beat again—as if they are jump-starting a car. From above I barely recognize my swollen and mangled self. Fallingtree assures me that all of the torture is about to end but that I still have work to do within this place before I can leave. Although I believe her, I really can't imagine what value I have because I am so beaten down.

After they cut the plastic ties, I slowly move my arms and legs to get the circulation back into my limbs. My ribs are bruised, but, by some miracle, I don't feel any broken bones. Everything is superficial and will heal in time. The door to the room opens and this time it stays open. I am able to adjust my eyes to the light, and I see a man enter. All this time I have not once seen my captor in the light. Now I anticipate finally putting a face to my tormentor. I can tell by the familiar sound of his footstep that it is the man in the black leather shoes. Finally... I look up and see his face... it's... Henry, DJ's brother? No... I blink, because maybe my eyes have not adjusted to the light, but I look again, and it is definitely Henry. My jaw must have dropped open because, just for a moment, a nasty victorious smile creeps across his face when he sees my look of surprise.

All I can think of is how he has violated my body and touched me in the most cruel and intimate fashion. He has caused me unbelievable mental and physical pain, taking me to the brink of death several times. Thinking of all of this makes me want to throw up and my stomach churns and clenches in anticipation. I wonder what DJ's role is, but I know he loves me so I believe he knows nothing about this. Still, our relationship is forever destroyed after what his brother has done to me. This is exactly what Henry wants. He most likely didn't expect me to survive, so his brother's relationship with me never mattered to him. Why? Henry must feel he's about to inherit everything, and he doesn't have to worry about DJ anymore. This is the only logical reason I have for why he would risk alienating his brother forever.

Henry hasn't said anything, but he motions to the two guards in the room to pick me up out of the chair. I notice my clothes are in shreds, covered in blood and looking like something a zombie would wear. My shoes are gone, and the guards are forcing me to walk barefoot across the cold, concrete floor. Every step is horribly painful due to the taser burns on the soles of my feet.

"Take her to a cell, and get her some clothes. Christa, you will have a visitor today."

A visitor? I can only imagine what that means. The two guards lead me into the brightly lit hallway, I look one way and then the other to get my bearings. I see a familiar silhouette at the end of the hallway—caught in my line of sight like a deer in a riflescope—DJ. He looks at me, drops his eyes, turns, and quickly walks away. Is this a trick of my mind? No… It was him. A tidal wave of betrayal, hopelessness, and abandonment sweeps over me and is more painful than all the torture I have endured. One thought pounds in my brain, demanding to be let in and fully acknowledged, did DJ know what was happening to me? All this time I assumed he had been going crazy with worry and searching for me. I had actually considered confiding in him earlier because I believed he was different from his family. I still believe DJ loves me but evidently not enough to save me. He has let his brother do horrible things to me. DJ is no better than the rest of them. He may not have participated, but his cowardice makes him complicit. Once again, waves of nausea come over me as the truth of what is happening begins to sink in. I am lost and will not be found.

I guess I have been standing frozen in the middle of the hallway because the guards are pulling at me trying to get me to walk to my cell. I start moving, but I can't stop the tears that are beginning to roll down my face, I feel broken. I hear a voice fighting to be recognized over all the crazy suicidal thoughts in my mind, and it is The Nomad. This is the first time he has communicated with me since I've been here.

"Christa, you will hear some news that will be very upsetting. Don't believe what you are told. Don't give up, remain calm and centered, the truth will be revealed shortly. Most of all—and this will be difficult—practice forgiveness." I try to hold his voice in my mind and respond to what he's just told me, but he is gone.

It makes no sense, but I know better than to question his directive. Fallingtree is with me again, talking to me and comforting me as the guards put me in the cell. She reminds me that I am surrounded by allies and not to be fearful. She says, "Listen with your heart and not your ears." She steps into the shadows of my mind, but I can sense her presence is still there, and it settles my feeling of desperation.

I slowly and painfully pull on the clean clothes that have been left for me. I wash my face and run some water through my hair, but I can feel that my curls have turned to knotted dreads. Finally, I give up and twist my hair into a bun. In the distance, I hear the clang of a metal door and the uneven step of someone approaching my cell. A woman appears at my door. She has shoulder-length black hair that has been shaved on both sides of her head just over the ears. Multiple earrings track up the sides of her ears and a spider web tattoo graces the length of her left arm. I can see more tattoos showing through the collar of her t-shirt. Her face is hard despite her beautiful green eyes. Any potential beauty she might have had, is marred by the right side of her face, which seems to be sliding down towards her jaw, and she has a noticeable droop to her eye and one corner of her mouth.

She leans into the cell bars and says, "Hello, Christa." The sweetness in her voice suggests she had once had been beautiful and knew how to use it as a weapon. "You don't recognize me do you? I can't blame you really."

I know I have never seen this woman before in my life. I'm sure of it. I strain to see what might be familiar about her, but nothing is coming to me.

"I saw a friend of yours today... Sparks."

Fear makes my body involuntarily shudder when I hear her say Sparks name. Maybe this is the news The Nomad has warned me about. I brace for whatever she might say next.

"He wasn't looking too good when I left him... Maybe it was the three bullet holes I put in him or all the blood that was messing up his pretty face."

My breath catches in my throat and the world seems to stop as I take in what she has just told me. My head drowns in horrible visions of Sparks shot with blood pooling around him. My face remains composed because I am listening to Fallingtree, calmly chanting a meditation and reassuring me that this is not the whole truth. Together we navigate this horrible moment.

"I'm sure he's dead by now—three bullets to the chest can do some major damage." She searches my face for a reaction, and when she doesn't see one, she changes the subject, "You really don't know me, do you?" She smiles a crooked smile with only half her face, "Phoebe... Phoebe Carlyle. You attended my funeral, remember?"

OK, that's it! The Nomad tried to prepare me, but this news is more shocking than what she said about Sparks! I look again at this woman's face and cannot see any shred of the elegant beauty I'd seen that night with Gary or at the compound. Instead, I see a twisted, malevolent looking creature with no trace of beauty inside or out. In her green eyes, I finally see Phoebe. The hair, the tattoos, the piercings, along with the lopsided face had thrown me. No doubt, it is Phoebe—but how? I'm certain she died that night.

"You must be filled with questions, so let me tell you a little story. My tracking chip saved me. It sent a medical SOS and all my vitals to the hospital, so the doctors were ready for me when I arrived. Unfortunately, I was in a coma for quite a while, and as you can see by my face, there was neural damage. Once I came to, I was able to fill Damien Marshall, Sr. in on all the goings on with you and the OTP movement."

Oh God! This is bad. I remember what The Nomad just told me, and I know Phoebe doesn't have the whole story, not even about Sparks. Phoebe (and Henry) anticipate this news will rattle me and put me in a hopeless state—it almost did too. I am determined to steady myself, even though I am unnerved by everything I'm hearing.

Phoebe continues with her story, and I admit I am hanging on every word. "Once I recovered, they put me into another OTP group to spy. This group had a station at the airport. When my group targeted Damien Marshall, Sr., I let security at Marshall Industries know. The rest played out exactly as I had hoped. The reward for me was having Sparks run directly into the barrel of my gun. As I squeezed off those shots, I imagined telling you that Sparks was dead." She stops and watches my face for a moment, and then says abruptly, "I'm done here."

Phoebe has already turned and begun to walk away when I feel the compulsion to rush to the bars of my cell and call out that I forgive her. The Nomad had said it would be difficult, but now I know I have to do it. "Phoebe, I forgive you."

She stops, drops her head for a second, turns back towards me with a hateful glare in her eyes, and says, "You forgive me? I should be the one forgiving you for what you did to my face. When you jammed that needle into my head you altered by life forever. You tried to kill me, and you almost did! But don't forgive me because I will NEVER forgive you! Instead, I will always be your worst nightmare."

"Still—I forgive you because we are all victims of the greed and ambition that is ruining all our lives."

"Bullshit!" Phoebe spits the word out, turns, and walks quickly to the metal door, insistently pounding on it to be let out.

*****

In a private OTP hospital, Big G is asleep, sprawled across a chair that is clearly too small for him. He snores loudly from total exhaustion and Gypsy is curled up next to him doing the canine version of his snore. G has camped out all night in Sparks' hospital room keeping watch. He could sleep because he knows for now they are safely hidden somewhere in East Los Angeles. The nurses have tried to make a fuss about a dog in the room, but when G rose to his full height and lowered his voice saying, "You'll have to go through me first if you want the dog to leave," the nurses abandoned their rules.

Sparks is finally starting to come around after a long surgery. As he opens his eyes, he can make out the creamy white of the plain hospital walls. He looks towards the window and sees bright sunlight working its way through the slits of the blinds. He is very, very lucky. Two of the bullets hit his chest without damaging any major arteries or organs and the third bullet passed through his left shoulder. The chorus of snoring draws Sparks' focus back to the hospital room and he smiles when he sees G's enormous body folded into the tiny hospital chair and Gypsy next to him. He summons some strength and says quietly, "G," but the snoring continues, so he tries again but louder, "G!"

G stops snoring and moves in the chair. He opens his eyes and immediately looks at the bed. When he sees Sparks is conscious he sits up and says, "Welcome back, man," smiling with relief because his friend is alive. "That was a long night, and I gotta say... you're one lucky MF!"

Sparks just laughs, but then he stops, remembering there were others on the tarmac that weren't so lucky. "Yeah, well... how many did we lose?"

"Four of our guys, and I'm not sure how many from the other group." Both men are quiet and G says, "I blame myself."

"Why?" asks Sparks. "We all agreed to the plan. Obviously there was a leak. You couldn't have seen that."

"I should have. I should have factored in what could happen if there was a spy. I didn't because I really thought we had the element of surprise on our side. I thought they didn't know about us. That was a fatal error in my judgment."

Sparks looks at G for a bit and says, "It was still the right strategy. Now, more than ever, we need to pull Damien Marshall, Sr. out into the open."

"I agree, and more than ever I want to get the SOB! You may not be able to fight Marshall in the field, but we can stir the pot from here. The Nomad said it's time for you to work some keyboard magic." G smiles at the thought of Sparks working his awesome hacking skills to bring down a multinational corporation.

Sparks smiles confidently and says, "No problem. Get me a laptop and Wi-Fi and I'll show you some magic."

******

Sparks sits up in his bed with the laptop on his hospital table. He types as fast as he can using only his right hand, since his left arm is in a sling. He taps into a network of hackers, all friends of his, that communicate through a hidden Internet portal or the dark net.

Sparks and his militia have made the news that day thanks to Damien Marshall's quick disinformation campaign. Marshall Industries has made it appear that an American corporation is under attack from terrorists, and they have averted a plot that would have costs thousands of American lives on homeland soil. It is a story devised to discredit OTP as patriots and endear the corporation to the American public. Of course, the truth is only Damien Marshall, Sr.'s men have taken any lives that day—not OTP.

As Sparks taps away, lost in a world of code, G who is keeping watch from his undersized chair, marvels at Sparks' talent. This is not his thing; he used to laugh that his hands are too big for a computer keyboard, and he wouldn't trust his meaty fingers to hit the right keys. But Sparks is a genius hacker, even with one hand.

They watch the evening news respond to the real time hacks Sparks and his anonymous team are making. They are planting online stories that refute the official news stories. For every story on national TV the Internet feeds have five that tell a different story. Soon UPI and Reuters News Service are picking up the Internet stories and reporting them alongside the stories Damien Marshall's people have planted. The entire news cycle has become a muddled mess of new facts and eventually it plays out. Nobody can find the true story, even if they wanted to.

Sparks is just getting started with his cyber attack on Marshall Industries, but Damien Marshall, Sr. is just getting started as well—this is war!

******

Chicago: 1pm the following day

A large, peaceful gathering has formed outside the Chicago Stock Exchange with the intent to draw attention to crimes against the people brought about by the banking establishment. Specifically these protestors want to follow the examples of other countries and make the bankers accountable for the mismanagement and gambling away of money that wasn't theirs to begin with. The protestors want equal justice in the eyes of the law.

Damien Marshall, Sr. wants the opposite. He believes those who can afford it can buy justice and he can afford it. This is exactly the type of movement he needs to end immediately. A plan has been struck to create a violent diversion. A cold wind blows in from Lake Michigan, adding a chill to what is an otherwise beautiful day. The protestors form a line in front of the police. They link arms and chant protest slogans. The police stand at the ready, tense, in full riot gear. The crowd has been well coached on how to conduct themselves and not provoke the police.

A woman protestor, with a distinctive severe black hairstyle shaved at the sides of her head and tattoos on her arms, muscles her way to the front of the protest line. She has a canvas bag slung over one shoulder, into which she reaches for a second then lays the bag on the ground in front of her and gives it a kick. A small metal canister rolls out of the bag and a moment later, a flash bomb explodes. The police immediately react as if they are under attack, and several of them shoot into the crowd. There is screaming and panic as half the protestors run away and the other half surges towards the police line. Two people are wounded but neither is fatal. Several people are arrested that day, including the woman with the severe black hairstyle. One hour later, the same black-haired woman with the tattoos strolls out of the Chicago Police Station free; the Carlyle Corporation posted her bail.

Damien Marshall, Sr. knows he has dealt a severe blow to the safety and credibility of the movement. He doubts their march on Washington DC will be very well attended now or perhaps not materialize at all.

*****

Sparks is outraged when he sees how the police have been provoked and a peaceful protest has turned into a violent encounter. He knows that was never the plan of the protestors and this appears to have Damien Marshall's hand all over it. He has watched the news coverage several times and spotted the black-haired woman leaving the back of the crowd. He recognizes her from the airport hanger as the same woman who shot him. He needs to put a stop to her mayhem.

Although he is confined to a hospital bed, he can still do some damage with his laptop, and, along with his hacker network, they start digging and breaking past the firewalls of Marshall Industries' computers. Of course, the most sensitive material is offline but, that doesn't matter because what they are after is right there in the open—emails. Thousands of executive emails, which when pieced together, create an ugly picture of the inner workings and manipulations of this company. Emails that show how Marshall Industries has defied Federal and State Laws, evaded taxes, funneled money overseas to fund small wars for their profit and much more. Once the emails are found, the hackers post them publicly on different online news feeds. They are deleted as soon as they go up, but not before some lone conspiracy theory blogger gets ahold of them and blasts them to all of their followers. With each new email, the damage is accumulating.

"Big G," Sparks calls to the hallway of the hospital, and G appears, filling the doorway. "Get ready to wipe this place down because as soon as I finish this hack all hell is gonna break loose. Don't forget to disable all the security cameras and no cell phones when we leave."

"On it," G disappears from the doorway.

***** *

Damien Marshall, Sr. is enraged now. The email hack has gone too far. He blames every member of his internal security team for the breach, and fires all of them. He needs to bring in a trusted person from outside the company, so he reaches out to his contacts in the FBI for the name of the best cyber agent they have. He wants to track this hacker, or hackers, and crucify them. His FBI contact gives him the name of an independent contractor, a former agent and army intelligence officer, who lives offline and off the grid on an Indian reservation in Arizona. He personally vouches for this agent as brilliant and top of their field in cyber security, but the only way to get to them is to physically go to the reservation.

Marshall immediately dispatches his private helicopter, along with Kimball, to bring Melanie Fallingtree to Marshall Industries and set her up to hunt down whoever is hacking into his company.

CHAPTER EIGHT

A QUIET MOVE

Phoebe emerges from the prison into the bright California sunlight, feeling very good about her encounter with Christa. Nobody in OTP knows who she is, and, with Sparks gone, she is determined now is the time to go after The Nomad. If she can get to him, the group will fall apart, and she might be able to find the other OTP group leaders as well. She needs support for this idea so she decides to approach Damien Marshall, Sr. She works out her strategy as she drives to Marshall Industries corporate headquarters. Once there, she is shown to Damien Marshall, Sr.'s private office where she waits for him to arrive.

He strides in and says brusquely, "What have you got for me?" Walking past Phoebe, and settles into his leather chair behind his ornately-carved desk.

Phoebe is relaxed as she proposes her idea. "Well, Mr. Marshall, I would like to go after The Nomad. He is the leader of the West Coast OTP group, which Christa is affiliated with.

I suspect they led the attack on you and your company. I can get inside. I was there before as Phoebe Carlyle, and I am there now under the name of Lou Mercer."

"Phoebe, you are a valuable asset to us, and you know I want to pull that group apart, but this sounds risky and could lead to some embarrassing exposure if you are caught." says Damien Marshall, Sr.

"It's not, I visited Christa in prison, and she had no idea who I was. The only other rebel who could identify me, died in the airport attack."

"Well, I will admit the airport incident played in our favor, as did the disruption of the protest rally. The flash bomb was handled well." He gives the idea a minute to grow on him and then says, "How will you find this man? This... Nomad."

"I believe they are at a place called 'The Farm.' I know that was the plan to retreat there after the airport operation. I've never been there, but if I work my back channels in the group, I can find my way. All I have to tell them is I am a survivor of the airport ambush and that I have been on the run since then. They will take me in no questions asked."

"You are sure they can't trace you to your previous identity as Phoebe Carlyle?"

"Not unless they run a DNA test."

Phoebe watches Damien Marshall's face and decides he requires one more push. "This will break the back of the OTP movement on the West Coast. Once I discover the location of The Farm, you can go in and destroy it. That compound is an important piece of their identity and their future. It's their model for a new society and the antithesis to a society run by corporations and bankers. It is a cooperative, sharing economy and there is no room for Marshall Industries in that model." Phoebe is confident her last statement lands the punch she is looking for.

Damien Marshall, Sr. leans forward as he listens to every word Phoebe says. He is surprised the OTP movement is so well organized and innovative. He wonders how they have come so far and stayed off his radar all this time. Phoebe has told him all he wants to hear. "All right—go ahead. Just be absolutely certain there is no link to us."

Phoebe (or Lou as she is known now to her new OTP comrades) nods. She smiles to herself at the thought that they will never see her coming, and when she is done with all of it, she'll go back to the prison and take out that smug little bitch Christa. It really bugs her that Christa is still alive, but the consolation is she'd have the pleasure of killing her.

******

Big G has dropped Sparks, against his wishes, for a few days of R&R at an OTP safe house in Santa Barbara. Then he cuts east and is headed up north to meet the group at The Farm. While he drives the endless stretch of Interstate 5, the only break in the monotony is when a big-rig truck whizzes by, causing his jeep to rock slightly. G is completely alone on this drive—he sent Gypsy with The Nomad to The Farm. She wasn't happy about leaving him behind, but he didn't want to worry about her while he reviewed the recent events in his mind. Now, he is free to replay the airport attack in detail and analyze every incident and person he can recall. He replays the game and all it's moves in his head, over, and over.

He knows there is a spy because Sparks identified her, but Sparks was shot so quickly that he had no time to focus on her face and couldn't give a good description of the woman. Only that she had very black shaved hair, multiple piercings in her ears, and a spider web tattoo on her arm. That is all he could remember. G thinks this woman should not be too difficult to spot among the

OTP members. However, he does question how she infiltrated the organization in the first place. The OTP is very tight on initiation and security. That is a question he can't find an answer to right now. G starts to replay the strategy again. The highway is hypnotic and he is the only car for miles—it is the perfect place to think.

He turns on some jazz, Miles Davis playing his haunting "Sketches of Spain." The melancholy sounds of Davis' horn playing has G's mind drifting and relaxing. He finds himself interjecting moves from the ambush with complex musical structures, layering musical outcomes with battle outcomes in his mind. Suddenly, the music begins to reorganize his thoughts into a new pattern, and he sees the holes, the things he has missed—he sees the next move on the board!

G knows without a doubt that the next move will be to take out a major piece—The Nomad! In the game, the queen, the one with the most mobility, is able to infiltrate the other side's ranks and threaten their king. The queen is probably the spy who shot Sparks. He feels the urgency to get to The Farm now.

"WEE WUP, WEE WUP." G looks in his rearview mirror and sees a police cruiser has sneaked up on his bumper while he was lost in thought. The flashing lights and beeping siren signal him to pull over. He looks at the empty passenger seat and thinks, "I really could have used Sparks' pasty white face right about now. He would diffuse this situation." Big G knows the drill, and he knows no matter what, this is going to be a humiliating experience that might not end well for him.

Two officers walk towards his car. One approaches on the passenger side and the other comes to the driver-side window. "License and registration," the officer says. G cooperates and hands him what he's asked for and then keeps both hands on the steering wheel in plain sight. The officer looks at the paperwork, looks at G, and asks him where he is headed. The officer also comments that G's all-terrain truck is a "very nice vehicle." G assumes the officer is fishing to determine if it is stolen, since a black man wouldn't drive a car like this unless he's stolen it or is a drug dealer. Meanwhile, the other officer was waits for the results of the background check on G's license and registration to see if he has any arrest warrants. A moment later, a voice comes over his com saying his license has come up clean. The officer looks genuinely disappointed.

The police officer on the driver's side of the car asks G to step out of the vehicle. When he unfolds his six-foot-four-inch frame—all 250 pounds of it—in front of the officers, the tension in the men was evident. No matter how docile and submissive G makes himself, the officers still see him as a threatening black male and their hands move immediately to rest on the hilts of their guns. G freezes—he doesn't make a single move—if his nose itched in that moment, he wouldn't scratch it because it probably would get him killed.

Finally, the officer holding his license and registration breaks the tension by ordering G to lay face down on the pavement. Without complaint he does as he is told. "You were speeding, and we suspect that you may be transporting illegal substances so we will be inspecting your vehicle," he says.

The officer reaches inside the car and releases the trunk. As he walks to the back of the car, he has to pass G lying on the pavement. G moves ever so slightly to give the officer room to pass, but as soon as he does, he knows he has made a mistake.

The other officer pulls his gun and was points it at G yelling, "Don't move, don't move! You think you're gonna try something? Huh?"

His partner looks down at G and says very calmly, "Now you shouldn't 'ave done that, boy." Just to punctuate his statement he kicks G hard in the ribs—hard enough that he stops breathing for a few seconds. "Now were gonna have take you in for threatening a police officer and resisting arrest. You just created a whole lotta paperwork for me... and I hate paperwork."

It seems the officer is about to go to town giving Big G a beat-down when a semi-trailer truck comes cruising by and slows down as it passes.

G is breathing hard, each inhalation stabbing his ribs. He can feel the uneven pebbles of the pavement pushing into the skin of his face as one of the officers puts his boot on G's head and presses hard. The driver of the truck, a white man, stares out his window, taking in the whole scene without any shame about the abuse he is witnessing. Then he waves at the officers and is gone. G sadly realizes this man is just another "oppressor" and the rescue he'd hoped for isn't happening. His mind crashes into shutdown mode, a dead space of no thought or emotion, all in an effort to save his life.

G is handcuffed and put into the back of the police cruiser. It could be hours before he will get to call from jail and hours after that before his lawyer will be able to secure his release.

Then he'll have to get to The Nomad immediately and hope he isn't too late.

******

After the airport ambush, the members had scattered to other OTP groups for safe haven. Phoebe had followed four members north, to The Farm, where she suspected, and later confirmed through her traveling companions, that Sparks' militia group was staying. When, as Phoebe, she had been seeing Sparks, he had spoken about The Farm often, and although she'd never been to it, she was familiar with the territory and knew what to expect.

She had arrived the night before, dropped off on the side of the highway. She had to walk in from there—this is OTP safety protocol for The Farm. If you are not in an approved vehicle, you have to go in on foot. This prevents members from being tracked to The Farm by their car's GPS location systems. Another protocol—no working cell phones. At the highway, Phoebe had pulled out the sim card and battery to her cell phone and stuck them in her jacket pocket.

She knew she was taking a chance walking in unannounced and that security would track her every step the moment she left the highway. If they found anything out of sync with her, she would quickly be surrounded and taken into custody. It had been a five-mile walk into The Farm. The main complex is encompassed by a grove of Eucalyptus trees and scattered oak trees that successfully hid the buildings from the highway and the air.

Phoebe trudges along the dirt road knowing she is being watched. Once she arrives at the main gate, her identity had already been verified by several of the airport battle survivors, and she is allowed to enter. "I am in the belly of the beast," she thinks, "no turning back now."

******

Phoebe—now Lou—walks into The Farm confident that she won't be recognized. She is sure her identity as Louise, "Lou" Mercer hasn't been compromised since she killed Sparks. Nobody at the airport has any idea that she is a spy or that she instigated the ambush that resulted in the death of four OTP members. If they did know, there is no way she'd be walking onto The Farm right now.

"Now I wonder where The Nomad's quarters are." She thinks she had heard Sparks describe it as an outer building somewhere behind the old farmhouse. She begins to wander, trying to get the lay of the grounds.

As she rounds the back of the house, a guard she recognizes from her days as Phoebe, walks right into her. "Hi," he says, "Can I help you? Are you lost?"

"No, I'm just trying to get my bearings and figure out where everything is. This place is huge!" She smiles at the guard waiting to see if he recognizes her. She quietly slips her hand to the handle of her knife hidden in her jacket pocket.

"Well, it is a big place, so I can see how you'd get lost. Most of the compound is behind you, and there are only a couple of buildings up this way. But if you want to wander around the open land, that's fine, just watch out for rattlesnakes, especially the babies—they don't have a rattle yet, and their bite is more deadly. But you should be OK."

She relaxes her grip on the knife and says, "Thanks, I'll follow your advice."

With that, he continues on his rounds never once seeming to recognize Lou as Phoebe.

Continuing toward the outer buildings, she hikes up a small grade and sees two bunkers when she gets to the crest. The door to one of the buildings opens and she drops to the ground to hide. The Nomad and two other men come out and stop briefly to speak. The men walk away, and The Nomad turns and goes back inside. She can see him through the window, moving about the room. Phoebe whispers triumphantly to herself, "Yesss!"

******

I can hear every voice, each as clearly as if I am talking to them on the telephone. The voices of The Nomad, Fallingtree, and

other members of the Council have been with me throughout this ordeal. The time I have spent alone in this cell has allowed me to uncover my unique abilities. Unlike The Nomad, and other walk-ins on the Council, I have come into this body at a very young age, and I've been repressing my soul's memories all this time. Now as I communicate with other ISHI walk-in souls, like myself, my purpose is becoming more defined. I feel I have a capacity to forgive and heal, to stand outside of myself and be compassionate, and to rise above my emotions.

I certainly didn't start out that way. The night I tried to kill Phoebe, I was angry and determined to protect myself. Even when she showed up at the prison, I felt hatred and was disappointed to still find her alive. I was self-righteous because I knew I was on the side of 'good' and she was clearly "evil."

My time alone, isolated from the rest of the world, has allowed me to go deeper into my consciousness. I see the world through a different filter now. As an ISHI, the people I know are not so clearly defined—it is difficult to judge them as I would through my human experience. For example, as Christa I have lost all respect for DJ and feel that I hate him. But, as an ISHI, I see only his energy and it is pure. DJ is coping with his life lessons, but not intentionally trying to harm anyone. In this moment of clarity, I can forgive him. As an ISHI I know we have the same energy from the same source. I understand, that on the material plane, our spirit is challenged and shaped and we learn lessons that we cannot learn in the next dimension. As awful as my prison cell is, it's exactly where I am supposed to be to "wake up" to my ISHI path and learn how to use my new found skills.

Although I have the same ability to communicate telepathically with other walk-in souls, I also have my own telepathic gift. I can speak to people even if they are not openly telepathic. I can 'broadcast' ideas and images of what I want to say directly into their minds. I can do this with just one person or a large group of people. I need to watch myself; I am like a teapot boiling over and finally blowing off steam. The "steam" from my thoughts has the power to influence people, and I can't allow myself to boil over. If I do, my anger may have wide reaching repercussions. The isolation for my spiritual awakening also has served as a protective measure.

My first awareness of this additional telepathic ability occurred while talking to the guards. I noticed that when they brought me food I would think that my meal was missing something or I wanted something extra, like a salad or dessert. Ridiculous thoughts that I would never voice aloud because I was a prisoner and you eat what you are given. With each of those thoughts, the guards would disappear and, for no reason, reappear with whatever I was missing. This happened a handful of times and I realized these were not chance incidents. I began to experiment to determine how far I could go with the power of suggestion—it turned out, quite far.

I had continued to practice with the guards and turned them into my friends. They would have released me without a problem but the Council had reminded me that my work at the prison wasn't quite finished. Not everyone could be influenced by my telepathic suggestions. I found Henry's mind impossible to break into. When I spoke and my voice began to weave its charm, I would hit a wall with Henry. I felt like a bee taping against a window—I could see the other side, but I couldn't get through. He had shut down his emotions and I learned my telepathic gift seems to link to the part of the brain that processes feeling and emotion. Henry is a insensitive wild card in my world. I wonder if his father and maybe even his brother have the same trait.

Today I tell the Council, and The Nomad, about Phoebe's resurrection and our conversation. I describe her new appearance, how she has been affiliated with the airport OTP group, and that she is the one that shot Sparks. Nobody takes this information lightly because lives have been lost due to her. Possibly many more will be too if she isn't found soon. Looking back on my talk with Phoebe, I see I had not tried to influence her or change her mission. Why? This seems like a missed opportunity, but, in retrospect, I understand that I couldn't go into her mind after she told me she'd shot Sparks because *my* emotions had been engaged. It would have been too much for me, and I had feared the outcome.

******

Lou lifts her head from the bathroom sink and inspects her new hair color, a soft golden brown. She has cut her hair into a shaggy pixie cut with longer hair in the front. She looks around the bathroom for a washcloth. Dousing it with cleanser, she begins to scrub away the spider web tattoo from her arm. It slowly disappears. She has already taken out all of her earrings. After she removes the semi-permanent tattoos, the only things left to do are change her makeup and insert brown contact lenses.

She pinches the sagging skin on the side of her face, pulls it up towards her scalp, and uses facial tape to hold it under her bangs. The desired effect is to even out her features and make her look different again. She puts on some makeup and a sweet flowered dress with white sneakers. For now Phoebe is gone and Lou has taken her place. All of this, the hair color, tattoo removal, and the dress were calculated to make her look as unthreatening as possible. However, hidden under the little flowered dress, is a small but deadly knife, and her signature hypodermic, filled with the paralytic drug. She's rehearsed in her mind how she will smile sweetly and approach The Nomad with fake information regarding Christa's location. Lou knows this will get her in the same room with him. She also knows if she can get close enough to kill him, she will deal a major blow to the entire movement. Her preference is to take The Nomad alive because he knows what the OTP's bigger plans are. That isn't an option though. It will be hard enough to get out of there after she kills him. She smoothes her newly-shorn hair and presses the wrinkles from the front of her dress with the palms of her hands. She is ready to go after The Nomad.

******

Jasmine Reveles walks into the tiny local police precinct and demands to see the officer in charge. She is the "go to" attorney for the OTP when their members are in trouble. With her flashing black eyes and confident smile, she projects so much authority it is almost impossible to deny her whatever she asks for. Her goal right now is to get Big G out of that holding cell. Jasmine is a petite woman, but her perfect posture and steady gaze make her seem quite formidable.

As the officer in charge approaches the front counter, she scrutinizes him and says, "Officer…[looking at his badge] Carson, I am Jasmine Reveles, attorney for Gerald Fowler." With this statement, she extends her hand, but Officer Carson just stares at the uppity Latina lawyer and is determined not to give her anything he doesn't need to, which includes shaking her hand.

Jasmine thinks, "OK, I can see how this is going to go." Then she says loudly, "I would like to hear the charges against my client."

"He assaulted a police officer." Officer Carson answers very dryly.

"Really? Are you aware that there is a second video of the incident in addition to the one shot by the police cruiser? This one has a much closer angle."

Officer Carson continues to stare unblinking at Jasmine, but she knows she has scored a blow because he shifts his feet uneasily.

"So would you care to revise your reason for holding my client?"

There is a long pause while Jasmine assesses the situation. She already holds her own cell phone in her hand but she suddenly fishes a second phone out of her bag. She flips it from side to side in front of Officer Carson but doesn't say a word.

Finally she speaks, "I respectfully ask that you immediately release my client and drop all the charges against him. That's the easy solution, or there is the hard way... I release the video of your officer kicking and beating my client while he's in custody and he is not resisting arrest. This will go viral, put your department under scrutiny, put you under scrutiny, and probably destroy a lot of careers. So what will it be, Officer Carson?"

His face is ashen, even if he doesn't openly register any emotion. It is obvious this scares the hell out of him. What Jasmine doesn't tell Officer Carson is how she got a second video. G had a lucky break that night. The big rig that passed during his beating happened to be an OTP truck that was transporting a group of the airport members to The Farm. When the driver saw Big G on the ground, he recognized him from the airport ambush. He pulled out his cell phone to film the encounter, but held the camera at a low angle so it wouldn't be seen. He'd slowed his truck as if he was checking out the officers to make sure they were OK. Then he had waved in a false show of support as he drove off. He hadn't stopped because he had militia members in the back, and everyone was looking for the people involved in the

the airport "terror attack." Once he arrived at The Farm, he'd found Jasmine, told her what he had seen, and gave her his phone with the video on it. Jasmine had known what to do from there.

Officer Carson now has no choice, his back is against the wall, and he has to release Big G.

It takes a very long time to bring him from lock-up and Jasmine begins to worry that something awful has happened. Finally, a door opens and an officer escorts Big G to the front lobby where Jasmine waits.

When she sees him, she is shocked by his physical condition. His right eye is swollen shut and his cheekbone has a huge bruise. His lip is split open and still bleeding. He holds his side and walks very slowly because obviously he is in great pain.

"What has happened to this man?" Jasmine demands.

Three officers stand behind the front counter, and all of them just star at her without answering her question. Finally one of the men says, "I guess he slipped and fell." All three conspiratorially smile at one another.

Jasmine is about to launch into a tirade when G says, "Let's just get out of here… please?" She looks at his bruised and beaten body and understands but vows that one day she'll get justice with these officers for what they have done to G.

"Where is his jeep?" Jasmine inquires in a very firm tone.

"It's in the impound…" The officer lets his answer just hang in the air with no offer to retrieve the car.

Jasmine glances at G and knows he is in no condition to drive. "Fine," she says, "I will send someone to pick it up."

She hustles G to her car and they start back to The Farm. Once on the road G says, "Jasmine, don't break any speed limits, but you need to get me to The Farm as soon as possible. The

Nomad is in danger, which I should have told him hours ago, but they never let me make a call. I just hope I am not too late."

Jasmine doesn't say a word but punches the gas petal a little bit harder.

******

The Chicago riot, with its ensuing violence and looting as a response to the police shootings, is still playing out in the media. Sympathy marches have sprung up all over the country and the world. While civil unrest dominates the news, there is also a wave of strange incidences involving major leaders of industry and finance. To the unpracticed eye these events seem completely unrelated and just a run of random bad luck: a car accident, a botched surgery, a sudden heart attack, a robbery gone wrong— but the result for the victim is always the same—they nearly die, or do die for a minute or two and are revived.

Damien Marshall, Sr., loosens his tie and pours himself an expensive bourbon, neat. He is on edge about all the unrest and doesn't like the direction it is going; there is a lack of control, and he no longer has the public conversation working to his advantage. Distracted by the protests, he fails to see the correlation of bad luck befalling only one particular group of highly influential people.

Melanie Fallingtree is brilliant and has become indispensable to him; as she sorts out any potential cyber threats and shores up his servers' security. He has to agree with the FBI director, she is a miracle worker.

While Melanie Fallingtree does her job for Marshall Industries, she is also digging around into the company's private real estate holdings trying to determine where they might be keeping Christa. Although she is in telepathic communication with her, it does not help establish the location because Christa can't see outside and never saw the surrounding area when they brought her in.

Finally, Fallingtree's digging seems to pay off. She finds some files that Damien Marshall, Sr. keeps on the server labeled, "Laura Marshall," after his wife. When Fallingtree opens them, she finds hundreds of documents for property held in Laura's name but this is confusing. Everyone who knows Laura Marshall, knows she is a major consumer of fashion, but real estate doesn't fit; this is out of character. Fallingtree digs a little deeper into the files, and after an hour of reading endless real estate documents, she thinks she has found what she is looking for. In one file, there is information about a warehouse used to store drilling equipment. The drilling equipment raises a flag in her mind because there are no oil holdings in Laura Marshall's portfolio. Everything else is residential or commercial property. She writes the address on her inner arm and rolls her sleeve over it. Fallingtree closes the file on the server and goes into the security code to erase any trace that she has been snooping around there.

She exits the building and starts walking up the street. She looks for the nearest pay phone with a blue handset cord. Fallingtree knows it's urgent to get this information to Sparks, and the only way to do that safely is via the phone because he isn't telepathic. Once she finds a phone and calls the lab, it just rings and rings because she doesn't know Sparks is hiding out in Santa Barbara recovering from his injuries.

Fallingtree hangs up the receiver and decides she has to use her backup option—reach out telepathically to The Nomad. This isn't her first choice because she knows that precise information such as phone numbers and addresses doesn't always translate perfectly when she connects telepathically. She has to risk it, though, because she senses that Christa may have outgrown her usefulness to Damien Marshall, Sr. They are running out of time to get her out of prison. Even though Christa can probably save herself if Henry tortures her again, she cannot stop him from killing her.

CHAPTER NINE

KARMA'S A BITCH

"Christa… , Christa?"

I hear my name, but I can't quite wakeup. I'm still trying to focus my eyes when I realize Henry is standing in my cell. I sit up quickly on my little bed and instinctively cross my arms over my chest.

"There you are," he says with an almost tender note to his voice. This is unnerving. "Today we are going to have a little fun. You are going to tell me everything you know about The Nomad."

I am surprised—this is the first time he has named anyone specifically, and I have to wonder what he knows about The Nomad. I remember Phoebe's visit, and I feel sick because, now, he probably knows everything about OTP.

"Oh… and, Sparks."

He waits and watches for my reaction very closely when he says that name. "That bitch!" I think about Phoebe and how she must have given Henry this name knowing I would be emotionally vulnerable since she has just told me his is dead.

I try to keep my body and face completely neutral, although inside I am really scared.

Henry leans towards me and says with a threat in his voice, "I want to know all about his inventions and his communication methods for the group."

Obviously, Phoebe has been very informative. Panic and anger take over and I am not sure that I can go through his torture again without breaking. I am afraid I might actually give up my body forever. I am out of strength. It has been a while since Henry has interrogated me, and I have been able to push it to the back of my mind. Now visions of recent events rush into my head: with ugly detail. DJ… there he is again, watching them drag me from the interrogation room—knowing his brother has done this to me—and he did nothing! The anger that vision generates gives me a bolt of survival energy, like an electric shock to restart the heart.

The guards come in and lead me to the interrogation room while Henry follows behind, which makes me very uneasy because he is not a man I want to turn my back on. "Christa, I warn you—if you don't give me something I can use I'm not sure what good you are to me." With that he walks up behind me and slowly strokes my hair, fondling it even. Then he leans in very close to my face and says, "At this point there really is only one use for an attractive woman like you. Death would be too easy; I could sell you to the highest bidder and end my Christa problem just like that. Plus, I'd get the satisfaction of knowing you were finally doing the job a girl like you was born to do."

There is so much I want to say in response to that comment, but if words fail me, I could just kick him in the balls. How I wish I could influence him, I want to make him turn all that evil on himself. The man is a black hole and completely impervious to any of my telepathic attempts to access his mind. I brace myself for what might come next, and I think something I have never thought before, "I need rescuing." However, I know nobody is coming for me.

There is a knock on the door to the interrogation room and a guard enters. He whispers in Henry's ear and the guard watches as Henry rushes out of the room, then he turns to me and says, "Looks like this is on hold for now."

The guard unties me and returns me to my cell. I try to push the guard to tell me what he said to Henry, but we are continuously interrupted by other guards, and I cannot get a decent hold on his mind. It didn't really matter anyway; I am still stuck here. I am very grateful, though, that I don't have to go through whatever Henry had planned for me.

It is night now—the only way I know this is because they served me dinner. I can't see out of a window, so I determine the hours of the day by the meals they serve me, or when the guards change shifts. Sometimes one of them will offhandedly mention the weather outside or the traffic, and I will have a little more information. Otherwise, the time passes in a surreal manner. I lie down to sleep when I guess that I should and wake up the same way. Tonight as I try to get myself to fall asleep, my throat feels tight with potential tears, I feel the desire to breakdown, but I know if I do, Henry will have won and broken my spirit. I'm not quite ready to give that up yet.

My mind is unusually quiet without Fallingtree talking to me. I am all alone. I search for a memory that will make me feel happy and hopeful, and I remember the drive down the coast with Sparks. The thought of his face as he laughed and talked with such passion about his work makes me smile. I can feel his genuine caring for me, and, in light of DJ's betrayal, I need to feel his goodness right now.

The more I focus on Sparks and the memory of that day, the more I can feel him, and I am drawn to him. Without warning, I find myself lying in bed next to Sparks in a room I don't recognize. He is asleep. I look at his bare chest and see bandages, and then I remember that Phoebe told me how she shot him. I know this is real. I watch him quietly breathing and feel so relieved that he is alive. He rolls onto his side and is facing me when he slowly opens his eyes. We look at each other for a very long time—as if we are saying, "hello." Sparks reaches out, pulls me to him, and we kiss. A deep, slow, soulful kiss.

I open my eyes and try to comprehend where I have just been. I hope that Sparks didn't feel that kiss because I certainly hadn't planned to end up in bed with him. I feel a little embarrassed because I know he experienced every second of it. I smile and finally drift off to sleep thinking about the kiss.

******

Sparks wakes up slowly and reaches across the bed saying, "Christa." He rubs his eyes and looks around the room. It is still the middle of the night—he must have been dreaming. It was so real, though, he could have sworn she was in the bed with him. Seeing her makes him anxious to find her. It is time to leave Santa Barbara. He needs to get to The Farm and find Big G and The Nomad. He has an idea of what their next move should be.

******

Phoebe walks across the grounds of The Farm smiling and saying, "hello" to everyone she encounters. She moves with authority so nobody will question why she is there or where she is going. She grabs a large basket from a pile on the front porch of the main house and heads around to the back. If anyone stops her, she'll say she is harvesting wild herbs for the kitchen. She walks down the little dirt path toward the rise on the hill where she'll have the perfect vantage point of The Nomad's quarters.

She wishes she had a gun—a scope rifle specifically—so she could shoot him from a distance but it would be an obvious assassination attempt, and she knows the attention that would garner is not what Damien Marshall, Sr. wants. No, she is going to have to get up close and personal. She grabs her basket and heads off.

Phoebe approaches the building and walks off to the side to sit under one of the windows. She can hear voices inside and thinks, "Damn! I'll have to wait until he is alone." She settles down and gets comfortable in her little spot under the window, and listens for the visitors to leave. One of the men slides the window above her open and she can hear their conversation perfectly. They are talking about The Nomad and his protection. How someone may want to kill him. One of the voices is off in the distance—she can't hear him as well, but the other voice is definitely Big G.

She recognizes that rumbling bass. "Look, I worked it out. The obvious next move would be to get rid of you," argues Big G. Phoebe has to admire what a brilliant strategist he is and how easily he's figured out that point.

"That may be true for all of us on the Council. What do you propose I do?" asks The Nomad.

"At the very least, put a 24-hour security detail on you as long as you insist on working in this isolated location. I'm just sayin'... look what happened to Sparks."

Phoebe smiles at the mention of her handiwork. Then another voice comes from the other side of the room but it sounds as if it is on a speaker because of the way it breaks up a little.

"Yes, look what happened to me and the men we lost at the airport. This is war and you are one of our generals—we can't lose you."

Phoebe closes her eyes and holds her head in her hands. She cannot believe what she is hearing—Sparks! Alive! This blows all her assassination plans apart, but she continues to listen to their conversation to learn more.

"I don't know where that woman is or who she's working for, but what I do know is she will hit us again, and she's deadly. I agree with G, you are the obvious next target," says Sparks.

She could tell that none of them seemed to know that she is the woman who shot Sparks. That's what she thinks until she hears what The Nomad says next.

"I've been in touch with Christa."

Both Sparks and Big G must have been surprised because they are quiet.

"I won't tell you how, but she is fine for now. However, the woman who shot Sparks paid Christa a visit where she is being held captive."

Sparks starts to break in but Big G says, "Let him finish, bro."

Phoebe thinks, "Yeah, let him finish—I want to hear this."

The Nomad continues describing what Christa had told him telepathically, "The woman's face was disfigured, and she has jet black hair, which is shaved over the ears, piercings, and a spider web tattooed on her arm."

"Yes, yes... that was her," Sparks says.

"That woman is Phoebe," said The Nomad.

Dead silence takes over the room. Outside, Phoebe is floored and wonders how the hell Christa got that information to The Nomad when she was being watched 24/7. She makes a mental note to tell Henry.

Sparks asks, "How did she survive the fight with Christa?"

"I don't know the details, but I do know that G, you're probably right, she'll come for me next. I left this place more open than usual to draw her out."

Phoebe stands up and knows she has to get out of there before she is discovered. The last words she hears as she sneaks away from the window are, "I think she may be here already."

******

Once she is back in her room at The Farm, Phoebe paces the floor—the Council, they are the key. That thought keeps repeating like a mantra. She finally has the big picture, the militia is a hydra—a many-headed snake, cut one head off and another takes its place. They would have to take out the whole Council.

She calls Henry Marshall. The guard at the prison tells her he is busy in the interrogation room, but Phoebe insists that he interrupt him. She says it is of vital importance. Once she gets Henry on the phone, she tells him he needs to compel Christa to divulge any information she knows about the Council. This is Phoebe's new objective. She lets him know that Christa is still communicating with OTP—specifically with The Nomad. She doesn't know how she is doing it, only that she's passing information to them.

When Phoebe leaves The Farm she decides to join the Detroit OTP group, where she has never been seen. There is an informant embedded in that group who can vouch for her. From the safe distance of Detroit, she could continue to look for the names of the Council members. She knows if she can dismantle the Council, it will create chaos in the movement.

Phoebe can't help but be pleased with the thought of taking down OTP's internal structure.

******

Henry Marshall charges into Christa's cell with two guards trailing behind him. "Hold her down!" he says. Christa struggles against the guards as Henry approaches her. He has a hypodermic needle, which, without mercy, he sticks into her neck. Christa screams in pain and starts crying because she has no idea what he has just pumped into her.

Henry says spitting with anger, "I'm tired of screwing around with you. It's time you answered some questions. In a minute, the injection I gave you will make it impossible to not answer me truthfully and tell me what I need to know." He looks at the guards and says, "Take her the interrogation room, and wait with her."

They each grab an arm, and as the drug kicks in it causes her to feel drowsy and weak. They drag her down the hallway to the interrogation room with Christa muttering the entire way, "No, no. Don't do this." But her resistance is futile.

Henry sits on the edge of Christa's empty bed for a moment. He doesn't like using drugs; it takes all the fun out of it for him, but he needs to get answers fast. Phoebe had called him asking for information about "The Council." This is the first time he's heard of it, but both he and Phoebe are certain Christa probably knows something. Phoebe said any intel will help her get started hunting them down.

Henry stands up, straightens his clothes, and walks down to the room where Christa is being held. "Time to take the gloves off," he thinks.

******

I know this isn't good: my head feels like it doesn't belong on my body. Voices crowd my mind like a packed auditorium, but not a single one comes forward. Not even Fallingtree. I think she is there, but whatever Henry shot into my neck makes it difficult to focus or receive messages. I am completely helpless.

My head keeps dropping forward—it is impossible to hold it up. I am drifting and spinning. What an awful, out of control, feeling! Not the same as when I had to deal with the pain Henry would inflict upon me. When he physically tortured me, I could easily separate from my body; but in this case, the drugs trap me in my mind—I can't leave.

Henry enters the room like a predator with complete control over his prey. Grabbing a chair, he places it in front of me and sits down, then he reaches forward and picks up my chin to stare directly into my eyes. I have no idea what to expect from him right now—this is not his normal MO and he seems angrier than he's been in the past.

"Christa, I am going to ask you some questions, and I highly recommend you don't fight the truth. In this case, the truth doesn't hurt—the lies do. This drug is quite powerful and not without side effects. From what I understand the more you fight it, the more likely there will be a residual impact on your brain. Do you understand?"

I find myself nodding "yes" but I know I don't want answer any of his questions.

"Good. Shall we start? Tell me about the Council. How many members are there?"

As soon as he asks the question, my head fills with voices, each telling me different numbers in an effort to distract me, but my brain knows the truth, and the drug is compelling me. "Twelve." Oh my God! That felt horrible... I have just confirmed the existence of the entire Council.

"Wonderful!" He smiles in a horrible triumphant manner. "We are off to a good start. Where can we find the Council members?"

"They are everywhere." That is the truth, as I know it, because they have never been anywhere but in my mind. Henry doesn't understand that, so he isn't satisfied with my answer. He keeps at me, trying to get an actual location. Finally, he decides to change tactics and asks, "Christa, I'd like the names of the Council members."

"I don't know all of their names," I am trying to stall, but it's making my head hurt to be evasive. I only know two names, and I don't want to give them to him.

"Christa, that is fine... just give me the names you do know."

"I only know two." I am resisting, but the words kept escaping my lips anyway.

"Then, tell me the two you know." The irritation in Henry's voice is obvious.

I push against the drug's influence, but my head feels like it's going to explode. I can hear my pulse in my ears as my heart speeds up trying to frantically throw off the effects of the truth serum. I don't want to comply, but the more I resist, the more intense the pressure on my brain—as if a vice is slowly being tightened.

Fallingtree is here. She tells me, "It's OK Christa, you can give them our names—they can't hurt us."

Oh my God, what a relief. Without hesitation I blurt out, "The Nomad and Fallingtree."

"That's it? Do they have any other names than those?" Henry knows about The Nomad but thinks that is a code name. He wants their full names. I have given him all I know.

"Yes, that's it." I can feel the pain start to back off because I am telling the truth. I'm still bothered about what I've just done., though. The one thing Henry Marshall doesn't know, and would never know, is that the Council has been a telepathic witness to his interrogation of me, and they are already preparing to ramp up a response to the inevitable attack he will try to make on them.

"Well, it's not a lot to go on, but it's a hell of a lot more than you've given me the entire time you've been here." Henry leans back in his chair and studies me for a moment then jumps up and leaves the room with a businesslike stride, eager to get whatever plan he has in mind into motion.

******

Damien Marshall, Sr. ends his phone call with, "We will be in touch," and then urgently calls for Kimball.

Marshall Industries head of security walks into the office immediately, almost as if he has been waiting outside the door. "Kimball, get down to the server floor and bring me Melanie Fallingtree," orders Damien Marshall, Sr.

Kimball rushes out and calls two security officers to meet him on the server floor. He steps off the elevator, and the two officers are waiting for him. He motions them to follow him to Melanie's office within the server complex. They charge into the office prepared to grab her immediately, but all they find is an empty room and her cell phone sitting in the middle of her desk. Kimball calls to the garage to see if anyone has attempted to take Melanie's car out, but it is still in its parking space. She is gone and they have no means to track her. They could go to her place on the reservation in Arizona, but Kimball assumes it will be empty as well. From her agent training, she knows how to become a ghost.

"Damn it!" Damien Marshall, Sr. yells when Kimball reports the disappearance. He has been losing his temper frequently these days and he does not like the feeling of being out of control. He phones a friend with government connections, and within the hour, Melanie Fallingtree is on the FBI's most wanted list with a nationwide manhunt launched to find her.

Melanie anticipated this would be the response, so she has already gone into hiding but not before giving The Nomad a specially designed back door code to by-pass Marshall Industries' security. Even if they change everything, the code will remain like a dormant virus within the system. She has conveyed the code telepathically to The Nomad so there is no record of it, no IP address that it was sent from, and no way to track who received it. There is no evidence at all of what she has done to compromise their system. Melanie Fallingtree is secure with the knowledge that The Nomad will know exactly what to do with the code.

******

Sparks, just released from the hospital with his arm in a sling, is already at work setting up a laptop station in an empty apartment next door to an Internet cafe. His computer is linked to another computer inside the café, which is receiving data via Wi-Fi. Sparks has mirrored the café laptop's operating system onto his computer, so he simultaneously receives the same information. The webcam on the cafe computer is activated, and if they are found out—which they will be eventually—he will launch a code to destroy the hard drive.

While he has access, he uses Fallingtree's back door code to get into the Marshall corporate servers and access their bank accounts, siphoning off hundreds of millions of dollars into Damien Marshall, Sr.'s private offshore accounts. He knows the company shareholders will overlook some stealing, but Sparks made the amount so egregious that it will be difficult to ignore. His goal is to have Damien Marshall, Sr. thrown into protective custody or placed under surveillance and rendered unable to move without eyes on him. He can still flee the country to a less protected environment. Either way the strategy is to throw Marshall off his game and get him somewhere they can force a walk-in exchange. They have watched and waited, and know they need Damien Marshall, Sr. at any cost. Currently he is a very dangerous man. Once the exchange takes place, they will explain his personality shift is due to a brain tumor. After the fictitious tumor has been removed, his position will be restored with the Board of Directors.

Sparks has just launched the OTP's first serious attempt to bring Marshall Industries down.

*****

The world is blowing up, and violence is erupting everywhere. Demands for fair banking practices, social justice, and consideration for the environment, are all front and center in the news. The safety of the citizens is at risk because of militarized police. It is their right to protest, but the police still pursue the instigators. No matter what, the voice of the people doesn't want to be silenced anymore.

For the first time in US history, the country is asked to explain it's human rights violations, being perpetrated at the hands of the police, to the UN. The legality of the private prison system is brought into question as well: isn't this just a new name for legalized slavery?

All over the world people are angry as they watch their water appropriated or fouled, their food supply rendered biologically inedible, and their skies saturated in chemicals that poison everything. The world court questions the crimes that "corporate governments" are committing against humanity, and they want justice.

Countries bordering the US are turning away brown and black immigrants who seek asylum from their violent police states. Other US citizens hide in fear of being spied upon or falsely reported for crimes they may not have committed.

People have begun to rally in large numbers all over the globe. Stepping out of the shadows, hoping it isn't too late to take their countries back. A revolution is happening in the streets and the cry is to restore true social democracy.

******

Gary has hit the end of his rope! Days and days have gone by and no word from Christa. Nobody from OTP has contacted him either. He'd watched the airport debacle play out on the news, but he still has no idea what is going on. He decides it is time to take matters into his own hands and confront DJ again.

He pounds on the front door until DJ answers, looking hung over and gray.

"Where the hell is she?" demands Gary.

"I don't know," answers DJ, but he won't look Gary in the eyes when he says this.

"BULLSHIT! I can see the lie in your eyes. Bullshit! Where is she?" Gary is irate because he can tell something big is going on but he is being kept in the dark. "What have you done, DJ? What bogus, cowardly, f'd up, self-serving thing have you done?"

DJ's guilty expression makes it impossible for him to hide his shame and depression. Gary moves in for the jugular…

"Tell me what you know you spineless prick!" Gary practically growls the words when asking the question.

DJ walks to the living room and collapses into a large chair. On the floor is an empty Vodka bottle and on the coffee table, half a bottle of Jameson, some weed, and some rolling papers.

"Tell me you didn't do all of this alone," Gary says as he eyes the remains of DJ's pity party. He's never seen DJ go off the deep end like this before, and he begins to genuinely worry that Christa is dead and DJ is hiding it from him. "You need to start talking now. This looks like a slow suicide, and it is making me very scared for what you have done with Christa. Don't try to deny it—clearly you are involved with her disappearance."

DJ doesn't deny Gary's accusations, but he also doesn't speak right away. He just keeps shaking his head. Gary waits patiently because he might finally get the whole story.

"You don't understand—I didn't have a choice. Then I saw her, and I saw what he did to her and... and... Oh god, what have I done?" DJ's voice starts to tremble as he tries to choke down the emotion building up inside of him.

"Who?" Gary asks insistently. "Who did what? To Christa?"

Gary feels manic now. He senses he is on the verge of getting the information he wants but DJ is having a total meltdown. He feels powerless to get DJ to pull himself together. All he can do is control his feeling of repulsion for whatever betrayal and vile acts DJ must have brought upon Christa. He could try to reassure DJ so he'd reveal more to him. The good news is that it sounds like Christa is alive, but he worries for how long.

Gary sits down quietly next to DJ and places a calming hand on his arm while he soothingly speaks to him like a child. "I know you love her. You probably were in an impossible situation."

"I do. I do love her. Henry gave me no choice. He called it family business, and all I had to do was look the other way." DJ genuinely sounds full of disgust and self-loathing.

There is a long silence while Gary waits for DJ to compose himself and unburden his guilt on Gary's seemingly sympathetic ear. It is obvious his knowledge of Christa's situation has been festering inside of him and he needs to talk.

"I don't know how it came to this. It's all ruined now—she saw me." DJ stops as he remembers the moment, so Gary encourages him to keep talking.

"Maybe, maybe not." Gary says, "Tell me what happened."

"I wasn't supposed to be there at all, but Henry asked me to bring Christa's computer to the facility."

The facility, thinks Gary, he wants to know where this is, but he has to be delicate and patient with DJ right now. He waits for him to continue.

"I had just dropped it off with one of the guards and was walking down the hall to leave—I was steps from being out of there—she never would have seen me… and there she was. She was standing in the middle of the hallway being held up by two guards. Oh…," DJ shakes his head and it seems he might break down completely, but Gary knows he will only do that alone. "She was really, really beaten up…."

Gary clamps his mouth shut tight, because he is filled with anger and fear for Christa when he hears this. For a moment, DJ straightens up and seems aware of what he is saying, and Gary thinks he might stop talking, but he continues.

"I swear, Henry arranged it. He can be so cruel. He knew Christa and I would never be able come back from that encounter. He knew I didn't want any part of this. Henry insisted that I had to personally bring her laptop, saying we couldn't risk it falling into the wrong hands if there is sensitive material on it. He insisted! All he really wanted was to destroy me and Christa—forever."

Gary is so wound up inside that he is ready to force the location of the facility out of DJ, then pass it on to OTP so maybe they could rescue her!

There is a clicking sound in the front hallway and Gary turns around to look, but DJ is too out of it to care. Henry Marshall appears at the living room entrance with Kimball, and, in that moment, the bottom falls out of Gary's stomach, he knows he is totally screwed.

"Gary, Gary, Gary. You know the old saying, 'curiosity killed the cat,' I think we just caught a curious little pussy." Henry is very smug as he strides into the room and walks up to his brother. He slaps DJ hard which makes Gary jump, but DJ barely responds.

"Pull yourself together! I knew it was a good idea to put you under surveillance. With all your drinking and drugging it was only a matter of time before you said the wrong thing to the wrong person." Henry shoots a look at Gary.

"Kimball, can you please escort my brother upstairs, put him to bed, and make sure he sleeps off this high he's on?"

"Certainly." Kimball puts an arm around DJ's waist, helps him out of the chair he's slumped into, and walks him out of the room.

"I think Gary and I will have a little chat while you do that."

Gary's heart races and he feels glued to his chair. He has always had the upper hand with Henry Marshall, but that is all gone now. He has not revealed to DJ that he knows about the movement but somehow he thinks Henry strongly suspects him anyway.

"So, now you know your friend is being held against her will and she's hurt. I'm sure you are very concerned for her, so when Kimball returns I think it would be best for all of us that we take you to see Christa right away," Henry says, his tone dripping with false concern and sarcasm. He knows Henry is talking about "disappearing" him or worse, interrogating him about OTP. Gary knows there is no way out and that he will never hold up under interrogation. He begins to shake because he fears for his life. He doesn't want Henry to notice so he takes a very deep breath and holds it while he wills his heart to stop racing. Then lets his breath out slowly. Whenever he had a difficult exam, this always has did the trick. It worked—for the moment.

One hour later…

The black bag is pulled abruptly from Gary's head, and he can see where he is. In front of him was a prison cell, and inside is Christa. When she sees him, she cries out, "Oh Gary, no! What are you doing here?"

"Don't worry sweetie." That is as much cheerfulness as he can muster, under the circumstances. He is trying to keep Christa calm even though he is truly disturbed by her appearance.

Henry walks forward. "Gary got a little too curious, and it occurred to me that he might be just the motivation you need to give us more information. You may be willing to die for this revolution but are you willing to let your friend die for it?"

CHAPTER TEN

CAUSING RIPPLES

They put Gary in the cell next to me. It is almost comforting knowing he is there because I haven't seen a friendly face in so long. But I am scared for him. Gary has no business here at all. I haven't heard a peep from him, and that is completely out of character—normally you can't shut him up.

I've walked up and down the length of my cell so often, I can count the exact number of steps with my eyes closed and turn before hitting the wall. I analyze my options and possible outcomes as I pace. The pacing calms me down. Gary is a new variable, which I need to factor in. He definitely makes me vulnerable to Henry's sadistic ways. I will never let anything happen to Gary. Already Sparks has been hurt, and The Nomad told me Big G has been attacked too. Enough is enough.

I am ready to find my way out of this place. I continue to pace back and forth, searching for answers when the Council crowds its way into my head. Fallingtree speaks, "It's time." She doesn't have to say it twice—this is what I have been waiting to hear, permission to expand the use of my power—if you can call it that. "Just a little more waiting," she adds. I am fine with that—as long as there is an end in sight, I can tolerate this a little longer.

******

Standing in front of his bank of screens, which display various satellite feeds, Damien Marshall, Sr. watches the action outside of his corporate offices like a big game hunter surveying the African landscape for his prey. It seems that Marshall Industries' internal servers have been breached, and, of course, he knows Ms. Fallingtree is responsible. He walks slowly across the plush carpet of his office, the nap of the heavy wool absorbing the sound of his shoes. His blood pressure rises with every step as he thinks about that woman and what she has done. There will be hell to pay when he finally gets his hands on her!

A quiet crowd of gawkers and protestors gathers outside, filling Marshall Plaza. Some carry signs asking for an investigation into the company, others have signs of a more general nature protesting the uneven distribution of wealth in the world. Videos, internal memos, emails, and other sensitive documents have been released to the public via various Internet outlets, each piece of information more damaging than the last. Payoffs, bribes, blackmail to cover-up a multitude of crimes.

Marshall has manipulated the agricultural industry in an effort to control all food resources, has privatized the water industry, and has even tried to manipulate the weather through seeding the atmosphere with chemical compounds. He knows if he controls the very sustenance of life, he controls the world, and he is just arrogant enough to feel he can achieve this. Now all of his lies are out in the open for the public to see, making his job far more difficult—not impossible—just difficult. He thinks of how to quickly change this, after all, he controls much of the media as well.

******

"Each time any one person stands up for an idea,
or acts to improve the lot of others,
or strikes out against injustice,
they send forth a tiny ripple of hope.
Together, those ripples build a current which can sweep down
the mightiest walls of oppression and resistance."

Robert F. Kennedy

One lone man stands in the middle of Marshall Plaza as the crowds stream in. He is dwarfed by the behemoth building that rises behind him like a black onyx monolithic shrine to capitalism. He is a nerdy blogger who was the first to manage to download all the documents that were leaked from Marshall Industries before they were pulled off the web. He had read as much of it as he could digest and became increasingly agitated as the full picture of the company's transgressions became clear. The documents are so damning that he could think of a host of federal charges for which the company should be prosecuted immediately. Yet, nobody is talking about these documents—none of the political pundits, talk show hosts, or mainstream news outlets, NOBODY! Either they aren't reading the material or they are too afraid to go up against this corporate giant.

This lone protestor, blogger, and law student from Berkeley, California, Anthony Davis, decides to take a stand. He has packed a box with copies of the documents he's downloaded, put on some comfortable clothes, and grabbed some food and a plastic storage crate. Anthony threw everything into the back of his old Toyota truck and made the trip to Marshall Industries corporate headquarters, leading him to this moment, where he now stands on his plastic crate in the middle of the plaza. From his informal pulpit, he pulls out and reads one document after another to the crowd—or rather, to anyone who will listen. Generally, people pass by and ignore him as a crazy zealot. Here and there, people stop and listen for a while, as he reads the inflammatory material out loud. The words are so damning that those who hear them know he is reading the truth, and they are shocked.

Mr. Davis' protest stretches towards evening and a squad car is sent to ask him to leave. The police officers say that someone has called in a complaint about him creating a public nuisance—he might even be intoxicated. Even as the two officers stand there asking him to leave, Anthony keeps reading. It is twilight on the plaza, and the officers become impatient and take a decidedly more stern approach with him.

"Sir, we have to ask you to vacate the plaza immediately," says one of the officers.

"I have the constitutional right to assemble and practice free speech," answers Anthony.

"Not here. We must insist you leave now, or we'll have to arrest you for creating a public nuisance."

"If you arrest me you'll be violating my civil rights. I'm not hurting anyone except Marshall Industries. Are you working for my tax dollars or Marshall Industries' payroll?" Anthony asks the officer.

Ignoring his question, the officer stands staring at Anthony with a completely neutral expression and says, "Sir, I need to see some identification, now."

Anthony reaches into his coat pocket, but at that moment the other officer, who had been watching the street, catches the movement out of the corner of his eye and yells, "Gun!" Only a moment passes and he has his gun out, firing several rounds into Anthony. The impact propels him off his crate. He falls to the ground and blood begins to spill out beneath him. Anthony Davis is dead by the time he hits the ground.

The crowd, which has assembled around the edges of the plaza, closes in when they see what is happening. Half a dozen phones have been held up overhead, filming the incident as it unfolds. One witness, after another, uploads video of Anthony Davis' death. The videos spread like wildfire on the web and focus unwanted attention on Marshall Industries. Anthony has succeeded, creating, with his tragic death, what he couldn't accomplish in life: He has shed light upon, and created interest in, the crimes of this large corporation.

******

The death of Anthony Davis triggers a furious public dialog about corporate corruption with Marshall Industries at the center. The public has proof that willful crimes as well as the ensuing damage have been covered up. Evidence of political lobbying in Washington, corporate terrorizing of farmers, manipulating the media, and turning the local police into a domestic military—is now available online for anyone to read.

Other sins are mentioned in the documents too, such as Marshall's collusion with the finance industry (specifically the Carlyle Corporation). These two corporations have sought to diminish the middle class and gain control of real estate throughout the country. They have forced people from their homes and bankrolled developers; in some cases entire communities have been destroyed for profit. These market manipulations have left thousands of people homeless and scrambling to maintain their dignity.

The list goes on and on with sins against the environment, women, children—anyone but the rich. The arrogance of this company and the tone of the documents reveal a total disregard for any living thing but themselves and their progeny.

******

Damien Marshall, Sr. doesn't fully comprehend what he is viewing, but as more news surfaces, he gathers the police have shot a protestor. This event has crowds streaming into Marshall Plaza like tributaries to a river.

Damien Marshall, Sr. makes a call. "Yes, Damien Marshall for Chief Allen... Hello, Richard... Yes, I have been watching this; I think it is time to pull the plug on this demonstration. You can finally put all that new riot gear to good use. The crowd doesn't appear to be violent, but we both know there is no proof it will stay that way. Better safe than sorry, don't you think?...OK, we agree then. When this is over you'll find a little bonus in the Caymans for your trouble. Thanks Richard, and let's get a round of golf in next week!"

He clicks off the phone and sits down to watch and wait for Chief Allen to bring in the riot squad and put an end to this mess. He is satisfied that once again he is in control.

******

Chief Allen goes into action calling up the Commander of the Riot Squad. A newly outfitted detail, these men and women are highly trained in the latest in military tactics and have the equipment to implement any procedures. They are not trained in the art of peaceful resolution—they are trained to shoot to kill and ask questions later. It really doesn't matter if their targets ware ordinary citizens; all these officers can see is a perceived threat.

Once Chief Allen has the police mobilized, he pulls a phone from his briefcase and reaches out to an informant embedded within OTP—it is time to instigate a riot. For him, the end justifies the means because the violence and destruction to come will clearly be blamed on the movement thus giving him carte blanche to go after them and destroy their organization. He sees his self-righteous point-of-view as an admirable character trait.

******

Sparks is back in the lab again, and it feels good to distract his mind with work. He loves to solve puzzles, and now he is on the verge of finally solving one that had plagued him for a while— how to get his reflective 3D nano-scales to flip simultaneously. This is the key to his cloaking device. He has created a plan to use the body's own electromagnetic field to "guide" the scales to flip. Sparks makes a simple glove from the scaled material and puts it on his hand. If the test is successful, his hand will disappear before his eyes. With his ungloved hand, he presses a panel on a wristband he wears. It transmits a magnetic pulse that surges across his nervous system and suddenly the scales flip on the glove and his hand vanishes! Sparks lets out an excited "whoop!" "It worked," he says aloud to an empty room. "Yesss!"

He knows the implications of this new fabric and the edge it will give OTP to achieve a bloodless takeover. Next, he will build a prototype suit, and if that works, he'll be able to outfit a team. Along with his stun gun, they will have two unique under-the-radar advantages in this war. Sparks has already distributed the plans for the stun gun to the other militia groups and they are currently printing them on their 3D printers for the next big organized coup. The plans are top secret and only the Council members handle them. Once the guns are printed, the plans are destroyed. They cannot risk the guns falling into the hands of the opposition.

The scale-covered suit—once he fully develops it—will remain a secret within his group. They have decided that if the enemy doesn't know about their stealth capabilities, they won't be prepared to combat them.

Sparks has been pushing hard for weeks, and although he'd just had a successful break-through in the lab, he isn't allowing himself to get too elated. The word has been passed along the pay phone network to all the militia that a concert will be given in an open field in California. This concert is to be much more than entertainment, it is where OTP plans to gather for "unification, a word The Nomad uses often but Sparks isn't sure what it means with regard to this event.

What The Nomad has told them, is the concert will be a peaceful demonstration. The leaders of many of the various OTP cells and some of their members will be there. The Nomad has alluded to the idea that "the unification" will be a powerful message which will bring them all together, focused upon one action. Sparks doesn't know how they will accomplish this or what the action will be—only that it will have wide-spread impact once it is implemented.

As a precaution, Sparks has made certain that some of the militia members will be armed with stun guns. He knows that if the corporate or government powers chasing OTP get wind of a gathering this size, or it's intent, they will view it as an uprising and move to shut it down. Sparks hopes that OTP will be in and out before anyone gets wind that something is happening because a gathering this size will make them an immediate target.

Sparks has leaked damaging corporate documents pertaining to Marshall Industries, thanks to Fallingtree's back door code. He is waiting for the repercussions from that, and an event such as this concert could provide the perfect opportunity for Marshall Industries to retaliate.

His wounds provide a vivid reminder of how dangerous his enemy is. They are well financed, ruthless, and have no regard for ethics or human life.

Phoebe is a living, breathing example of that mentality. Sparks can't believe he'd once been romantically involved with her, slept with her, cared about her, and trusted her enough to bring her into the movement! In the end, he didn't even recognize her the day she shot him. That demonstrates how little he knew about her. On that day, though, he did learn quite a bit about how his enemy functions.

He isn't upset—he is doing a psychological inventory of all the things that have gone wrong to date because he is determined they will not be repeated. As for Phoebe, now that Sparks knows she is alive, he'll never underestimate her ruthlessness again.

Exhausted, he falls onto the black couch in his lab and indulges a memory of the last time he sat there with Christa. The day he drove her to the San Francisco Airport was the last time he'd seen her and she's been missing for weeks now. The Nomad steadfastly maintains she is alive, but through a strange encounter the other night he has proof of his own. The dream of her visit is still fresh in his mind. He shakes off the memory because now is not the time to be distracted by things he can not control. He picks up his headphones and plugs them into his ears, determined to cancel the world out for a bit by getting lost in some good music. Sparks needs to escape into his head because he knows they are in for one hell of a firestorm if they can't pull this operation off smoothly.

******

Chief Allen positions his men in a row with their shields in front of them, assault rifles at the ready, helmets and flack jackets on. The police face their "enemy," the American people, ready to do battle.

Big G knows this is a volatile situation, and he is on high alert as he guides his people to the front of the line of protestors. Each member of G's group is armed with a stun gun. They position themselves one-to-one, each in front of an officer. All of them appear to be praying as they bring their hands together in front of their faces and bow their heads. The crowd behind them is agitated from the shooting of Anthony Davis and growing more so by the minute. The police chief climbs to the top of the entry stairs to Marshall Industries corporate building and takes a microphone to address the people.

"Hello. May I have your attention please! We are here today to express our sympathy and tremendous sadness over the recent terrible incident..."

"Murder! It was murder! Tell it like it is!" yells an anonymous voice from the crowd. All across the plaza, murmurs of support rise for the man's charge.

The chief ignores the heckler and continues, "I want you to know everything is being done to have a fair and transparent process around this investigation."

"Have you arrested the officer who shot Anthony Davis? Yeah... he had a name, Anthony Davis!" shouts a second demonstrator.

"Is he in jail?" comes another question from the crowd.

"Where's the video from the shooting? Why haven't you released it to the public so we can judge for ourselves? You say you want to be 'fair and transparent...'"

A new voice rises from the crowd, "What about the 361 other UNARMED citizens shot by your officers? What about justice for them? I'm sorry—not shot—KILLED—by the police. What about justice there? Not a single officer has served a day in prison for those killings!"

The crowd really starts to bubble over with anger at this last statement. They surge forward against the front row of praying OTP members. The members hold firm. Each of them keeps one eye on Big G—waiting for a signal.

Captain Allen yells out to the crowd to settle down because they don't want any more violence today. As the demonstrators continue to surge forward, he gives the signal to his officers, and they point their rifles at the crowd. Over the microphone, Captain Allen warns the people to move back away from the police barricade or they will use force.

"You can't keep shootin' us—pretty soon there'll be nothin' to protect!" yells a protester to cheers from the surrounding crowd.

Big G raises his voice and the boom of his bass can be heard above all the others, "Take their guns away until they know how to protect us without killin' us!"

This is the signal. At this moment, all militia members part their praying hands to reveal Sparks' stun guns. Before anybody knows what has hit them, each officer is frozen. The OTP members calmly walk forward and disarm the officers, quickly passing the guns to other members waiting in the back of the crowd. In moments, the guns have disappeared completely. A couple of minutes later the officers are mobile again, but without their weapons and with the momentary loss of time, they appear deeply confused. They face the crowd with fear now because they are unarmed, and they know some of these people want to tear them apart.

Then an unusual thing happens, the front row of OTP members link arms to form a human chain and protect the unarmed officers. From out of the crowd strides The Nomad, and with complete authority, he makes his way to the top of the stairs, followed by Big G. Chief Allen stands glued to his spot at the top of the stairs and speechless in the wake of what he has had just witnessed. He holds the microphone limply away from his face. The Nomad calmly approaches him and gently removes the microphone from his hand, then turns to address the crowd.

"Please… Listen." There are cries of "Shhhhh!" from all over the plaza, and then a pure, peaceful silence settles on a rapt audience. Two words, and The Nomad somehow has total control of the moment.

"I stand here as a witness to the violence that has been done to all of you in one way or another. Be it environmental, financial, or emotional—we have all been subjugated to a society that is no longer serving us. What you have witnessed today is the movement of people, just like you, taking back their power. Quite simply—we matter. All of us. We are 'Of the People.'"

The crowd is mostly quiet but some cheer. The Nomad put his hand up, and there is total silence again. The moment is almost holy in the way the crowd shifts from violent to cooperative. He looks at the police officers and says, "We are you. We have families, children, jobs, dreams, struggles, and values. We are no different. We are you. You can no longer fight us—it makes no sense. Even though I may have a reason to be angry about the shooting that happened here today and other shootings, I forgive you. I invite you to join us." He gestures to the crowd that is still quiet and now in fascinated shock over what is unfolding before them.

"Do you really want to continue beating and killing your neighbors because they are just trying to tell the truth and bring some decency back into their lives?" The Nomad pauses.

"Lay down your helmets and flack jackets, or walk away with Captain Allen. The choice is yours. Either way, nobody will be hurt today." The Nomad stops talking and G steps to his side protectively because he isn't sure what will happen next. Finally, one young police officer takes off his helmet and his flack jacket and lays them on the ground. Then he walks into the crowd unprotected. Nobody puts a finger on him and the atmosphere remains peaceful.

The crowd cheers and applauds the young man's courage. Several more officers do the same thing and they are embraced as well. Other officers walk away from the crowd, following Captain Allen back to the precinct. They have their reasons, money, fear, or simply not being able to make a decision in the moment. The Nomad watches them leave, but he is confident that today has raised serious questions in everyone's mind, especially Captain Allen's. As the Captain leaves, followed by a handful of his men, he isn't quite sure what he has witnessed, but he is definite he'll find out eventually.

******

My head is resting on the wall of my cell when I ask softly, "Gary?"

"Here," he answers. "Wherever 'here' is…"

"Is it crazy that I am actually happy you're here?" I ask.

"A little," He laughs lightly.

"Gary?…"

"Yes?"

"A lot has happened since I've been in here, and I really need to talk about it."

"I can only imagine."

"No—actually, I don't think you can."

"Christa—time to spill."

· 203 ·

"I know, but you have to promise me that you will not think I am delusional. I am in my right mind, I swear! Promise?"

"Yes, of course. Now, talk."

I tell Gary everything about my "awakening" and how I can communicate with the Council. I describe Fallingtree, how she stood by me during my darkest moments of torture and interrogation by Henry.

"I need a Fallingtree if Henry interrogates me," Gary says thoughtfully.

I can tell he is truly terrified at the thought of whether he would survive being tortured.

"He won't," I say.

"How can you possibly know that?"

"Because we are leaving here soon."

"How? By the way, NOW you sound crazy!" Gary gives a more hopeful laugh this time.

"When I first met The Nomad, he asked me if I knew who I was. While I've been in here, I've remembered where I came from. I haven't always been Christa McCaffrey. My spirit, for lack of a better term, is part of a group of beings called, ISHI. We live in what would be called, the 'soul dimension.' We also can exist within a material body on the soul level. The ISHI have been watching over humans since they first appeared on Earth thousands of years ago. We are good—of course, but there are always exceptions. Even though we can inhabit a human body, we can't enter it unless we are invited by the existing soul. We aren't like human souls that can reincarnate at the point of death and birth into another human body. In my meditations and conversations with Fallingtree, I've discovered an entire other world that I came from but had forgotten because I arrived in a six-year-old's body. It has taken me 20-plus years to remember who I am. As Fallingtree pointed out, some ISHI never remember until they move on to another human body or go back to the soul dimension."

"As if that isn't enough, I've also discovered that I have one more level to my natural ISHI telepathy that the Council doesn't have. Not only can I read the minds of other ISHI, but also non-ISHI. In addition, I can project my thoughts to anyone I choose. I know this is what The Nomad was referring to when he asked me the question, do I know who I am."

"That was one hell of an answer..." Gary's voice trails off in thought. It is clear he was trying to digest all of this information.

"My telepathic ability has taken some adjustment. It is odd to see how easily I can influence the way people think. I can mentally communicate with anyone, even you. That's pretty heady stuff!" The makes us both laugh.

"Really? You can mentally communicate with anyone? Prove it," challenges Gary.

"OK..." I close my eyes and concentrate by imagining Gary and I are sharing a rare 1998 bottle of *Krug Clos d'Ambonnay* champagne. I am specific about the vintage to be able to verify the thought I send him.

"Oh yes, that is exactly what I want right now—a bottle of champagne! How did you know?" Gary giggles at how fun this feels.

"Was it a 1998 bottle of *Krug Clos d'Ambonnay*?" I ask— knowing it was.

"Oh God! That is creepy, girl! I'd scream if I didn't think it would bring the guards running. Geez..." Then Gary is silent. I fill the space by sharing my thoughts about this newfound ability.

"I know it's pretty crazy. So... now you know I can do this and who I am."

"You'll still be Christa to me even if you can read all my horrible thoughts or suggest it would be a good idea to run naked down Sunset Boulevard," Gary laughs at the thought.

"The good news is, during the time I've been here I've learned how to control my abilities. So you don't have to worry about me asking you to run naked down Sunset Boulevard— I'll make sure you wear some cute boxers." I laugh and Gary joins me. It feels good to be a little lighthearted. Things have been so dark and hopeless for so long. "When I first discovered I could do this, anything I thought would happen if I wasn't careful. Fallingtree worked with me and helped me to focus my energy on what happens when I use my telepathic transference. Now I can target who will receive my suggestions and exactly what I want them to receive. At the same time, it is a horrible responsibility."

"Oh honey, that super power is so wasted on you! You'll do the responsible, ethical thing. You'll try to change the world. Ughhh! Give me that super power, and I'll show you some fun! Oh yeah!"

Gary finally has me laughing outright at the thought of this "power of suggestion" in his hands. We both let loose until we have tears in our eyes. It is a great release of tension, it has been so long since I have felt any joy—I have worried that I might die without smiling ever again.

Now that Gary knows I can get him out of here, he isn't scared anymore. Suddenly he asks, "But if you can do this mind control voodoo, why didn't you stop Henry from... you know...?"

"He is the one person, so far, with whom I can't get past the blackness in his mind. I can't get past the hole in his spirit. I need to make a connection with the person on an emotional level to transfer energy and thoughts, but his energy is so dark I don't want to—or I can't—connect to him."

"I see," says Gary, "Well then, I'd say we need to get out of here before he comes back."

"Don't worry—I'll know when the time is right to leave, and we'll get that bottle of champagne afterwards."

"Deal," says Gary.

******

Damien Marshall, Sr. watches the protest from the protected sanctuary of his corporate perch, like a predatory bird. Watching the satellite feed stone faced, he waits for the game to play out with the expected violence and destruction of an all-out riot. It is his opinion that these angry mobs usually devolve into violent behavior and it won't be difficult to provoke it. Today is different though, he saw something that completely shook his confidence—a weapon he had not developed and knew nothing about. He thinks about redirecting one of his drones to destroy the entire assembly in the plaza but he calculates the loss of life, the loss of the weapon, and decides it would not be prudent. The scene downstairs continues to unfold, and he watches as some of the police disband into the crowd while others return to the precinct.

This gives him pause and he hits the intercom to speak to his secretary. "Bring the chopper to the roof, and find out if Henry is in the building."

She checks her computer screen, "Yes sir. The log says he swiped in at the back entry about an hour ago. Do you want me to get him for you?"

"Yes. Have him come to my office immediately." Damien Marshall, Sr. goes back to watching the drama outside but without sound. He needs to think. What next?

The OTP movement has been developing all along right under their noses. He understands the implications of this group working outside the grid—outside digital surveillance. How else can he explain so much advancement on their part? He thinks about how the scene on the street played out with the officers frozen in place and disarmed so effortlessly—without bloodshed. Most of the crowd had their view blocked of the front line; only he had the perfect vantage point from above them. He saw the weapon in action and he had to admit it was pure genius, which also scares him. He wants that weapon and the person who developed it.

There is a quick knock and Henry walks into the room. He looks at the silent monitors following the movements of the crowd and is about to make a comment when his father holds up his hand for him to be quiet. He says, "Just watch." With that, he replays the entire incident with the weapons freezing the police and the protestors disarming them. They watch The Nomad address the crowd.

"What the...?" says Henry incredulously. "How did we not know about this? That Bitch! I've been pushing Christa all this time, and she probably knew about this weapon. I need to put her through another round. What else isn't she telling me?"

Henry is furious, he doesn't like that Christa has made a fool of him. He yearns to squash that high-and-mighty attitude once and for all and really teach her a lesson. Only then will he feel that he has regained the upper hand. He does not like to lose control of any situation.

"No." says his father. "You don't have time. It's too risky. The chopper will be landing on the roof in a minute, and it will take us to the airport. We need a safe, protected place to regroup and decide how to quell this thing. Christa is fine where she is for now. She's not going anywhere. When we get back, you will know exactly how to proceed with her, even if it means disposing of her permanently.

"What about DJ?" asks Henry.

"I'll have him meet us at the airport."

The men leave for the rooftop as the helicopter hovers to land. A moment later, it is on the pad and they run to board it. Once inside Damien Marshall, Sr. addresses the pilot: "Bert, can you swoop the crowd? Not too low, but I'd like to get a closer look as we leave."

"Certainly, sir."

As the chopper begins to lift off from the landing pad, the rooftop access door opens and Sparks rushes out along with a group of OTP soldiers. He sees Damien Marshall, Sr. and Henry on-board the helicopter, and he isn't about to let them get away. He orders the group to aim their stun guns at the helicopter pilot. Sparks isn't sure, but he hopes that the combined power of all their guns focused on the same target will allow them to immobilize the pilot from a distance. The chopper is barely inches off the ground, so this could give them a minute to board and try to commandeer it.

They fire their guns in unison at the pilot, but the chopper continues to rise off the helipad. The OTP train their stun guns on the target and follow the ascent of the helicopter, but Sparks is disappointed that it seems to have no effect. Then, the chopper begins to wobble, does a half spin, and starts to drop. As it comes down, Sparks can see the horrified faces of Henry and his father trapped inside. Damien Marshall, Sr. reaches forward and shakes the pilot who is clearly unresponsive. Sparks doesn't have time to be happy that his theory has worked because the helicopter comes crashing onto the ledge of the roof, hanging half on and half suspended over the plaza below. The spin the helicopter has made has moved it away from the central pad. The blades still rotate but the entire aircraft teeters precariously. There is a creaking noise as part of the roof ledge gives way. Almost in slow motion, the helicopter drops down the side of the building bouncing off the steel structure here and there, until it comes to a fiery crash on the street below.

Miraculously, it completely misses the plaza, and there are no serious injuries within the crowd of protestors, but no survivors on-board the helicopter. Nothing can connect the militia to the crash—not even the security footage from the rooftop camera, which looks as if they were aiming at the craft, but did not fire. The investigation would later blame the crash on pilot error.

******

Standing in a room a few floors below the rooftop, Kimball witnesses the company helicopter careen past one of the windows. Seconds later, he is looking down on a burning mess of glass and metal.

He rushes upstairs to Damien Marshall's office to find his secretary at the window crying and shaking. He walks over to her, grabs her by the shoulders, and forcefully turns her to face him.

"Who was in the helicopter?" he asks.

"It, it, it…" She breaks down hysterically again. Kimball waits a moment and then, still holding her by the shoulders, says calmly and firmly, "It is very important for the security of the company that I know exactly who was on that helicopter. I will ask you again—who?"

The secretary takes a deep breath to try and stop crying long enough to say, "Damien Marshall, Sr., Henry Marshall, and the pilot." She bursts into tears again because her words make real the deaths she has just witnessed.

Kimball knows the protocol—he has to get to DJ immediately!

CHAPTER ELEVEN

YOUR MOVE

D J got the call on his cell while he was on a run to pick up more drugs. His brother and his father are gone—just like that. The news blindsides him. He parks his silver Porsche on a dimly-lit side street in a warehouse district. The area is completely empty, so nobody will hear him as he rages and cries. DJ thinks of the horrible, dark, distasteful, or painful things his father and brother have twisted him into doing over the years in the name of the legacy. Now they are gone and none of it matters.

He stares at the streetlight in front of him and thinks that he doesn't understand anything anymore. He has destroyed his relationship with Christa out of fear of his father's rage if he defied him and fear of being cut off from the money. Now he doesn't have anyone and he has no one to fear. The idea "you can't take it with you," means something to DJ now. His father and brother are gone, but the object of their greed, Marshall Industries, didn't go with them. It is all his now but he doesn't want to carry the heavy load of all that wealth—or at least he isn't going to think about it right now.

DJ has been on a downward spiral ever since Christa saw him in the hallway and realized he knew about her abduction and had left her there. He can't recover from the look on her face. Drugs and alcohol are numbing the shame and pain he feels but he'll always be a loser in his mind. So who gives a damn—from now on, he can do what he wants. He has nothing to lose anymore. Although things are different because he will inherit everything that Marshall Industries controls, he knows he was ill-equipped to handle the change.

He looks around the floor of his car and finds a half-smoked joint from earlier that day. He lights it up and takes a long, deep drag, holding the smoke for a bit to get the high going and numb his feelings again. DJ leans back in the leather seat and closes his eyes, but there is a rush of images through his mind: his father, his brother, the company, Christa when he met her, and Christa the day he saw her at the facility. Life is just speeding by in his mind. From this dark place, he can't see what he is worth anymore and he is sinking into an emotional abyss that he isn't sure he can crawl out of it.

A knock on the passenger side window breaks the meditative silence of the car, and DJ looks over to see his dealer, a young man with a hoody shading his face.

"Hey man, I got your stuff." DJ keeps the window closed and just looks at the kid. "Seriously dude, roll the window down, and let's get this over with. I wanna get outa here."

"One good thing… if I could do one good thing, I might be able to save myself," DJ thinks. He debates for a second whether now is the moment to save himself. He decides it isn't and rolls down the passenger side window.

******

Wait... that's all I can do: be patient and wait. Fallingtree told me that soon I would be free and to trust her, which I am doing. I am beginning to understand how being incarcerated while I explore my new gift has been a blessing. If I had come into my ability to influence people while out in public, I might not have had any control or understanding of the long-term effects of my actions. Even the pain and torture have taught me to have greater empathy for human frailty. This insight helped to refine my ability, and the isolation has been a necessary component.

I am finally ready. I know there is something I need to do when I emerged from this prison, but I am not sure what it is—yet. What I do know, is everything that was my life before is gone. DJ, my home, my law practice, everything.

Gary sleeps in the other cell. I am surprised he can sleep at all, but I guess he really does believe me when I say we'll be leaving soon. Once I assured him of our escape he had a rapid letdown and now I hear him quietly snoring. I laugh at the thought of telling Gary he snores—he'd be mortified to think that any of his former lovers may have heard him.

Off in the distance a door opens and clangs shut again. The sound of shoes on the concrete floor echoes through the quiet holding area. The heavier step is obviously a man and he is walking toward my cell. I am waiting at full attention for him to arrive, and then he is standing in front of me—DJ. He is limp and spent, with a vacant look in his red-rimmed eyes, his hair is uncombed and his clothes are dirty and wrinkled. He is a mess, and I almost feel sorry for him.

He mumbles, "They're all gone. I need to redeem myself. This is my one good thing."

"Who is gone?" I hear Gary up and moving around in his cell—he is obviously listening to this conversation too.

"Dad..."

DJ stops and I take a deep breath wondering to myself, "Did I hear him right?"

"Your dad? Your father?" I ask trying get clear what I am hearing. I probe carefully, "So... he's 'gone away' or 'gone'...?"

"He died." DJ says with quiet finality. But then he starts to lose it emotionally, "No, no, no, they can't be gone. I can't do this alone."

"They?" I ask.

"Dad and Henry," he says simply.

Before I can say anything Gary, blurts out from the other cell, "Henry is dead?"

DJ doesn't answer with words but confirms this with his sudden emotional breakdown. Despite the anger and hurt I feel toward him, in this moment I see a man I once loved and I want to ease his pain. He is extremely unstable, and I realize I can try to gently push his mind and at least prevent him from harming himself.

Entering DJs mind is as if I walked through the front door of my home. I know I've been there before because of our intimate connection, but everything is different. He has become darker, like his brother. There is a voice in DJ's head asking him to do "one good thing." He is searching for a way to redeem himself, but it is obvious he's failing and feels hopeless. So I push...

"DJ you can do one good thing... you can let Gary and Christa leave the facility." I plant the conversation in his mind and wait. I do have pity for him, and I may even forgive him somewhat, but I don't trust him because his cowardice controlled his judgment when it came to protecting the people he loved, that is unforgivable—and he knows it. So perhaps this push will help him redeem himself a little.

I wait a moment and then DJ turns to the guard and says, "Let them out."

The guard quickly complies and, just like that, Gary and I are standing in the hall with DJ. He silently walks us out to the front of the facility and pushes open the heavy metal door. We emerge, squinting into the bright sunlight, and I realize that I have absolutely no idea where I am. The entire area is unfamiliar to me. Not a single landmark to orient myself, only open land for miles. It doesn't matter—Gary and I are walking away from this place, and a day ago I was not so certain that would happen. Looking at DJ, I can see tears welling in his eyes, and I feel his pain. So I ask him with my mind to be calm. I suggest that he go home, get some sleep, and I tell him when he wakes up he will be ready to cope with his new life.

DJ's face appears to relax a little and he mutters, "I am tired… so tired."

He is spacing out and staring at the ground. I shoot Gary a glance, and he looks as worried about DJ as I am. I am tempted to follow DJ back to our house to make certain he's OK but I know that would be a bad idea. I need to get as many miles between him and myself as I can.

I am thinking about getting away when DJ starts to dig around in his pocket and pulls out the keys to his Porsche. He hands them to me and says, "Take it—get out of here. Get as many miles as you can between you and me. Don't look back— you won't be missing anything."

Dropping the car keys into my hand, he wraps my fingers around them so I can't give them back. He stands there for a moment holding my hand in his and we both know this is goodbye. He then pulls out a wad of cash, a Platinum AmEx card with my name on it, and a phone—all with the intent of giving me what I need to escape. He has come prepared to help me whether I had pushed him or not. That gives me some faith in him.

I take one last look at DJs face searching for any sign of the man I had loved, but he is gone—destroyed. I can't put him back together either, all I can do is hold onto some good memories of who we had been. Then I say, "Thank you."

Gary and I climb into the silver Porsche, put the car in first gear and never looked back, as DJ has asked—except I do glance in the rearview mirror to see him standing motionless for a moment, then he turns and goes back inside the facility.

******

DJ has finally done his "one good thing." Getting Christa out of this place eased his conscience a bit, but now he is exhausted. He is coming off his short-lived high and he wants to get back home to his Whiskey and whatever. He doesn't know if he can call the house he shared with Christa a home anymore… There is nobody there to meet him. It is just a house, not a home.

DJ leans up against the wall of Christa's empty cell and thinks as he looks around, "What did I do? How could I have left her here?" He feels completely alone—everyone who had balanced his life is now gone in less than 24 hours. He pulls out his phone and calls Marshall Industries to have a car to pick him up. Then he waits because he knows it will be a while before it arrives.

An hour later…

A town car pulls up in front of the private prison, the driver opens the passenger side door, and DJ crawls in. He immediately rifles through the mini bar and downs, in rapid succession, as many little bottles of alcohol as he can lay his hands on. He needs to get drunk and quickly. DJ does not want to think about Christa or what a spineless jerk he'd been or anything at all. He digs around in his pockets but can't find another joint. He'll have to wait until he gets home to top off his high. He suddenly knows, though, that he can't go back to that house, so he says to the driver, "Take me to the Marshall jet, and phone ahead to let them know I will be flying to Connecticut." DJ wants to put some distance between himself and this day.

By the time he arrives in the driveway of the Marshall family home in Connecticut, he is suitably drunk and ready to collapse. Walking from the car to the house required assistance. Once he stepped inside the front door, grief floods over him—the undeniable truth that his father and brother are gone. He'd never hear them again. DJ's grief becomes overwhelming. He walks into the living room pulls out his stash of weed and looks around for more alcohol. As he lights a joint, tiredness sweeps over him with each inhalation of smoke. All he wants is to crawl into his comfortable bed—which he does—without even bothering to undress. Within moments, he is in a deep sleep, dead to the world. Peaceful—finally.

******

Kimball shows up at the Marshall's Connecticut house per protocol once he was informed that DJ was going there. Since the accident he'd only spoken to DJ once—to deliver the news about his father and brother. He had told DJ to stay put while he wrapped up details at the corporate headquarters. However, he hadn't heard from him in hours and now he is infuriated that DJ has not followed his orders. This makes his job much more difficult during a vulnerable time for the company.

Kimball had been given very specific instructions for what needed to happen in the event of the death of Damien Marshall,

Sr. or Henry Marshall, but he never has expected to have to handle both at the same time. It has taken quite a bit of doing, but finally Kimball feels assured the company is locked down—for the moment.

Now it is time to get DJ a new security detail. He goes from room to room on the lower floor of the mansion checking everything. He posts men outside because he knows DJ will be an instant target for kidnappers or militants once the word gets out that his family has died leaving DJ everything.

DJ is nowhere downstairs, and Kimball worries when he sees the remnants of a drug-filled evening still on the living room table. He strides upstairs and finds DJ passed out, fully clothed, in his own bed, so he leaves him undisturbed.

Kimball reviews the security footage to be certain the house is secure. DJ's vitals are online and in the footage; he sees him stumbling through the front door with the driver helping him. Obviously, he'd been somewhere, and Kimball will have to find the driver to find out where he had been. He sees DJ stumbling around the house, smoking a joint, pouring himself a drink, then another, then pick up the bottle and drink from it. He grabs the bottle, weaves up the staircase, and makes his way to his room.

He'd fallen asleep with a photo of Christa in his hand. The photo reminds Kimball that Christa is a loose end; her absence must be explained, and then she needs to be "taken care of." Christa goes on Kimball's mental "to do" list.

As he watches the video he thinks he has a big job ahead of him, getting DJ straight and ready for all the responsibility that is about to be thrust upon him—board meetings, money decisions, and, of course, the funerals of his father and his brother will be no small task. That's what Kimball is trained for—to clean up messes like this one.

******

Big G and Sparks reconvene at The Farm to go over what has happened at Marshall Headquarters. Everybody certainly is worse for wear after the events of the last several days. Things have spun out of control and a new plan needs to be worked on, now that Damien Marshall, Sr. is gone. Two significant unexpected deaths do not garner the type of attention they want to draw to OTP.

Big G paces the room followed by Gypsy. She keeps an eye on him as if he is one of the herd and must be kept in line. Pace, pace, turn—dog and man in unison. The Nomad and Sparks watch without speaking, they know G is formulating his next move. He always says he needs to "see the board."

"The game is always over with checkmate and that can only happen when the king is in checkmate. Technically, with the death of Damien Marshall, Sr., and Henry, we should have checkmate, but this is not conclusive. Everything has continued along undisrupted… the game is still in play. What am I missing?" He turns as he speaks and Gypsy matches his steps.

"The king is the key—the king is always the key. If he is not in checkmate, then all the forces continue to move to protect him." Suddenly G's entire face lights up, "I've got it! The king is just a different person—that's why the game is still on. It's DJ we need to capture, and we need to do it quickly. He is our key! He is the king now."

"I agree," says The Nomad. "DJ will inherit his father's empire and all the sins that go with it. It will swallow him up unless we can get to him first." Sparks and The Nomad immediately see the favorable long-term implications of a walk-in ISHI taking over DJ's body and they set out to make a new plan.

Sparks stops to raise a question, "What about Christa, how will she feel about this? After all she loves DJ."

The Nomad answers, "She did love him, but he betrayed her along with Henry. DJ is part of her past now. Trust me, she will agree to this plan."

Sparks feels an urgency now and starts to speak again, but The Nomad stops him saying, "Sparks, you don't have to say anything. I know what you want. You should hurry and pick him up. DJ has headed to Connecticut, and Kimball will be on his way there to put him on lockdown before the reading of the will."

"Then we have to try and get DJ out of there," says Sparks.

"He'll have a tracker implanted, so unless you can disable it Kimball will follow you."

"I've got that solved," says Sparks. "After Phoebe, I am all over that tracker business. They won't get me with that tech again."

"Well then, you better get moving." says The Nomad.

G and Sparks grab their team, head to the lab for their cloaking suits and stun guns, and drive to a private airstrip. They will need every advantage to pull of this mission.

******

I push the gas petal on DJ's Porsche, and I almost laugh from the giddiness of feeling free. The car takes off, carrying me away from that horrible place like a plush magic carpet. I need to be in control again, and the act of driving gives me a sense of freedom. Yet I am not completely in control of my destiny at the moment. Since I left the facility, the Council has been in my head directing me towards the central coast of California.

"Where are we going?" Gary asks.

"I'm not sure, but the Council wants me to head to a place in central California. They're guiding me."

Gary laughs and says, "Your own personal GPS system."

"I guess, but I don't get to pick the place."

"I still can't get used to the idea that you are traveling around with ten other people in your head."

"Twelve, if you want to be exact, and they aren't there all the time."

"Well, thank goodness for that! I would expect there are times you don't want a crowd watching what you are doing. Or maybe you are the type that likes an audience," Gary teases and we both laugh. Gary goes on, "You are lucky I trust what you've told me because if I was anybody but my fabulously understanding self, I would say you are schizophrenic."

"I know, and right now I'm glad you're with me and safe."

"Yeah, well…" Gary looks out the car window to watch the landscape flash by and doesn't finish his thought.

We fall into silence as we watch the highway edge us closer to our freedom with every mile that passes under the car. After awhile, Gary starts to rub the leather seat and says, "Well, I'll give you this… when you make a jail break you do it with style!"

"I know… Right? Don't forget I still have that platinum card burning a hole in my pocket. I think we should make a little shopping side trip." We both crack up at the idea, and I say, "Find us some good traveling music—it's been a while since I've heard any music, and I really miss it."

I'd caught sight of my appearance when I first looked in the car's rearview mirror and I don't recognize myself. My brown skin is pale and ashy from weeks with no sunlight. My hair—well my hair is an undesirable knotted mess verging on dreadlocks. I've always wanted to cut it all off but never had the guts, now is probably the perfect moment and the only option. I've become a little thin and I still wear my nondescript prison outfit; my own clothes were completely destroyed. Before I show up anywhere, I will need some serious TLC.

Gary starts to fiddle with the radio and soon he has an old blues station playing BB King's "The Thrill is Gone." Something about the plaintive guitar riffs fit the moment perfectly, and we relax into the drive. Because we don't know what to expect once we arrive wherever it is the Council is guiding us to, it's good to just let the music take over the moment.

******

The black sedan winds it's way through the tony neighborhood of the very rich. Only the car's headlights, on low, are barley visible. Big G and Sparks lead a crew into the pitch-black night of the winter landscape around DJ's Connecticut house.

As they approach a stone wall with an immense iron gate blocking a long private driveway, they turn off the headlights and pull to the shoulder of the road. Only two lamps, on the sides of the iron gate, provide any light. However, in the quiet of the countryside, there is a subtle, barely-there humm—the sound of electricity powering the motion sensors of the security system. If they trip one, the floodlights will immediately illuminate the area. Sparks, two men, and Big G emerge into the dimly-lit scene. G is rolling a chess piece, the black queen, between his thumb and forefinger while he sizes up the area. After a moment, he looks back and tosses the chess piece into the car and shuts the door.

Each of them is wearing Sparks' new suit made from Graphene, a special conductive carbon-based material. He has "painted" it onto reflective nano-sized scales, which cover the suit, hood and gloves. They tap a wristband and suddenly all of them are white from head to toe, allowing them to blend into the snowy landscape. Night vision goggles have been embedded into their hoods and obscure their faces but give them total mobility in the darkness.

They approach the iron gate undetected and scale it, quickly dropping to the other side. The motion lights go off for a moment. The security guard on the other end notices, and he studies the scene for intruders but attributes it to a rabbit or some other creature triggering the system. Because of the cloaking suits, he never notices Sparks, Big 'G,' or their team, huddled in the snow beside the gate.

Once the guard turns off the floodlights, the group starts off, at a low-to-the-ground trot, towards DJ's house. Sticking to the shadows so the cameras will not spot them, their footprints are camouflaged by the darkness. They are silent with each other, all communication is with hand signals, and head nods. Arriving at the house, the team fans out to all four sides, and each person stops in front of a door or window.

Sparks attaches a small metal box with some electrode discs on the frame of a window. A computer screen comes alive, and a rapid scrolling of code is evident. The screen flickers and displays the entire security setup for the house along with the bypass codes. Sparks starts tapping and swiping the screen, and within seconds, he has hacked the system and disabled the alarm and motion detectors. He's left the cameras on, so the guards are unaware that anything is wrong.

Sparks raises his fist and does a five-fingered countdown. On one, each person enters a door or window. Once inside, all of them tap a strap on their wrists, and their white suits turn to a reflective gray material that mirrors whatever they are standing next to and effectively makes them invisible on the security cameras. Sparks brought the computer box into the house and is using it to scan for heat signatures to locate the guards and DJ. They wait as the guards make their rounds of that wing and then move quietly up the stairs to the northwest corner of the building and to DJ's bedroom.

******

DJ sleeps undisturbed, still fully clothed, in his opulent six-hundred-thread-count Egyptian cotton sheets and silk comforter. He's dreaming of rocking gently in a little sailboat on a lovely Tahitian sea. The mood of his dream starts to shift and the rocking becomes more violent, as if a storm is stirring up the waves. Somewhere in his dreaming mind, he realizes that he is no longer dreaming—the shaking is real. He wakes with a start and wants to sit bolt upright, but someone has a hand over his mouth and is forcing his head down on the pillow. He tries to focus on his attackers, but his eyes are blurry and he can't make them out—only the outlines of their bodies. Everything else is gray. He can see there are four people, but that is all. He wants to scream, but even if they did uncover his mouth, he is certain no sound will come out.

They pull him from bed and Sparks scans his body for the tracker. Once he finds it, he attaches an electrode to the spot on DJ's skin where the tracker is embedded. He begins to download the tracker's code and within seconds has cloned it. He then creates an identical tracking signal and shuttles the signal from the security office computer to the new tracker. He puts all the information on DJ on a digital loop, causing it to appear as if DJ is still asleep in his own bed. One of the men inflates a life size mannequin, and they place it in the bed with the new tracker attached to it.

Big G throws a lightweight cloaking blanket over DJ, and they spirit him out of the building the same way they came in.

Once outside, all four of them touch their wrists again, and their suits, as well as the blanket covering DJ, become white once more. Walking confidently through the snow, they know the guard watching the monitor will never see a thing.

They hope that DJ's abduction won't be noticed until the following day, if they are lucky. By then he will be back in California.

******

Computer screens filled with scenes of mobs of people and protest marches from all across the globe illuminate the dark room. People are shown flowing into the streets in Madrid, London, Paris, Dublin, New York, Berlin, Istanbul, Athens, and other cities. A dark figure seated at one monitor focuses on several different street scenes with pay phones that have blue cords on the handsets. A faceless "suit" stands up in the dark room and reaches to tap on one of the computer screens. The sound goes on in the room, and the street noise becomes audible in real time. In all of the scenes, the pay phones are ringing. Different people answer them, and the pictures start to multiply onto a much larger screen until there are thousands of images all portraying the same thing—an unseen analog network of pay phones being answered by thousands of different people. The same "suit" taps the screen again, and the room is silent. Faceless people watch as world events unfold from what appears to be a control room. One says, "It is much, much bigger than we had any idea and this is just a small sampling of what we found." The other man nods in agreement. They continue to tap and swipe the screens searching for clues about the OTP movement.

******

Phoebe walks onto the concert grounds with the other members of her new OTP unit. They have arrived in a large open field, surrounded by rolling hills and oak trees, in the middle of nowhere. She observes people streaming in and thinks, "I had no idea the movement was this widespread. I'm sure Mr. Marshall will want to know about this." She can't contact anyone, though, because all Wi-Fi devices have been banned. She can't even take a photo. The entire event is "underground" and by the time the word gets out that the OTP had a major meeting they will be long gone. Phoebe does think this is a highly unusual gathering. From her experience, OTP members never reveal themselves in large numbers, precisely so the opposition can't get an eye on how big an army they really have. She wonders what has prompted this event?

Phoebe and her crew make their way through the crowd until they are under the stage that has been set up in the middle of the field. Some protest musicians are playing, filling the air with their words about seeking justice through revolution.

"This is so boring," thinks Phoebe. "How long do I have to suffer through this whining and moaning event? I really thought something important was going to happen. God! Shoot me now!" She rolls her eyes in boredom while the crowd chants and claps along like a herd of sheep. "Mindless followers," Phoebe thinks to herself, "Not a single one of you would truly be missed if I were to blow up the whole thing." The thought of a drone strike making a direct hit to the center of this crowd of loyal OTP followers, while they sing peaceful protests songs, actually makes her smile.

She looks around trying to figure out how to entertain herself for the next several hours. Finally, she has had enough and thinks, "Maybe I can trek down to the highway and hitch my way back to town. At least from there I could get the word out about what is happening here, not that they would find it all that interesting."

Just as Phoebe turns to begin working her way out of the crowd, the music stops and everybody becomes quiet. She looks toward the stage to see what is happening.

Twelve people walk on stage and Phoebe starts to get very excited, "Now, this just got interesting," she thinks to herself. She suspects that the 12 are the OTP Council that lead all the groups from around the country, but she can't be certain until she sees him, yes—The Nomad—there he is! This is the Council! This is big. They have never appeared together in one place. She asks herself, "Why now?"

The Nomad steps forward to greet the crowd, "Welcome."

The crowd is so quiet, the only sound you hear is that of birds chirping as they fly overhead. The Nomad's voice resonates across the field, "While we wait for the arrival of our main speaker, enjoy the music and the message. We are here to spread Peace and Justice by any means possible."

He turns and joins the line of the other 11 members of the Council and they walk off stage, while a band from Nashville sets up to play.

Phoebe feels a rising sense of urgency to get a message to someone at the Carlyle group. They need to know what is going on here! This is an opportunity to disrupt the militia's core leadership. The entire Council is present and by tonight every group might have representatives here. How can she get a message out now knowing tomorrow will be too late?

As Phoebe examines the area, she realizes the organizers have been very smart about the location. She has absolutely no way to get in contact with her people. Satellite communication is the only possibility out here because there are no cell phone towers for miles and miles. "Good luck finding a Sat phone among these clowns," she thinks.

She has been so deeply pondering her dilemma that it takes a moment for her to finally notice a sound she's been trying to ignore, a car driving into the middle of the field. The crunch of the tires on the dirt road makes a distinctive gritty sound, which pulls her attention towards its approach. She wonders who has enough clout to be allowed to drive in because everybody else has had to hike in. The car, a silver Porsche, comes to a stop at the side of the stage. The door opens and Christa McCaffrey emerges, along with Gary. "Oh, this day just keeps getting better and better!" thinks Phoebe.

She almost doesn't recognize Christa from her last visit to the prison. Gone is the matted hair and prison clothes, and, instead, Christa emerges from the Porsche with a radically shaved head, new clothes and makeup. "She cleans up well," thinks Phoebe. She wonders how Christa has escaped because she assumes Henry would have killed her by now. "Henry is such a pussy," she thinks, "of course he didn't kill her. He probably wanted to hold onto her as a personal sex toy." But the big question is not why she escaped but why she is here.

Phoebe slowly starts to maneuver toward the side of the stage but keeps undercover by merging with different groups within the crowd. "Too many people, too public," she thinks. "Unless I want this to be a suicide mission, I need a plan." Looking at the silver Porsche she suddenly gets an inspired idea. She creeps over to the car.

The band has begun to play, and the music has everybody's attention focused on the stage. The sun is dropping behind the hills, and twilight has dimmed the scene considerably. The OTP members begin to sing along with the band, it is like a tribal war dance with the music bringing the crowd to a higher level emotionally. They are getting ready for the "reclamation," something she's heard discussed many times at OTP meetings.

> *"Raise your voice, express your dismay*
> *Don't be a slave so the rich can play.*
> *United we'll rise, divided we'll fall*
> *Take back our country for one and all.*
> *This nouveau aristocracy knows who we are*
> *An independent nation not slaves for a war.*
> *Of the People, By the People, For the People.*
> *Of the People, By the People, For the People.*
> *OF THE THE PEOPLE, BY THE PEOPLE,*
> *FOR THE PEOPLE."*

This is not some friendly hippie love-in of the past. It could easily be mistaken for an artsy desert gathering masquerading as a spiritual music festival, but instead, it is a call to arms for OTP. Word has gone out over Sparks' pay phone system for weeks, culminating with this gathering. Because there has been no internet chatter, no Wi-Fi interceptions, the movement cannot easily be followed by outsiders and hasn't been picked up by the opposition, the NSA, the FBI or CIA, or even local law enforcement—nobody knows about this gathering.

Nobody, with the exception of Phoebe. Sure, there have been other embedded operatives, and they had all been discovered and taken care of. Only Phoebe remains. Now she really feels and urgency to get this information in the right hands as soon as she can. She has positioned herself by the driver side door of the Porsche, and tries gently flipping the handle—hoping and praying the car has been left unlocked and the alarm has not been engaged. She is in luck—the door is opening!

She glances toward the stage and can see Christa, Gary, and The Nomad standing to the side listening to the music. The 11 other Council members stand with them too. Convinced that everyone is distracted by the music on stage, she drops down to her knees below the sight line of the crowd and carefully pulls the car door open with a quick movement, trying not to attract any attention. The interior light flashes on so Phoebe has to act fast, she quickly rolls into the car, pulling the door shut, and the interior goes dark again.

She sits motionless inside the dark car with her head pressed to the leather seat. She waits until she feels it will be safe to look up. Raising her head slightly, she peeks out the front window of the car. The Nomad is looking directly at the car! Phoebe freezes. "Did he see me?" Her mind races to various escape scenarios and none of them rule out killing to get out of there. Especially The Nomad, "I wouldn't mind putting a bullet in that pompous ass," thinks Phoebe. After a few seconds, he turns his gaze away from the car, and she can breathe easily again.

Phoebe lets a few more minutes pass and begins to execute her plan. She rifles around the car for the ignition wires jimmies them together to turn on the battery. The car is equipped with a satellite-tracking and communication access system in case the driver has an emergency in a remote area. Lucky her! "GPS system access." Phoebe says into the car's speaker while adjusting the volume to its lowest setting.

"How may I assist you Mr. Marshall?"

"Mr. Marshall," Phoebe thinks, "I wonder which Mr. Marshall this car belonged to?"

"Mr. Marshall is unable to speak. Can you patch me through to a number?" Phoebe knows the GPS emergency operators have high level tracking access to assist local police and the FBI.

"Certainly, is this a law enforcement issue?" asks the GPS voice.

Phoebe is about to answer when she glances out the front window and sees The Nomad and what looks like militia security walking towards the car. She isn't sure if he can see her but she must act—she can't risk being discovered.

"Hello? What agency…" the operator's voice disappears behind Phoebe as she slips from the car and into the crowd.

"Damn," she thinks. She had been so close to getting a message out. She moves very quickly deep into the crowd to hide from The Nomad who is now scanning the scene for whomever had been inside the car. Meanwhile one of his security people drives the car away, and she presumes The Nomad has figured out the risk of leaving it parked in the field. There goes her chance for anyone to find this gathering in time. She slips further and further into the crowd until she can run away into the nighttime landscape.

Now that it is dark, she has to carefully pick her way across the open field; she is using the sky to navigate towards the highway. Eventually, she makes it to the pavement and begins to walk along the shoulder of the road until a large freight truck stops and gives her a ride. Phoebe thinks about going back to The Farm, but decides it is too dangerous and she heads to her motel room instead.

By the time she throws the door to her room open, she is covered in desert dust, exhausted, and all she can do is collapse on the bed. Phoebe is furious at herself that she has to let this opportunity pass, but she finds her cell phone and calls DC, even though many hours have passed and she is sure the OTP groups have moved on by now.

******

Sparks drives the black SUV like a bat out of hell. Tearing down the highway toward the turnoff to The Farm. Big G says,

"Slow down dude, the last thing we need is to get pulled over for speeding!"

Sparks lightens his foot on the gas pedal to make sure he is driving the speed limit. He keeps checking the rear view mirror to see if they are beng followed. "Is he alive?" he asks about DJ.

"Yeah, I think so," answers Big G. "Barely. I don't know what this guy took, but he is pretty fucked up."

By the time they land in California, DJ has is showing signs of slipping into a coma. Big G had administered Epinephrine, which revived him for part of the trip, but now they are losing him again.

"Just don't let him die on us... at least not yet," Sparks says.

Finally, the turnoff for the dirt road to The Farm appears and Sparks feels a huge weight lift as they turn off the highway. Leaving a cloud of dust in their wake, he punches the accelerator and tears down the road to safety. He parks in front of the medical facility, and they carry DJ in, laying him on one of the examining tables. DJ isn't moving. Sparks checks for a pulse while Big G prepares another syringe of Epinephrine in an effort to prevent him from going comatose, but the shot only makes him conscious briefly. They continue to work on DJ, hooking up an IV to keep him hydrated while they try to figure out just how serious his condition is. His eyes are barely responsive. They determine they need to watch him and wait to see if he pulls out of it. At least he is still alive.

Suddenly DJ starts to code and immediately Big G rushes to his side with the paddles to start his heart again. G knows what he is doing after his time with the gangs. He's patched many a member up so they wouldn't have to go the local hospital. He is a "medical hobbyist" as he likes to put it.

He yells, "Clear," and Sparks steps away from DJ while Big G pumps him full of electricity—nothing. "Clear," G yells again and puts the paddles to DJ a second time.

There is a sound from the heart monitor and G says, "Thready, but he's still with us. Look, we need The Nomad to know what's going on here, and we need a real doctor. I can stay with him while you do that. I think I can keep him alive long enough for you to make a couple calls."

Sparks nods, looks at DJ, and says sternly, "After all we went through to get you, you better not die on us!" With that, he leaves to call The Nomad and find a doctor.

G settles into a chair next to the examination table. He knows it is going to be a long night of playing medical watchdog. Gypsy trots in and settles by his side to keep him company.

******

Kimball turns into the driveway of DJ's Connecticut home and goes straight to the guard's office to review the security video for the night. He taps his fingers on his cell phone as he waits for the guard to pull the feed up on the monitor. As he watches multiple cameras looking for anything out of the ordinary, he notices one scene with a black car, which is barely visible, parked in the distance on the road. It strikes him as odd. Since all the estates in the area have plenty of private parking there is no need for a car to park on the street.

"Can you zoom in on that one there?" Kimball says, pointing at one of the screens.

The guard enlarges the picture for Kimball. Suddenly there is some movement of the bushes by the side of the road, but nobody is around the car. Then the car doors pop open and the interior lights go on, but still no people are visible. A moment later, as if by magic, the car is full of men and driving off! As the car passes their security cameras Kimball can just make out a face in the back seat.

"There! Freeze that!" He yells at the guard, "Was that DJ?" The guard stares at Kimball, fearing his wrath because he doesn't have an answer.

"Pull up Mr. Marshall's status—I want to see his location." The screen moves into several graphs and GPS coordinates tied to DJ's internal tracking device. They all indicate he is sleeping peacefully upstairs in the house.

"How the hell?" Kimball storms out of the security office and tears upstairs to DJ's bedroom. Without bothering to knock, because he suspects what he will find, he barges into the room and throws back the bedcovers to reveal a mannequin sleeping in DJ's bed. Lifting the doll from the bed, he examines it closely until he finds what he is looking for—a cloned tracker taped to the thigh of the doll. Kimball rips it off and smashes it with the heel of his boot.

Calling the security office he says, "I want you to shut down DJ's tracker for two minutes, then reboot it and do a new signal search. Let me know when it's back online."

Kimball makes a second call, "I want a ten-man team fully armed and ready to go immediately."

Kimball stands staring at the doll, and the crushed tracker, and he thinks to himself, "You think you know who you are messing with but you have no idea." He walks out of the room to meet his soldiers—and get DJ back at any cost.

******

The cool air hits my newly-shaved head and I am reminded that I no longer have my mass of curls. It was a strange moment when I sat in the barber's chair and told that little old man to

shave my head. When the hair dropped to the floor, I felt an unseen weight drop from my body. It was symbolic of my new freedom—my image is reinvented, and I face a new life as I walk toward the stage. Looking at the huge crowd of OTP members that have gathered in this field, I feel their energy rolling towards me like waves on a beach. Gary instinctively grabs my arm to steady me. "So many people," I think. It is sensory overload after weeks of solitary confinement. Fallingtree leaves the stage and heads straight towards me. I've never met her in person, but she is unmistakable with her long flowing black hair. She isn't wearing the Native American clothes that I usually visualize her in, just a plain leather jacket, t-shirt, and jeans. Still, I know it is her.

"Christa, finally." Fallingtree smiles and gives me a warm embrace while saying, "The moment has come. This is the unification." She turns and points to the crowd, and off in the distance still more people are emerging from the dirt road that leads to the field. "All of these people are here through the efforts of many OTP groups. Fifty years of planning, training and placing operatives within the government and business have come to this moment—the unification. We are ready. All we need is you. You can send a clear message—one that everyone sees the same way. The visual you plant will keep the message from being doubted or diluted. That is the value of your time in confinement—you were able to hone this skill for exactly this moment."

I should be overwhelmed by the position Fallingtree and the Council are thrusting upon me but I'm not. I have a memory of my moment of "walking into" my six-year-old self and another memory of who I was in my previous life. In that life, I stood before people to guide them away from dark forces and was a leader of integrity and courage. In that life I'd been cut down too soon—before I could accomplish the change I wanted to see happen. What I remember now is my purpose. I know who I am—I am ISHI.

I say, "I'm ready."

Fallingtree nods and takes her place on stage. I stand on the side, gathering the will to walk out in front of an audience—after weeks of only speaking to people in my head. I have cleaned myself up and feel I look rather striking with my shaved head, but I am somewhat self-conscious that I don't look like myself. However, none of them know this. The lights are blazing on stage, and I study the crowd, looking at individual faces. I feel an enormous responsibility to use my power with humility and awareness. I glance at the Council, seated at the back of the stage and waiting for my entrance. Although we have never met until now, they are friendly and familiar faces because they were my protectors and guides while I was incarcerated. I can see Gary, giving me the thumbs up and making me smile as I turn to face the crowd again. Fallingtree hands me the microphone, and as I take it, I run my hand over my shorn head one last time just to remind myself that I am a new person tonight. There is still some chatting and buzzing conversation, but as soon as I say, "Hello" the crowd quiets down.

They have no idea who I am, but they feel the emotion I am transmitting as I "live stream" my sense of peace into each of their minds.

"My name is Christa McCaffrey. Like all of you, I have traveled many roads to arrive here tonight." The crowd remains quiet as I continue, "We have all come because we are committed to seeing the human race and all living things not only survive but thrive. There is an army of higher consciousness and they are fighting a good war. That army is you! You have raised your conscious vibration to a level that is in tune with nature, peace, and love. You have experienced the sense of balance when you are no longer striving or thinking with your survival or greed-based mind."

I look out at the sea of faces looking back at me and every one of them has a peaceful expression. As I speak, I give them images of a new world. A world where we care for each other, live cooperatively, and decisions are made for the greater good. I show them how we can head back into our communities and stop consuming and valuing money above all else. How we can make better use of the land and be more responsible with our impact on nature. The vision I project of The Farm as a model community floats into the crowd. Another vision of the Council governing with true democratic representation of the people fills their minds. A mental switch flips on, and I can hear the collective hum of every mind unified to make decisions for the good of the world. There is no difference between the energies of these minds, no race, no rich or poor, no smart or stupid, no male or female. It is exhilarating to feel their collective unified power! Then The Nomad taps me lightly on the shoulder and the spell is broken.

He whispers in my ear, "You must ask them all to leave immediately. Our security has been breached, and they are in danger. Encourage them to leave quietly and peacefully. We don't want anybody hurt."

I turn to the crowd and say, "Goodbye, I wish all of you every success in your part creating a new society." I push an image of an orderly exit into their minds and they quietly get up and start filing out—no pushing, shoving, or rushing.

The Nomad guides me off the stage, and I ask once nobody could overhear us, "What do you mean we have been breached?"

"Somebody turned on the GPS tracking system in your car. We don't know how far they got, but we can't risk the safety of all these people. Still it bothers me that we have someone in one of the groups who is a spy and witnessed some, if not all, of this entire event. Your secret may have been revealed."

The Council gathers around to say hello in person, and Gary comes up with a serious look of awe on his face. I look at him and say, "Gar, it's still little ol' me."

"I'm not so sure about that. Seriously, where is my girl Christa? The one who hates crowds and loud music?" We laugh but it is short-lived because Fallingtree wants a moment to talk to me.

"Christa, you have just witnessed firsthand how powerful your, for lack of a better name, two-way telepathy is. None of us can do what you can do. We can only speak with other telepaths, but you can "send and receive" with anyone.

"Not anyone," I add remembering Henry. "Some energy is too dark."

"I understand, but because of this, we need to protect you and judiciously use your ability. If the opposition truly knew what you are capable of, they would do everything in their power to use you for their own gain or failing that— eliminate you."

Both of us are quiet as we take in the gravity of what Fallingtree has just said. It is obvious I will never live a normal life again and I will forever be on the alert for people who want to use me, or eliminate me.

The Nomad breaks in, "It's time to get Christa to The Farm where we can protect her."

******

Kimball and his group of soldiers arrive at the outskirts of The Farm in record time. Just as he had anticipated, once DJ's tracker rebooted, the signal reverted to DJ's real location and gave them coordinates for a rural area in California.

Kimball knows his group of elite soldiers, all ex-military, can easily take this compound. What they really need to do is rescue DJ. He instructs them to spread out and enter the compound from multiple points. They advance across the barren dark landscape to insure their approach will go unnoticed.

The tracker, which Kimball carries, blinks silently showing the location of DJ within the compound. He instructs the men to converge on the center of The Farm. He hears some soft PFFFT, PFFFT of the silencers on his men's guns as they pick off The Farm's security forces. Kimball approaches the building in which DJ is being held; four men come running out of the door. Kimball and one of his men duck behind a tractor as the men run past. Kimball points at the building in front of them saying, "DJ should be in there." They make their way to the entrance, but just as they are going to enter Big G fills the doorway, coming face-to-face with the Marshall Industries' Security Director.

Kimball can see DJ lying on the table inside the room, and he is determined to force his way in there. He already has his gun pointed at G when the rest of the events seem to unfold in slow motion, like action scenes in a Kung Fu fight movie.

Out of nowhere, Gypsy came flying through the air, teeth bared, and lunges straight for Kimball's shooting arm.

Big G yells, "Nooooo!!!"

It is too late; she has already grabbed a hold of Kimball's arm and is ripping at his jacket sleeve. She pulls him off balance with all her force, but Kimball shakes his arm furiously, simultaneously firing the gun and flinging Gypsy against a wall, knocking her unconscious. The little dog falls into a crumpled heap on the floor; a giant gash opens up on her head and blood streams down her face.

In the background, there is a loud clanging sound and then a thud, and Kimball turns to see G fall backwards into some folding metal chairs and crash to the ground.

"Well," he says callously, "it seems my bullet found its mark anyway."

Blood streams out across the white tile floor as G lies there dying. Kimball decides not to waste another bullet on him since he can tell he will be dead in a few minutes anyway.

Kimball rushes to DJ to pull him off the table but finds he isn't responding at all. He tries to revive him, but it seems he is in a coma. DJ is dead weight, so Kimball has to hoist him up and carry him out. As soon as he moves towards the door, Sparks appears.

Sparks sees Big G on the floor with rivers of blood streaming around him, and the rage that sweeps over him is uncontrollable. He sees Kimble with DJ in his arms and rushes at him with the intent to kill. One of Kimball's men appears from behind and fires at Sparks but misses. Sparks whirls around and fires his stun gun freezing the man before he can get off another shot.

Kimball freezes too, but out of shock. He has had first-hand experience with that weapon and he still wants to get his hands on one. Sparks spins back to face Kimball and is ready to stun him too when Kimball throws DJ at Sparks with all his force. Sparks goes down like a bowling pin, hitting his head on the floor, he is knocked out cold. Off in the distance, Kimball can hear voices shouting and he runs for the door but as he passes Sparks, he kicks him hard in the head for good measure. He looks over at his security soldier, still frozen from the hit from Sparks' gun, and knows he can't risk the OTP will catch him and interrogate him. He can't move him, so he does the only thing he can do—he puts a bullet between his eyes, which solves the problem and Kimball starts to run for the door again. But he stops and turns to look at Sparks body on the floor and see if he can spot the stun gun. It's there—still in his hand! He starts back into the room but there is no more time, the voices are almost at the building. Kimball disappears into the night leaving DJ and the stun gun behind.

When Sparks regains consciousness, he is filled with rage and adrenaline. He throws DJ's body off him and gets up to chase Kimball, but he stops short, horrified by the sight of G's body in front of the doorway. He stands there for a minute processing the loss of his friend and then collapses on top of G's lifeless body. He isn't crying—he can't—he just says goodbye and tries to hold onto his friend a little longer.

Several OTP soldiers rush into the room, but they stop abruptly and stand in silence when they see the grim scene. Then it starts... a sound that could cut through your heart and all the way to your soul.

"Howlllllll, Howlllll..." Gypsy has regained consciousness and she knows immediately that the man who once saved her life is gone. She whimpers and limps over to G's body and snuggles up close to him, putting her blood-soaked head on his quiet chest. Nobody tries to move her.

******

The medical building has a large crowd around the door, so I know something is wrong. I want to push my way to the door, but I can't see past The Nomad who is blocking my view. Finally he steps aside and I can see the horrible scene inside. Big G is dead on the floor, blood everywhere. Sparks looks shell-shocked and is trying to tell The Nomad what happened. Another body is lying on the floor but no blood around it. I look more closely and realize it's DJ! How did he get here?

I rush to DJ to see if he is still alive. Kneeling beside him, I pick up his wrist to take his pulse, and I find that not only is he alive but his spirit immediately reaches out to me.

"DJ, you're alive."

"Yes, but I don't want to be."

"You can fight. You don't have to die."

"I need to leave—really I do. I screwed it all up."

The heaviness of his spirit is very apparent to me. The whole conversation takes only a few seconds, and then I turn to two militia guards and ask them to put DJ back on the table where I cover him with a blanket to keep him warm.

Surveying this scene of devastation, I steel myself because the shock of the moment hasn't really sunk in yet. G's dog starts to howl, and we all feel her grief and pain. With that, hot tears fill my eyes. I work my way outside so I can be alone, but Sparks follows me, and I don't mind.

We stand there in silence, what can we possibly say right now? We have not seen each other in weeks, and then I come back to find him leaning over the dead body of his closest friend. I do the only thing I can do—I reach out, draw him close, wrap my arms around him, and hold him as tightly as I can. Then I release him and with my eyes say, "I am here for you."

He speaks very softly. "This is my fault."

"How could this be your fault?" I ask gently, wondering where this is coming from.

"I thought I had disabled the tracker, I was overly confident about my skills and it got G killed."

"You don't know that for certain."

Sparks just stares at me with disbelief in his eyes. He doesn't cry and I don't expect him too. He will do that in private but right now, we are at war and he seeks retribution.

The Nomad walks up and motions me to walk with him. I reached out to Sparks one last time, and give his hand a squeeze, while wishing I could erase the pain I see in his face. Then I walk away.

"DJ is unresponsive," says The Nomad.

"Why? How did that happen?"

"We found him like that. We think he overdosed, but now he won't wake-up."

"His spirit spoke to me when I went to take his pulse. He doesn't want to live. I think he is not waking up because he's given up."

"Hmmm," says The Nomad, "Christa, I am about to suggest something that may be hard for you to hear, but we must consider it because—as Big G would have said, DJ is the white king now."

CHAPTER TWELVE

THE ENDGAME

Ileave the devastation behind me and walk towards the open space of The Farm. The Nomad has proposed they make DJ a walk-in, an ISHI. Despite the fact that he'd abandoned me to be tortured by his brother—I still didn't know if I can condone his death. Night has taken over the sky, and the stars shine with their ancient light. I sit down on the ground and focus on nothing, trying to make sense of everything. It is a movie reel in my head, playing out picture-by-picture all the events that have led me to this moment: running away from home as a little girl, college, meeting Gary and eventually DJ, falling in love with DJ, meeting The Nomad, reconnecting with Sparks, being taken by Henry, my release, and here I am. So much has changed in such a short period.

In the midst of it all, I've found my place and remembered why I walked into this body so long ago. I know what I need to do and I can't stop myself even if I wanted to. The Council is strangely quiet except for Fallingtree. I feel comforted by her presence because we have already been through so much together.

"Christa, you did a great thing today. You showed people a different picture of their future. You pulled them together, and they are returning to their communities to spread the word. I know all of this has come at a great personal cost to you."

I can't hold back anymore, I have too much grief after seeing Big G's lifeless body on the ground and then a comatose DJ whom I still care about, even though I know that relationship will never be again. The tears freely roll down my face. It is the right time to mourn these losses.

"If we don't honor the part they play in our lives we are doing ourselves and them a disservice," says Fallingtree. In the ensuing silence, I can still feel her, but she is giving me some space. The cool night air calms my tears and fills my lungs. Eventually I come back to center and focus on the present moment.

Fallingtree speaks, "You know what needs to be done. DJ has destroyed himself, and although he runs the Marshall empire now, he isn't ready and probably never will be. His soul wants to move on. He does not want this life anymore. Christa, do you remember what it was like to need so urgently to come into a body to do the work you needed to do? Well DJ feels that same urgency to leave his body. You know you need to guide him and help him transition."

I hang my head and look at the dark ground. Of course, she is right. I'd felt it earlier when I touched DJ. What Fallingtree doesn't want is DJ's soul to leave his body and to lose the opportunity for an ISHI to enter and make better use of the life he is leaving behind. It is not a time to be emotional or equivocal. I need to make a hard decision now.

With that, I say a silent "thank you" to Fallingtree, take one last look at the stars, and allow their ancient light to flood my mind. Then I walk back to the medical building determined to guide DJ's soul to a better place.

******

Sparks enters the room and notices that G's body has been moved to a table and covered with a sheet. The blood has been cleaned up and the scene made a bit more tolerable. He looks over by the wall and sees Gypsy shaking and injured, so he scoops the dog up in his arms and says, "I know girl, I know how you feel. Let's take care of that wound."

Sparks feels a need to stay busy otherwise he doesn't know what he might do. He wants to kill someone—especially Kimball. While Sparks works on Gypsy's head wound, he looks over at DJ's comatose body and wonders how he is going to be of any use to them like that. He knows the plan is to force DJ's soul to want to leave his body, but how can they be sure his hasn't left already?

The alarms suddenly go off on DJ's medical monitors, and the room is filled with a cacophony of beeps and buzzes. He is coding. Sparks would prefer to see him die and leave this earth forever, but instead he jumps up and starts to work on DJ's heart to get it beating again. Even The Nomad has made it clear that it is imperative they keep DJ alive. Once Sparks is certain DJ is stable, he sinks down into the nearest chair. He knows he is in for a long night, and although he feels drained, he digs down deep and finds a second wind.

The door to the medical facility swings open, and Christa walks in followed by a blast of cool, clean night air that clears the staleness and memories of the night out of the room.

*****

As soon as I see Sparks slumped in the chair next to DJ's body, I am connected to his mind and can hear what he is thinking and feeling, but I shut it down immediately. It feels criminal to experience his deepest grief without his permission.

He stands up as I walk in, but I know I don't have time to talk. I need to get to DJ and reach out to his spirit before he leaves his body forever.

As I walk past Sparks, I give him a look that I know how he feels, but then I move to touch DJ's shoulder—I am immediately inside his body—I feel his life current but it is weak.

"DJ?" I ask with my mind.

"I'm here."

The energy is growing very dark around him. Something is happening... but what? This is new to me.

"DJ, do you really want to move on?"

Yes, I really do. I'm so tired. I can't do this."

"DJ, you can leave, but would you be willing to let another come in your place and use this body? Another soul that is strong and wants life so it can complete important work on the human plane?"

DJ doesn't answer, and I worry that maybe he's left already. Then I can see him walking towards me—smiling and shining. He is reaching out with both hands. I can feel a soul energy behind me ready to come in when DJ passes through. Out of nowhere, a dark curtain drops between us.

I can't see through it, and I can't get to DJ's soul. The room is filled with the sound of the alarm from the heart monitor. DJ is coding again, and I am pulled abruptly out of his mind and back into the medical facility. Sparks is up and applying the paddles. DJ's body jumps with each electric shock, then he takes a breath, and he is back. Barely, but he is still with us.

I need a moment. This is too much. I walk outside again, closing my eyes to compose myself when I hear a voice say, "Oh honey, you look like crap! Not that I can blame you."

I open my eyes, and Gary is standing over me. I grab a hold of him as if he is a life raft on the ocean. "Where were you?"

"You left the concert so quickly, and I had to wait to ride down with someone else... a nice someone else." Gary smiles. "I heard about Big G on my way in. Christa, I am so sorry. Really, he was a brilliant guy... what a loss. How is Sparks taking it? I know they were very close."

"It hit him hard, of course. He's trying to do his job. What you don't know is DJ is in there in a coma," I say pointing to the medical building.

"What? How did he... forget it... I don't even want to know. I can't keep up with events anymore." Gary looks at my face and assesses me again, " I know I said you looked like crap when I walked up, and I wish I were lying, but you do look stressed. What else is going on here?"

"Gary... DJ doesn't want to go on living, and I need to open the way for his soul to make a deal with a walk-in soul. I just tried, and it's not that easy. There is a darkness there trying to block his soul from leaving. It made me panic, not for myself, but for DJ. What if that dark energy traps him in his comatose body? Or worse, what if that dark energy takes over his body? We have no idea what that means, and I don't understand how this is happening. I didn't expect resistance from anyone except DJ, but he is ready to move on."

"Christa, you can't stop trying. You have to help DJ's spirit out of there. You can't leave him a living corpse the rest of his life.

Nobody, not even DJ, deserves that." Gary watches my face as I gather my determination, and finally I feel it, nod affirmatively, and walk back in to try again. On my way, I stop and hold out my hand to Gary saying, "Come with me. Just stand out of the way. Knowing that you are there will give me strength."

"You got it," says Gary and he forcefully grips my hand as we walk back.

******

I do feel stronger this time with both Gary and Sparks in the room. I can draw off their goodwill, and maybe it will help me see through the dark energy if it is still in there. I approach DJ and wait a second, and then I grab DJ's limp hand and attempt another telepathic "push" to contact his spirit. I can't shake the image of the dark curtain from my thoughts because I can sense that I'm not alone with DJ now. There is a malevolent force here, and I need to pay attention because I'm not sure what it wants.

I close my eyes and say, "DJ? Are you there?"

"Yes. Christa I saw you, but something tried to drag me back into my body and away from you."

"Was it Sparks restarting your heart?" I ask.

"No… it was before that. One moment I was walking towards you, happy and ready to leave, and the next there was darkness and I was pushed backwards."

"Can you see me now?" I asks DJ.

"No, I can only hear you."

I am worried. Something is off about this whole encounter. Usually if the soul chooses to move on, it steps off and smoothly exchanges places. That isn't happening here.

"DJ—can you follow my voice—can you see the light?"

"No, wait—someone is walking towards me."

I can't see a thing or feel a thing, but I can still hear DJ.

"Who? Who is there with you?"

"It's Henry!"

"Oh God no," I think. Not Henry! No wonder I can't get past that dark curtain, it's Henry's energy—the one I could never penetrate.

"DJ, what does Henry want?" I ask.

"He says he wants to say goodbye to me, that's all. He also says he left too soon."

I start to panic because it makes sense that Henry would come after DJ—they were brothers, so he has a natural connection to him. Why didn't I anticipate this? I know Henry has passed over. The idea that Henry might steal this portal to DJ's body is frightening. If he does, he will be telepathic and privy to all the conversations of the Council. We won't be able to block him—essentially, he'd be one of us. Or is he one of us?

"DJ, ,can you move towards me?"

"I can't see you, Henry is in front of me."

I am trying to think what to do when DJ says, "Christa, he's offering me the same deal you did, to swap… but with him."

"DJ, please don't do that! I don't know what the effect will be on your own soul."

DJ is quiet, "Christa, he's my brother. I feel like I owe it to him."

I am about to answer DJ and try to negotiate with him when what feels like a gale force wind blows past me and hits Henry's dark energy with such power that sparks of electricity fly. I can see DJ walking towards me and the light of another soul is visible as it entered DJ's body.

I embrace DJ and ask, "What just happened?"

"Another soul came in. It happened so quickly, I really couldn't tell you anything else."

"Must have been the soul that was waiting behind me," I say. "DJ, I do forgive you. Please, move on—let go of this life."

"Thank you Christa—but I can't forget all of this life. I will remember the good moments with you and that you fought to save my spirit in the end."

He smiles and a moment later, I am in the medical facility standing over DJ's body. He is resting peacefully, but I wonder, with more than a little trepidation, who is inside his body now? We won't know until he regains consciousness.

******

Sparks still holds the paddles in his hands, ready to hit DJ's heart with another jolt if he needs to. Christa has been standing next to DJ with her eyes closed—almost as if she is praying.

She opens them now and looks at Sparks holding the paddles and says softly, "You won't need those."

He puts them away and asks, "So, is everything OK?"

Christa looks back at Gary leaning against the wall by the door, and says, "Yeah. Fine. DJ is fine. An exchange happened—I just don't know who he exchanged with because it didn't go smoothly in there. But at least it's over. DJ's gone."

"Oh…" says Sparks, and then examining DJ's face, he thinks, "He looks the same."

"I know," says Christa, "but trust me, he's not."

Sparks stares with a questioning look into Christa's eyes and says, "You were in my head, I didn't say that out loud."

Christa feels so awkward at that moment. "I'm sorry. I know, we have a lot to talk about."

Sparks takes this in and asks, "Just tell me… are you like The Nomad, or DJ, a walk-in?"

"Yes, but I have been from a very young age, before I met you. I only recently realized it. I haven't changed if that's what you're asking. I am still the same soul you have always known. How strange does that sound?" Christa smiles.

Sparks doesn't know it, but this is exactly what he is asking—is she different? She is still Christa, except for the unnerving ability to read his mind.

*****

Sparks and Christa walk outside to relieve the tension of waiting for DJ to regain consciousness and reveal who he is. Christa tries not to imagine that Henry has succeeded in taking DJ's body because the result of that is too much to comprehend.

The two of them sit in the nighttime landscape not speaking, surrounded by blackness and a carpet of stars roll out across the sky. This is the first moment they have had alone together since Christa has been set free.

Sparks, trying to lighten the mood jokes, "You know, you will have to breakup with DJ now."

Christa laughs, "I suppose that would be awkward for both of us. But believe me, that was going to happen anyway."

"Really?" says Sparks.

"Really," she says softly.

"So… you're a single woman again."

"Technically, no… but,"

Sparks doesn't wait for the rest of her sentence; he pulls Christa to him, and brushes the side of her face with his fingertips. His thoughts linger on the touch of her skin and what her eyes look like so close to him. He remembers the dream of her in bed with him, and she is smiling at him because she can read his thoughts. He puts his lips to hers, softly at first. It is a kiss both of them have waited lifetimes to have. The passion grips them, and Sparks kisses her deeply holding her so tightly it feels as if their bodies are inseparable. They kiss for a very long time until they are satisfied and can just hold each other for a while. They know everything doesn't have to happen in one night; this is the first of many kisses to come.

Gary interrupts them, yelling from the medical building, "Get in here. DJ, or whoever he is, is waking up!"

Christa takes off running towards the medical building followed by Sparks.

******

DJ coughs and Sparks offers him a sip of water. He is blinking furiously and trying to focus on Christa hovering over him. He struggles to sit up, but he is clear-headed and calm. Sparks watches him closely. Christa can't feel DJ's thoughts and she is concerned because she could never feel Henry thoughts either. The other force, which had swept past her to enter DJ's body, was powerful enough to get rid of Henry's dark energy—that force is still unidentified.

While Sparks, Christa and Gary stand waiting for the new DJ to reveal himself, Gypsy jumps off the table where Sparks had left her. Christa looks at the dog who is now creeping slowly and cautiously towards them.

"What is wrong with her?" thinks Christa. Gypsy has her head lowered and her eyes are wide. She keeps stopping and smelling the air.

Now all three of them are watching the dog when Gary says, "What is she doing? Does she have rabies or something?"

"No," answers Sparks, "just a serious head injury. It's probably scrambled her senses. She's disoriented…"

Suddenly Gypsy takes off running straight to the bed where DJ is lying, jumps on top of his body and starts licking his face and whining.

Sparks rushes forward to pull the dog off when DJ says in a raspy voice, "Naw, naw man, leave the girl."

Sparks freezes, Christa gasps, and she hears Gary say, "Shut my mouth!"

Christa looks at Sparks and sees the shock on his face—he can't speak so Christa does, "Big G?"

"Oh yeah, it's me."

Christa starts to laugh and cry at the same time. The sound of Big G's street talk coming from DJ's mouth is incongruent. Sparks is smiling and then he leans forward and gives DJ—or rather Big G—a huge hug and says, "Welcome back man. Wow... this is gonna take some getting used to."

DJ/Big G says, "You're tellin' me!" He looks over at Christa and says, "I couldn't let that punk Henry wreck it all." Then he holds up his hand, twisting it from side to side, as he examines it, saying, "Well don't that just beat all... Now I'm the white king!"

All four of them have a much-needed laugh after a hell-of-a-roller-coaster-ride of a day. Then Sparks looks at G/DJ and said, "You don't get to die again for a very long time!"

"Deal," says G/DJ.

******

Phoebe smashes into her hotel room muttering, "I need to get out of this shit hole!" and she begins slamming her things into a bag. Every time she comes up against Christa the situation always goes sideways! Phoebe is over it. She just wants out!

She looks around the dingy little room as she packs, trying to spot her cell phone... nowhere. She needs to call her handler for extraction, but she can't use a landline. "Damn!" she thinks angrily, "This just keeps getting better and better. Now I'll have to head to the backup location to be picked up. I'll need a burner phone."

She pulls a chair to the wall, stands on it, and removes the cover to the air vent. Reaching in, she pulls out a gun, a wad of cash, a driver's license, and a passport in case she needs to leave the country. Dropping down into the chair, she sits twisting the gun around in her hands as she contemplates how much she wants to be rid of Christa. Phoebe isn't a very reflective type but right now she feels like a failure. She needs a purpose—she craves her next assignment.

She shakes off the moment of reflection, and sticks the gun in the waistband of her jeans, grabs her bag, and heads down the road toward the main highway. At one point, a couple of large, dark SUVs come careening down the narrow road and she has to jump into the bushes not to be seen. All she wants is get out of here all in one piece. No sooner has she stepped onto the highway and stuck her thumb out to catch a ride, than a large truck pulls to a stop. Phoebe runs to catch up and pulls open the door to the cab. The driver smiles at her with that "I'm a lucky SOB, look at this young girl I just picked up" expression on his face. Phoebe can feel the cold metal of her gun pressing against the skin of her back, and she is confident he isn't going to bother her.

She climbs into the cab, smiling sweetly and he smiles back at her with his nicotine and coffee-stained teeth. He starts in, "So... what's a young thing like you doin' on the road at this hour?"

"Oh, an emergency and my car died. I need to get to San Jose as fast as I can."

"Well, you're in luck sweetheart, I happen to be passing right through downtown San Jose."

"Great!" Phoebe forces a smile and hopes he won't ask any more questions. "Do you mind if we listen to the radio?" she asks.

"If you don't mind a little talk radio. I had the news on—turned it down when I picked you up." He smiles that brown-toothed smile again.

"No problem—I'm fine with the news." The driver leans across to turn the volume up, and as he does he lets his hand graze Phoebe's thigh. She wants to pull her gun out and blow his head off, but she needs the ride so she ignores him. If he tries anything again, at the very least she plans to break all his fingers. With that thought, she relaxes into the seat to listen to the radio.

The scratchy sound of the broadcast fills the night air, "Our lead story in this hour—after the untimely deaths of Damien Marshall, Sr. and his son, Henry Marshall, there have been arrests and multiple Federal indictments of several top officials from Marshall Industries, and The Carlyle Investment Group for racketeering and insider trading, among a list of other charges. This is expected to be the first in several indictments within the private banking and investment sector. The Department of Justice said damaging evidence had been turned over to them by a whistle blower and they are pursuing every allegation." The newscaster goes on to say, "Both companies have declined to comment."

Phoebe sits up and can't fathom what she is hearing. What happened? Now she isn't sure she should be headed home at all. She isn't even sure what her mission is anymore.

"Wow," says the truck driver. "That's something. They never arrest those bankers or CEOs! About time if you ask me."

"Yeah... About time," says Phoebe with much less enthusiasm than he has for this news.

She needs time to think—normally she has anticipated all the possible outcomes, but this has thrown her. She can't get to San Jose fast enough and find a phone to try to sort all this out. Then there is the question of whether she'll have a handler to contact. "Some music?" Phoebe asks.

"Sure, just as long as it aint rap," says the driver and he laughs. "Give me the Man in Black."

Phoebe looks at him quizzically, "The Man in Black?" Her mind immediately goes to the actor Will Smith in the movie, "Men in Black."

"Johnny Cash, baby! Haven't you heard of the "Man in Black" before? He's the best driving music there is."

Phoebe switches the dial to a country music station and settles in for a night of, in her opinion, twangy songs of lament from Peggy Lee, Willie Nelson, and lots of Johnny Cash.

After a couple of hours of driving, the truck pulls to a stop in downtown San Jose. Phoebe jumps to the ground and focuses on her surroundings. "This looks like a fairly crime riddled area," she thinks, "I'm sure there are lots of liquor stores selling burner phones. It's probably big business around here."

She starts walking across town toward the brightly-lit streets when she comes to a corner shopping center anchored by a liquor store. As soon as she enters, she spots the burner phones by the register and hands one to the cashier. Phoebe starts to pay the man when she can feel the hair on the back on her neck stand on end. She is being watched. As she walks out, she hears the beep of the door open again and two sets of footsteps follow behind her.

"Oh, you are messing with the wrong girl tonight," thinks Phoebe. She looks around and spots a shadowy street off to the side of the parking lot and heads there. "Perfect," she thinks.

As she cuts down the street, the footsteps follow her. Phoebe turns and sees two young men standing at the entrance to the street. They are punks—probably belonging to a gang. They have the requisite gang clothing—baggy pants, white t-shirts. One of them is covered in ink and has two tear drops tattooed by his eye. Phoebe knows the tear drops mean he has killed at least two people in his life. The other man hardly has any tattoos and he is much younger. The older guy starts to walk up on Phoebe while the younger one comes around behind her. She feels like wolves are circling her. Phoebe calmly drops the phone package to the ground to free her hands.

"Whoa, girlie, what are you doin' out here all alone," the older one asks. "Could be awfully dangerous for you." He smiles, but his face is full of cruelty. Phoebe can hear the guy behind her laugh. The older guy grabs his crotch saying, "Why don't we all have a little fun? Huh?" His false charm sickens Phoebe and she can't wait to teach this guy a lesson, but she has to let him get closer for her plan to work.

He walks up on Phoebe and pulls a knife, which he holds to her throat as he grabs one of her breasts with his other hand. He is almost salivating he is so excited by the possibility of what he thinks will happen next. "So you be nice to me and..." He gives her breast a tighter squeeze, "and I won't have to hurt you." Phoebe just looks the man coldly in the eyes and then she seizes her moment.

The young man reaches from behind to pin her arms, but Phoebe twists one arm free and flies into action. Neither of them sees what hits them. She grabs the wrist of the man with the knife, flipping it back so suddenly he is screaming in pain,

"What the... Bitch!" said the older man. He holds his wrist, but still lunges for Phoebe's neck. The younger man is behind her as she pulls her purse off her shoulder. Using the younger man's body for leverage, she pushes off him doing a round-house kick to the jaw of the older man who falls reeling backward. In a moment, she is behind the younger man and has looped her purse strap around his neck, choking him as she twists it tighter.

The older man backs up and pulls a gun from his waistband. Pointing it at Phoebe he says, "Let him go, bitch. I will kill your sorry ass! Let him go! And when you do, I am gonna fuck you up real good."

The young man is turning blue in the face and the older guy is getting more agitated as he watches his friend dying. He starts screaming and waving the gun and walking up on Phoebe. He is out of control with rage.

Phoebe slips her gun out, and when the older man is directly in front of her, she pulls it around the side of the younger man who she is using as a shield. She pumps one bullet right between the his eyes of the older man, the silencer making a soft "Pfft, pfft" sound. He falls where he stood. The younger man limply hangs from her bag strap and she lets him drop to the ground.

Phoebe picks up the plastic bag with the burner phone and starts to mess with the phone's plastic packaging, "Why do they always make these things so hard to open!" she says angrily. She is pulling out the phone, when she hears a cough behind her, and she whips around with her gun drawn. The man she choked is still breathing and she thinks, "Geez, why don't they ever stay dead!"

She starts to squeeze the trigger when she hears him say, "Phoebe." She cannot believe her name has come from the young man's mouth. She stops cold and a shiver runs up her spine. "No way I heard that," she thinks.

Then the young man speaks again, "Don't, don't shoot me," he says with difficulty.

"Give me one reason not to!" Phoebe says. "And how the hell do you know my name?" With that question, she gets down close to the man's face and pushes the gun to his forehead.

"It's a long story. Please... the gun..." He stops to gather his thoughts, but Phoebe can tell there is something different about the way he is talking to her. He looks around at the dimly lit street and the dead man behind Phoebe and says, "Let's just say I am not who you think I am."

"You mean you're not some low-life thug that would kill and rape a woman for some change and a burner phone?" Phoebe asks derisively as she continues to push the gun into the man's forehead.

"No, Phoebe, I'm Henry Marshall."

Phoebe stops breathing when she hears these words and slowly lets her gun fall to her side.

******

The Nomad enters the room with great expectations after hearing that G is the soul that walked into DJ's body.

"Well G I guess the universe plays a pretty good game of chess, too—wouldn't you say?"

"Ha! You could say that!" laughs G.

The Nomad smiles, but he knows serious work needs to be done now. It is time to move into the next stage of the reclamation. With G/DJ running Marshall Industries, OTP is going to have a big advantage. He turned to Christa and said, "We need to find you someplace safe to live. In the coming year you will be needed to deliver the message to the movement. There will be a complete rebalancing of all power structures from political to economic. We are about to turn the pyramid upside down and put the people on top.

Then The Nomad turns to the group—Sparks, Gary, Christa and G—and asks, "Are you ready for all of this?"

"Yes!" they answer in unison.

Big G speaking as his new persona, DJ, says, "Oh yeah, I know where ALL the bodies are buried now, and I'm gonna have some fun with this white boy's body! The universe does have a pretty good sense of humor!"

Taylor Barnes

Taylor Barnes has been, at different points in her life; a fine artist, publisher, book designer, illustrator, teacher, and journalist. She is currently painting and writing—searching for ways to create a heart-centered dialog within contemporary culture. She lives in Venice Beach, California.

Will Keane

Having stuck out the rat race in a corporate engineering and IT job for 38 years, Will Keane has released his creativity as a singer/songwriter and collaborating author. He spends his days in the quiet Irish countryside, living, dreaming, and creating works about current issues in society.

www.ingramcontent.com/pod-product-compliance
Lightning Source LLC
Chambersburg PA
CBHW060306260626
47160CB00007B/2522